Child's Play

Child's Play

a novel

CARMEN POSADAS

Translated from Spanish by
Nick Caistor and Amanda Hopkinson

HARPER

An Imprint of HarperCollinsPublishers
www.harpercollins.com

Originally published as *Juego de niños* in Spain in 2006 by Editorial Planeta, S.A.
First published in Great Britain in 2008 by Alma Books Limited.

FIRST U.S. EDITION

Library of Congress Cataloging-in-Publication Data has been applied for.

ISBN: 978-0-06-158362-9

09 10 11 12 13   OFF/RRD   10 9 8 7 6 5 4 3 2 1

Child's Play

Part One

Carmen O'Inns

"What a beautiful building," said Carmen O'Inns.

"What's more, it's a school with an excellent reputation," added Isaac Tonñu. "So prestigious nobody would suspect anything could have happened here."

The iron gates slid silently open. As Isaac pulled into the drive, the taxi wheels seemed to make each pebble on the gravel path crunch. The drive was circular, with the school on the far side, so you approached the building from one side and left from the other, after passing the rhododendron bushes, then a well-tended rose bed, and finally the green-framed sash windows of St Severin College.

"What do we know about the victim?"

Carmen O'Inns consulted her black notebook. Name: Oscar Beil. Age: 11 years. Time last seen alive: in the gym class at 10.30 a.m. Cause of death: apparently by drowning in the school swimming pool – yet what were those marks, those marks...

"What marks, O'Inns?"

"It's still too soon to say exactly. But, although we haven't seen the results of the forensic report, according to the boy's father there was a crescent-shaped indentation on his left temple."

"Anything suspicious about his death?"

Carmen O'Inns stretched her legs. She always travelled in the front passenger seat rather than in the back, so that she could comfortably extend the full ninety-two centimetres of her limbs in their Wolford tights.

"Who found the body?" asked Isaac Tonñu, but Carmen O'Inns didn't reply to this question either. She had taken her powder compact out of her handbag and was conducting the inspection that was a feature of every case she worked on: she needed to confirm she was looking as attractive as possible. First she examined her jet-black fringe, satisfying herself that it was neither too long nor too short; too thick nor too thin; that it set off her features to perfection, with its combination of indigenous traits and the jade-green eyes of her Irish ancestors. Then she checked her lips: a skilful blend of a natural outline enhanced by a touch of silicone, that made her look a lot younger than the thirty-seven years that featured on her identity card. The rest of her looks only added to her charms: she had the posture of a ballerina, and strong thighs slender enough to enhance her flat stomach, as she shifted in her seat.

When asked where she came from, Carmen O'Inns always gave the same reply: "From the land of rum, with a few extra drops of whiskey." "Whiskey" and not "whisky" she would add with a knowing wink. "No Scotch mists about me. In other words, I'm half from the Caribbean and half from the land of Erin."

She also liked to point out that she was a psychoanalyst rather than a psychiatrist or a psychologist, and that she believed in world peace, the forces of nature and man's innate goodness, but that for some reason she still couldn't fathom, she always found herself up to her neck in deep water. Like now, for example.

"Was it the boy's parents who came to you?"

"It was the boy's father," O'Inns corrected him. "Oscar Beil didn't have a mother, and he was an only child."

"It's such a dreadful tragedy! He was so young. And then, those marks on his temple..." Tonñu shuddered as he drew up in front of the main school building.

Isaac Tonñu was not his real name. He was born Isaac Newton, but when he arrived in Spain from his native Belize, he had decided to reverse the two syllables of his surname: Tonnew or, better in Spanish, Tonñu. It sounded less foreign and much more suited to his height and his colour: one metre, eighty-nine centimetres of sleek black male. It also led to fewer jokes, although he would never have let anyone make fun of him. Whether it was Isaac Newton or Isaac Tonñu, he knew how to look after himself.

When they pulled up outside the school entrance, O'Inns didn't move, but waited for Isaac to walk round the taxi and open the door for her. They had been working together for more than three years now and kept faithfully to their set rituals. They had faced danger together many times, as during *The Mysterious Balanchine Affair* and in the case known as *Death Dances to a Latin Beat*.

"Thank you, Isaac," said Carmen O'Inns, almost whispering into his ear as she glided out of the car. Both of them could feel the electric current flash between their bodies. "Not now," O'Inns told herself, "now's not the right moment." But her rebellious side couldn't stop two irresistible images from surfacing in her mind: first, the inky black of his skin submerged in her pale, Irish flesh; then the faint fragrance of musk that enveloped their nights together as they lay naked on the terrace of his new penthouse overlooking the Royal Palace, the two of them alone in the darkness, in the vast, slumbering city. "Why do we always think of sex when death is in the air?" mused Carmen. "Why is death so orgasmic?" She was about to answer her own question when...

"When... When what? When what, for God's sake?" Luisa asked herself, pausing at the keyboard and reading through the paragraph she had just written. "Can death be orgasmic?" That's what she'd written. And how about someone like Isaac Tonñu – or Newton? Could he be a taxi driver and be living in a penthouse? That was before she started getting into the other inconsistencies in what she'd just written, such as how unlikely it was for someone, however intrepid a detective they might be, to string together so many ideas in the short distance between the iron gates and the school entrance. And what about that school? Wherever in Spain would you find a school (a boarding school, least of all a co-educational one, and called St Severin to boot) so similar to du Maurier's Manderley, with a rhododendron drive and all the rest of it? Do rhododendrons actually grow in Spain? How do you spell them anyway? Rhodendros? Rhodedendrons?

Luisa put her hand over her mouth. It was a habit of hers, as if this was the only way to rein in her rampant imagination, the imagination which had created Carmen O'Inns in the first place. It's said the characters that writers create are their alter egos, the summary of all they might wish to be but aren't, and yet that was clearly not the case here. Perhaps thirteen years earlier, when Luisa Dávila, moderately successful as a children's author and with an even more muted track record in serious literature, had decided to create this sexy and inquisitive busybody of a psychoanalyst, the hypothesis might have held true. That is why she made Carmen several years younger than she was; gave her a physique similar to her own, but even more appealing, with green eyes she didn't possess; and invented an exotic background for her along with an equally evocative name.

Whereas she was called Luisa, came originally from the River Plate region and was Spanish by adoption, her character rejoiced in a name which in any language (with the possible exception of Spanish, in which she had become a world-famous author) signified beauty and a sense of adventure: Carmen. She had also been prophetic in selecting her nationality, because long before ethnic fashions came in, and before Latin music conquered the planet with its merengues and salsas, she had dreamt up the figure of Carmen O'Inns, who was Latin American like her, but Cuban and slinky. Isaac Newton had been introduced as a minor character in earlier novels, but Luisa now thought he could move on to play a major role. The fact is that in each new book in the series featuring Carmen O'Inns (this was the sixth), her heroine found herself torn between two lovers. One was generally sensible and conventional. The other was difficult, a dangerous rogue... Of course, Carmen didn't end up with either (whoever heard of James Bond in a couple?) but the love scenes recurred throughout her escapades, providing an agreeable counterpoint to the investigations. On this occasion, for example, Luisa suspected that Carmen O'Inns would find herself either in the arms of Newton or in those of the murdered boy's father. So far this was no more than conjecture, because one of the most enjoyable aspects of being a writer – in fact, the only one – was to be the first and most surprised reader of what she had written. This of course was a cliché, as she never tired of telling people whenever she was asked the classic question: "Tell us, Señora Dávila, do you know beforehand what is going to happen in your novels, or do your characters grow and escape from your control?" It might sound like a cliché to say she did not know what was going to happen twenty pages further on, but it was the simple truth. Though perhaps not the whole truth. To be more precise, Luisa Dávila was constantly surprised by what her characters got up to: not because they took on a life of their own (that was such nonsense), nor because she wrote following the dictates of some mysterious muse or other, as some of her colleagues affirmed, but because, as in real life, things happen, and as a result you have to improvise as best you can. It was the same with her creations: they reacted to whatever happened, and so the plot developed. Afterwards, if something did not fit, or if a character turned out not to be sufficiently interesting, she backtracked, killed off the unfortunate misfit, and then made sure she tied up all the loose ends. Nothing simpler.

The difficulties lay elsewhere. What was hardest of all was to make her writing seem true to life, to achieve the "suspension of disbelief" or, put another way, to tell a story that was accepted as real, however unlikely. That was it exactly: getting people to suspend disbelief and to join in the game was what most worried Luisa Dávila, and at the moment it was causing her considerable anguish. She wondered how likely it was that in Spain – a country where private detectives did little more than spy on adulterous spouses, where anyone in their profession met with so many legal restrictions on obtaining a gun permit, not to mention trying to check fingerprints on a database, or the impossibility of getting hold of DNA samples – a young Caribbean-looking woman, a psychoanalyst by profession, would be able to solve every perplexing variety of murder, assisted only by her impressive physique and – as Hercule Poirot might have said – her "little grey cells"? For years now, other European thriller writers had chosen to create detectives better suited to their times. They made them either members of the State security forces, former cops or agents who knew how to bug phones, use police labs, and were able to rely on all that technology can offer in the service of the law. Amateur detectives, with their magnifying glasses and bloodhound instincts, in the old-fashioned style of a Conan Doyle or Chesterton, were as incongruous nowadays as medieval knights embarking on their holy mission to right wrongs.

However, in spite of the myriad doubts which assailed her whenever she began a new novel, the fact was that until now Luisa Dávila had succeeded in *getting away with murder*, as a critic on the *New York Times* enthused, or – what amounted to the same thing – she had survived where so many other writers failed, and made her character's adventures believable, despite the fact that she was an extravagant mixture of Merimée's cigarette girl and Miss Marple.

So here we have Luisa Dávila, recently turned fifty-two, embarking on a new novel at the same time as she was moving into a new apartment in an old building close to the Prado Museum overlooking the Retiro Park. It had cost her a small fortune, but no matter: she finally had money, respectability and her independence. What's more she had won them all by herself, without any help from parents, husbands or lovers. The rest of her life could be easily summed up. She had arrived in Spain in the mid-1960s thanks to her father's job: he had been his country's consul in Madrid until 1969. Then, having lived in various other countries for more than a decade, Luisa had returned to the city of her adolescence. Behind her were two distant marriages of which the first (to a French author with an imposing name, one of those sunk by the events of May 1968) had left her with the convenient aura of being a left-wing writer; and the second, even briefer (this time to a crackpot Chilean, as handsome as he was sociable, whom she put down to her mid-life crisis), had left her with a taste for the good life, in sharp contrast to her naturally introverted character. That was all she'd inherited from her husbands, because even her daughter Elba, born when she was on the verge of turning forty, didn't belong to either of them, but was the consequence of another set of circumstances to which Luisa referred as little as possible. Why should she have to? One of the many advantages of being a woman at the dawn of the twenty-first century – words she had put into the mouth of Carmen O'Inns on numerous occasions and in the widest variety of situations – was that "We no longer have to explain or justify anything we do from the navel down". This, which might sound provocative when uttered by Carmen's Caribbean lips, remained just as true of the eminently sensible, conventional life led by Luisa Dávila.

Elba

It took Elba at least two days to thoroughly investigate the new apartment. Not because it was too big (and it was big, big and bare, according to her), but because it appeared so plain, with no nooks and crannies where she could find what she was looking for, a secret refuge like the one she had enjoyed in her previous home. A place where she could hide away, perhaps with a friend, in this new, cold apartment. There was no trace of animals either. Not so much as a fly. The only exception was the caretaker's cat, but she wasn't allowed to bring him into her flat, because her mother didn't like cats. According to Elba, she was afraid of them.

Right from the outset, what she liked best was the entrance hall, with its two facing mirrors, one large, the other much smaller. The second one appealed to her because of the way it reflected and cast shadows in the first. Elba was a little frightened by the larger mirror's frame, which was apparently made of twisted, ash-white wood. It reminded her of dead tree trunks washed up by the sea, like drowned corpses. By contrast, the mirror glass shone with a blue tinge, and made her look almost pretty. If she turned her head to one side, narrowing her eyes and tilting her face slightly to the left, she almost looked like a princess. Of course, Elba was too grown-up now to believe in such things, only silly little girls thought they were princesses, but she had her own reasons, or at least had them until quite recently, for wondering about her past. Not now though. Now, although the mirror reflected her in a frail, blue-tinged silhouette, Elba knew she wasn't a princess, because she'd asked Luisa and Luisa had explained it very clearly to her: "Sweetheart, it's very common for adopted children to think their biological parents are royalty or film stars or celebrities, but I can guarantee it never turns out that way. You only have one mother, and that's me. And remember, I love you very, very much."

Luisa had raised her voice when she mentioned the word *adopted* and again when she said *biological*, just like a teacher explaining something essential for the pupils to understand, however ugly or unpleasant it might be. It was the same tone a doctor might employ when he said the word *vaccination* or a cook, *spinach*. Elba knew it well. In her view there were two kinds of grown-up: those who used pretty expressions to describe horrible things, calling spinach "Popeye's lunch" and vaccinations "fairy nips", and those who preferred ugly words to describe ugly things, and raised their voices as if to say: "See? I don't regard you as a silly child any longer, so I'll tell you in plain language."

Elba couldn't remember the first time her mother had told her she was adopted. Perhaps she had been so small that she still hadn't worked out how adults use ugly words, and yet she clearly recalled the day when Luisa had insisted she wasn't a princess. That had been when she decided to call her Luisa rather than mum or mummy.

"How long are you going to keep this stupid game going?" her mother asked Elba, the third day she heard herself addressed by her Christian name. Elba simply shrugged and scarcely glanced up from the pressing task of feeding her dolls. "They also call me Elba now," was her only explanation, because she didn't know how to make Luisa understand that while she appreciated her refusal to speak to her like a silly little girl any more, she was also capable of telling the plain truth.

The frame of the big mirror Luisa had hung in the hall might have frightened Elba a little, but she soon learnt to stand on tiptoe to see herself in the glass. It was true: there was no way she could be a princess: she had short, straight black hair, and eyes to match. "Black as coals", as the geography teacher at her previous school had often said. Whenever she did, Elba would peer round the classroom, desperately searching for someone else who looked like her. But the nearest she found to her own looks was on a wall chart near the window showing "Peoples of the World". This included a photo of a little Laplander (she had just learnt the word in lessons and liked it a lot) who lived in Finland in a log cabin and travelled everywhere by sleigh. For some time, Elba thought she must be from the icy homeland of the Lapps, and made great efforts to read all about them, to discover what they ate and what their customs were. Elba wasn't the only adopted girl in her class. Irina, for example, wasn't sure who her real parents were either, but she at least did know she'd been born in Russia, and didn't have to spend all her time trying to discover her roots, searching on the Internet or the school's wall charts.

"Come on, Elba," her mother said to her one day, "why don't you stop thinking about all that stuff? I couldn't tell you where your family is from even if I wanted to. Adoption laws are like that, they prevent us knowing who the original parents were, my love." "What if it turns out I come from another country, Luisa? Couldn't I at least learn where I'm from?" But her mother shook her head: "All I can tell you is that you were born in Madrid, not in Russia or Ecuador, and certainly not in Finland. But that doesn't mean a thing. Your biological father could be Spanish, but might just as well not be."

For a long while, before they moved and Elba discovered the hall mirror, she had imagined herself as being many different nationalities. It was around this time that she appeared one day with a hideous doll under her arm, which she had bought with her own money in a pound shop. It had dark, mousey hair that matched its clothes. Elba swore it looked just like her. "Isn't this the prettiest dress you've ever seen?" she asked, carefully smoothing down the doll's skirts. The dress was made of a dull brown fabric which only a girl like Elba could ever have described as pretty.

"What countries do kids with thick straight hair and jet-black eyes come from?"

"From so many I wouldn't know where to start, my love. From Mexico down to Tierra del Fuego; from India right across to Ireland; in any case, you shouldn't be thinking about things like that."

This was what her former geography teacher told Elba when she had opened a huge atlas and asked her to point to all the places where children who resembled her might live. "It's easier to find a needle in a haystack," the teacher had added, after Elba explained that all she was trying to do was to learn what part of the world her family came from.

"Listen, my dear, you shouldn't worry about such things. None of the other adopted children in the school – and there are lots, I can tell you – are as worried about it as you. Besides, the person you resemble more closely each day is your real mother, the only one you have, Elba. Look in the mirror and you'll see: the same shade of skin and hair, eyes black as coals, you even have the same slightly square face. Hasn't anyone ever told you? Adopted children end up becoming the carbon copy of their adoptive parents."

This explanation failed completely to restrain Elba's geographical searches, or her fascination with atlases and dictionaries. Whenever she had nothing else to do, Elba pored over illustrations, her finger following the arrows which mapped the migratory currents, or else she'd study racial characteristics until she convinced herself she must be from this continent, only to change her mind a while later and decide in favour of another. Sometimes she felt like a Cheyenne, at others as if she came from the Persian Gulf. Yet again, she might be Finnish, Greek, Egyptian, Hungarian or Roma. She would rush off to look at herself in the mirror, holding the doll up to her cheek to compare their features. She spent hours scrutinizing the shape of her face, her snub nose, her high cheekbones, until she fell asleep still clutching the doll and dreamt of who she might have been had she remained with her real parents.

Mirrors. In her previous home they had all been small. The largest had been half-length, on Luisa's bedroom wardrobe. But there was nothing to compare with those in the new apartment, especially the vast blue-tinted one in the hall, in whose mysterious depths Elba thought she could see shadows which soon became more and more familiar to her, silent silhouettes lurking at its quicksilver edges. They kept Elba company and seemed to smile at her when she greeted them, or reached towards her when she ran to hide behind the door, as if they knew where she'd gone. Elba rapidly acquired the habit of telling them her secrets, whispering so that nobody would hear, bringing her mouth close to the glass, brushing her lips against its cold surface. She tried her utmost to make sure her body didn't touch the frame that so sharply divided the two worlds: the outside one in which Luisa and she lived, and that other world, inhabited by her friends, the shadows.

So what became of her secret refuge, the one she'd been looking for so anxiously when they first moved into the new flat? Bah, that was childish nonsense, babyish silliness. Who needs any of that when you have a special doll – thought Elba – and a magic world, a whole universe of my own, if I dare to plunge into the blue mirror? With a bit of luck – she thought – perhaps the caretaker's cat will also become my friend, then the three of us can stare at our reflections. As soon as they'd arrived, her mother warned Elba that she loathed cats, but Luisa couldn't really expect her not to have at least one friend, could she?

How to Write a Novel

"Isn't it rather depressing to write a novel about evil children, child murderers no less?" That's what Enrique Santos, the current Man of Her Life, had said. Luisa always had a Man of Her Life, because – according to Carmen O'Inns – and in this, Luisa was in total agreement – the important thing in these emotionally precarious times is to convince yourself, against all common sense, that each new love has come to stay for ever and ever, even if it only lasts a week. Enrique had already lasted eighteen months, quite a record, which made it all the more a shame that he belonged to the group Luisa dubbed "my philistine lovers", those who considered that culture and literature – and especially women authors – were absurd, over-concerned with matters they couldn't possibly understand, like pathos, Eros and Thanatos; in short, they were bloody useless. Or, in Luisa Dávila's case, bloody useless... but with a nice pair of legs. All right, so she didn't really care if he thought like that, because she also found him bloody useless... but good-natured. Besides, she told herself, it's one thing to be convinced that love will stay for ever and ever, even if it only lasts a week; it's something else entirely to pretend not to realize that, by the time you reach fifty, love is a bargain basement. Worse still, it's a shipwreck, every last one for themselves, grab the first solid-looking plank coming your way and make sure not to be the last one overboard.

Enrique Santos was seven years younger than her, with the kind of physique that, although there was nothing extraordinary about it, is usually described as pleasing. He was a self-made man: a mattress-maker. An excellent mattress-maker. A prosperous mattress-maker but not a superlatively rich one

19

– a bit of a nuisance, that. Not because Luisa Dávila was over-concerned with her lovers' finances: at this point in her life, she didn't need anyone to provide her with economic security or social lustre (in fact, one of her more recent lovers had been an extremely young and impecunious yoga teacher). But, as Carmen O'Inns had said in a recent adventure called *The Trials of an Opium-Smoker*, in which Luisa had immortalized the yoga teacher (changing him into a lifeguard for legal reasons): "As far as successful women's boyfriends are concerned, some win a round of applause, while others are deemed totally unacceptable". Nothing to do with morality, of course, it's been a long time since that ceased to be a relevant benchmark, but there are others just as exacting, if not more so. As O'Inns put it: "What can I say, *chico*? That's how things are, and it's stupid to pretend otherwise. The fact that a woman like me has a pool attendant or a Cuban spendthrift in tow, or even a postman or a serial killer, is super cool. Because it's seen as an independent woman's flight of fancy. What I absolutely can't allow myself is to have a 'nearly' lover. Get it, Isaac Newton?"

In response, Isaac Tonñu (the conversation is meant to be taking place in his penthouse, following a torrid episode of sexual gymnastics on his terrace overlooking the Royal Palace, etc.) had asked (tracing an erotic line with his long black finger dipped in vintage Jamaican rum down Carmen O'Inns's pale Irish skin etc.) why she couldn't allow herself this, and in any case what was a "nearly" man? So she explained: "Darling, you'll never understand women, will you? What do you think it means? A man who's nearly rich, nearly important, nearly handsome or even nearly young. Nothing more unforgivable in a successful woman's personal track record. And it doesn't matter if the guy is endowed with every virtue and is a tiger between the sheets, if they're the last of the great romantics, and a model father to boot – it's all the same, because what women like me can't permit ourselves is anything in the middle."

"You mean you're willing to go with a young kid or an assassin, but not a—" Isaac began (this time running his tongue down O'Inns's spine, pausing only to pay special attention to her beauty spots etc.), but Carmen O'Inns cut him short: "I mean precisely what I said, Newton. All or nothing, big winners or desperate losers, just leave the 'nearly' men to others. They're the curse of women like me."

This peculiar theory was also to blame for Luisa's concerns about the profession of the current Man of Her Life. She would never have admitted as much, even to herself, but Carmen O'Inns would have expressed it like this: "A mattress-maker in the personal track record of a woman like me is only acceptable if he's a millionaire, preferably a billionaire. It's the same difference as there is between having a lover who's a butcher or Mr Walls himself, get it, Newton? Only excess renders certain professions acceptable."

Yet, in Luisa Dávila's quieter and more bourgeois existence, between these two opposed theories about love – the one about having a "nearly" man and the other which declared that love at fifty is a rout where everybody had to look after their own skin – in the end the latter prevailed, so that here she was living a tepid but pleasant love affair with Enrique Santos. "A grown-up relationship" she told herself, whenever she let herself think – which didn't happen very often, as she had to do quite enough thinking during the hours spent at her computer and she had no wish to do overtime. As a result, her life was calm, and her literary career had blossomed to the extent that she had been able to move to the neighbourhood behind the Prado Museum, where only those with the deepest pockets were welcome. Her daughter Elba was starting at a new school that year too. After she finished at primary school, Luisa had finally decided to send her to the English High School, the same one she herself had attended years earlier. "Good grief, I get it now. It was when you went back to your old school all those years later that you got the idea of writing about child murderers, wasn't it?" Enrique had asked, with that air of his – halfway between patronizing and disrespectful – which he always employed when he mentioned her novels. (Patience: all the Men of Her Life were sceptical about her work for a while, it was a real labour of love to convert male incredulity into appreciation, but little by little…)

"…Those walls dripping with memories of the past," Enrique continued, "those cold classrooms smelling of chalk and hardwood where you rich people spent your childhood. I get it: so that's where all your bloodthirsty ideas about mysterious childhood deaths came from, isn't it darling?"

Roaring with laughter, Luisa replied that with his over-heated imagination, he'd soon be the one writing thrillers rather than making mattresses. Besides, the kind of building he'd just been describing was nothing like Elba's new school, which could only have been built ten or a dozen years earlier. Not that it even looked like the place she'd been to almost forty years before, although it was true that the other grey, dilapidated mansion, in which the traces of faded past glories were a dim and distant memory, lent itself more to intrigue and mystery. It was at this point that Enrique (who always took advantage of a chance to boast of his humble origins and his loyalty to them) told her that one of his childhood friends was now caretaker of the new English High School. "He's called José Peñuelas. We were born in the same street, and we still play cards together once a month. As you can see, darling, I'm someone who is faithful to friends way back from his schooldays. If you want me to, I'll call him. He must know heaps of stories about evil children."

Luisa told him not to bother, and that she didn't believe either that the fact that her daughter Elba was going to her old school could have anything to do with her sudden interest in childhood evil. Yet though she said nothing to Enrique at the time, from that conversation onwards, things began coming to mind that Luisa Dávila hadn't thought about in years. For example, the impression made by her first day at the English High School at the age of twelve, the same age as Elba would be at her next birthday. She also remembered her grey pleated tunic and red pullover. Then, little by little, other memories of that distant spring way back in the 1960s began to surface, less in the form of images than smells. "Spain smells of smoke," she remembered thinking the day she disembarked in Barcelona, and from that moment on, smoke of differing colours and textures best defined the country that would now be hers for ever. If a mingling of steam and soot evoked the port of Barcelona, the streets of Madrid in the early morning on her way to school smelt of a jumble of competing kinds of smoke. First there were the bars, with their dense smell of fried food, always accompanied by the loud murmur of agitated voices. Then, crossing the streets, particularly the widest and saddest ones, there was the essentially Spanish odour of drains, swirling around her legs until they indecently reached inside her skirts. Then came the smell of deep-fried churros and that of church candles; boiling tar, oily foods and burnt leaves; fearful foreign smells which insisted time and again: "You're not from here, you're an outsider, you'll never return home, your childhood is dead and gone." Then all at once, this hostile country with its strange smells offered up a friendly white vapour, and made her think that although she might be from somewhere else, she was becoming a little bit Spanish, since she could appreciate at least one of them: the gentle warm smell of roasting chestnuts.

She now realized that there were forty years between those memories and the present day, but that they only rarely came into her mind. While it was true that her school days were still a forceful presence after she left, and that during her early years at university she had more than once woken up with the unpleasant feeling that her life was a fraud and that she wasn't really an adult, but that someone had unmasked her pretence and was forcing her back to school – yet soon there was a first marriage; then later on a second; so that little by little there were more pressing anxieties for her nightmares to feed on. Then she began writing her book about evil children: the smoke and the dark walls of the former English High School; the grey-and-red uniform; the cold mornings; even the redemptive aroma of chestnuts, were as distant to her as the names of those girls and boys she had shared classrooms with for years.

What could have become of them? Luisa had never wanted to attend the old school reunions which had taken place after she had left, because her childhood was not a time she recalled with any particular pleasure, even all these years later when time had carried out its habitual process of sifting the good from the bad. Would she meet any old classmates now that Elba was starting at her school? Would they recognize each other? How had life treated them? Would the cleverest in the class now be triumphant and the stupidest a complete failure? Is it true what they say that childhood contains the seeds of the future like an oracle or a trial run? Delving a little deeper, did children adopt their parents' ways once they reached their age: did mean parents only have mean offspring; the intellectual, intellectuals; and the cruel, cruel children? "You and your imagination," Luisa Dávila scolded herself, then thought what a relief it was that Carmen O'Inns was childless. Otherwise, her readers were at risk of being lectured about some hare-brained theory of how events have a worrying tendency to repeat or imitate themselves, as happens in Greek tragedies, where whatever horrors that occurred in the parents' infancy get visited upon their children, because fate is mischievous and likes looking at itself in mirrors. "What rubbish," thought Luisa. "Something like that wouldn't be credible even in one of Carmen O'Inns's novels." In any case, even assuming she wanted to use one of her former classmates as a model for a story of this sort, it was more than likely she wouldn't find anyone suitable. (Enrique always reproached her for her inveterate mania of using her friends and acquaintances as literary material without bothering to employ the least camouflage. According to Enrique, this was not only tactless but downright rude.) "Remember, you are a late first-time mother," the Man of Her Life repeated to her more often than was strictly necessary, in that pragmatic way realists have of bringing anyone back to earth whom they regard as scatter-brained. This observation was usually only made when Luisa was spoiling or over-protecting her daughter, but now the memory of Enrique's words allowed Luisa Dávila to realize that if she wanted material for her novel set in a school, she would have to rely on her imagination. It was unlikely that there would be any child of a former classmate of hers in Elba's form. "You are a late first-time mother" meant the parents of her daughter's companions would be at least ten years younger than her. "By now my classmates at the English High School must have children in their twenties," Luisa told herself. It was a shame, because the sight of Elba in front of her bedroom mirror, trying on the same uniform Luisa had worn forty years earlier, had conjured up certain childhood shadows still lurking in the recesses of her mind.

The Truth about Elba

Luisa called her daughter Elba because she calculated that she had been conceived on the island of Elba. In fact, Luisa was unsure whether she had become pregnant on Elba or on the neighbouring island of Monte Cristo, but when she came to pick a name for the baby, there was little doubt which to choose. Her "mating trip", as she preferred to refer to that obscure episode, had lasted some months and at the time (around twelve years earlier), had seemed to her the best idea she'd ever had. By the time she decided to put it into practice, her second marriage was already a distant memory. She had just turned forty and could see her age as issuing her with an ultimatum: Now or Never. Or (in the words of Carmen O'Inns, a character she had brought to life only a few months before, despite a host of literary fears and doubts), "this is the last train to maternity, so be sure to catch it, idiot. Who on earth is going to enquire where the baby came from if your ovaries are on the case? Ovaries and little grey cells are all it takes, so make sure you don't forget the latter."

So, just as if she were Carmen O'Inns, that was exactly what Luisa had decided to do. The plan consisted first of getting pregnant by someone she met along the way, a partner she chose for nothing more than insemination. Then to return to Madrid for the early months of the pregnancy, announcing she was in the process of adopting a baby and, before her condition became obvious, to disappear for a while without offering too many explanations, apart from: "Yes, I'm going away for a few months. A friend of mine has lent me her flat on a quiet beach… It's a real luxury. I'll have endless time to myself, and I'm sorry but no, I can't tell you where it is. I've realized the only way to finish this damned book is to cut myself off completely – but don't worry, I'll stay in touch..."

This plan, like something out of a second-rate novel, had seemed a perfectly acceptable solution at the time. Crazy yes, a bit like a soap opera, but possible, as long as Luisa added the two ingredients mentioned by Carmen O'Inns. Now, twelve years later, and seeing how incredibly fast centuries-old moral judgements had evaporated in modern-day Spain, Luisa regretted not having done things in a much more straightforward manner: to have got pregnant and become a single mother as of right and without qualms. Yet she knew regrets came only with hindsight. In those days her mother was still alive, and Luisa liked to think that her roundabout manner of setting about the business had been a way to avoid upsetting her. There were also more practical reasons: to have a child with someone she knew presented other problems beyond the predictable gossip. Such as what to do about the father of the child. Because Luisa did not belong to that group of women so liberated that they considered it perfectly fine to use a man, specifically a friend or acquaintance, as a stud – today I'll have you, tomorrow I'll drop you – thus depriving him of any right to decide whether or not he actually would like to be a father. Her "mating trip" was quite different. It was a situation where no one was being deceived or losing out: you choose a man, if possible a handsome, young and healthy specimen; enjoy a romantic interlude over the relevant period; and then, ciao. Antonio, that Valencian near-adolescent with uneven teeth and a broad smile, whom she met on a beach near Portoferraio, would never even discover he had a daughter in Madrid. That was better for all concerned.

It seemed a perfectly acceptable idea at the time, and to begin with it had all gone according to plan. Nobody was surprised, for example, that a woman like Luisa should be given such a tiny baby for adoption, because people generally believe the rich can buy whatever they want. After a few weeks of gossip among her friends, they stopped asking questions, and Luisa decided to call her daughter Elba, as the one souvenir of the unusual manner of her conception. However this woman, who prided herself on foreseeing everything, was forced to recognize with hindsight that she had made a mistake with unforeseeable consequences. Like most people, Luisa thought you had to tell children the truth regarding their origins as soon as possible, and yet since everyone believed Elba was adopted, Luisa chose not to tell the girl the details of how she had been conceived until much later on. Because, she mused, how was she to explain to a four/five/six-year-old child that there is more than one truth: one for grandmothers and people in general, and another just for the two of them? How could she tell her that sometimes you have to tell white lies to go on living, and that some lies are preferable to some truths, because they protect us from even worse things? How could she describe a much younger man about whom she could only remember his name (Antonio) and a shining smile? Every time Elba's birthday came around, Luisa wondered whether the moment had finally arrived to discuss all this with her. Each year she decided it would be better to wait a little bit longer, at least until her ancient grandmother finally died.

So birthdays came and went. Elba turned eight, nine, then ten… By the time Luisa realized it, the grandmother had been dead a year and a half; Elba had begun calling her Luisa, and had started staring at herself in mirrors, fantasizing over her origins. Origins which, at least on Antonio's side, were so obscure she might as well have been adopted. So Luisa decided to wait yet another year. To wait, at least until they moved into their new apartment and the girl was about to enter secondary school.

However, when the moment finally came to tell her the whole truth, Elba was too intrigued by what she could see in her mirror to believe her.

"Why do I have to believe that, Luisa? Which story is the truth? This claim that you are my real mother or the one before, when you swore you didn't even know where I came from?"

The girl said all this without raising her eyes from her bowl of soup. The two of them were alone in the new flat, in the unfinished kitchen. Elba seemed so serious, sitting at the table on a packing crate that was so tall her feet didn't even touch the ground.

"I've just explained to you, my love: some truths can badly hurt others and so it's best to keep them hidden. Your grandmother..."

"Granny is dead. Perhaps the dead deserve truth more than the living?"

As had happened before on numerous occasions, Luisa wondered where an eleven-year-old girl found such weird arguments. From television or the cinema, perhaps? Elba didn't know what she was talking about, she was upset, wounded even, but she would get over it. It was only a matter of time, children forget so quickly.

"There's no reason for you to take it so badly, sweetheart. All that really matters," said Luisa without looking at her, concealing her mouth behind her napkin, "is that you are my daughter. Of course you always were, but now this new truth will be our very own secret, OK? No one else needs to know..."

"No one needs to know you're a liar, you mean, Luisa? Don't worry, I can keep a secret," she heard her daughter say, still not daring to look her in the face.

All of a sudden a slight catch in the girl's voice led Luisa to think she might be sobbing. She looked up and saw it wasn't so. Instead Elba, still seated upright on her crate, had begun a nosebleed. The blood was gushing down her chin, neck and chest: it stained her pyjama top, even running into her soup, where it made distractingly beautiful red swirls. This wasn't the first time Elba had had a nosebleed, the doctor had already

30

explained she had thin capillaries in her nostrils, but that it was hereditary, not worth worrying about. (Inherited from whom? Clearly something her father had bequeathed her.)

What was obvious, Luisa discovered, was that these haemorrhages only happened when Elba was upset. They came without warning, apart from the change in her voice she had mistaken for a sob. "Why didn't I realize this was bound to follow?" Luisa reproached herself.

"Good God, Elba!"

She ran around the table, and tried to staunch the blood with her napkin.

"Here, darling, put your head back, wait and I'll bring some cold water. Don't move, my love, please don't worry. It's nothing."

When it was all over, once the bloody napkin and the stained soup had become the last traces of the incident, Elba kissed her so tenderly that her mother breathed a sigh of relief. "Some truths can badly hurt others, so it's best to keep them hidden," Elba repeated like a good girl learning a lesson by rote. By now she was standing facing her mother. Elba's head hardly came a foot above the edge of the table: she was small for her age, yet her eyes had the same grown-up look about them as her mother's.

"Come here, Elba," said Luisa, dropping her napkin onto the table, and smoothing her straight dark hair back from her face. "It wasn't anything to get upset about, was it my darling? Don't worry. Look, I've got an idea. Let's look at ourselves together in the mirror, and you'll see we're as alike as two peas in a pod," she added, as if proposing an amusing game. She pulled her daughter away from the table and the bloodstained bowl. "Where is there a mirror? Ah yes, the big one in the hall. Let's look at ourselves in that one."

She had already clasped her daughter's hand, and was encouraging her with a smile as if to say: "Look, it's over, don't worry any more", when she felt Elba's sticky fingers (it must have been the blood, poor girl) digging into her arm. How cold and strong they were, as if she wanted to stop Luisa from moving.

"What's the matter, Elba?"

"I don't want you to look into the big hall mirror. Let's look into the smaller one, or into a window pane. We could use the kitchen window, Luisa."

"Don't you think you could start calling me mummy again, darling?"

"Well, if you want." Elba lowered her eyes, then added: "It's true we look a lot like each other. At least in the kitchen window we do. Don't you agree, *Luisa*?"

"Give her time, she'll forgive me," thought her mother. Children rapidly adapt. Sooner or later they forget everything, thank God.

The Suspects

"Don't try to demonize anyone by claiming that some people are born bad, Señorita Duval," said Carmen O'Inns, addressing one of the schoolteachers. "Obviously, some characters are evil by nature, but right now it's not as important to philosophize as it is to discover exactly how the phenomenon we call 'evil' operates. As we know, even the most perverse individuals are not evil all the time. Evil is an opportunist which lies in wait for the right moment in order to manifest itself, like a bacteria attacking a weakened organism, or a parasite deciding where to lodge in its ideal environment. Are you with me?"

O'Inns paused, waiting for the gym teacher Señorita Duval's response. But she was far too busy sobbing her heart out, apparently unable to understand a word of what O'Inns was saying to her. Seated in one of the many chairs in the now-vacated staff room at St Severin, Señorita Duval was staring at a photo of Oscar Beil, the dead boy. It was the same picture the newspapers had published. She was muttering to herself: "If only that day I hadn't sent him to get the blasted stopwatch from the changing rooms, perhaps he'd be alive now... Or, who knows, if I'd gone instead of him, then..." She shuddered, and her voice trailed off before she could put her thought into words, but her gesture left nothing to Carmen O'Inns's imagination.

"What nonsense, Señorita Duval, as if that could have changed the course of things in any way. As I was trying to explain, evil is an opportunist, who only shows up when success is guaranteed. I'm sure that your going to the changing rooms would not have averted the tragedy, still less that you rather than the boy would have become the victim. If they had not seized their prey in the pool, they would have tried time and again... It was him they wanted to kill, not you."

"My God! Who could possibly wish that kind of harm on an eleven-year-old? Such a sweet child who everyone loved? I know what you'll say next, Señorita O'Inns: it could be a sexually motivated crime, there are plenty of depraved people about these days, but there's nothing to show that..."

Oscar's father, Señor Beil, had sat silently throughout the interview with Señorita Duval. A man of around forty, blond and with a calm air ("The air of a married man," thought Carmen O'Inns, who had a mental card index of male types), somewhere between strong and domestic, as befitted a pater-familias accustomed to cooking the weekend barbecue. However, Jaime Beil was a widower and the managing director of a large company, who in all likelihood had never barbecued anything in his life, not even as a student. When he heard mention of a sexually motivated crime, he momentarily closed his eyes, then stared at the gym teacher blankly, as if they were discussing someone he didn't know. "What a strange man," Isaac Tonñu thought to himself. "It's as though the whole horrible story had nothing to do with him."

"A sexually motivated crime can be ruled out in this case, Señorita Duval, so let's drop the subject," replied Carmen O'Inns, staring daggers at her, as if to say: "Don't you realize, you silly woman, the harm your words could cause this man beside us? Shut up, you old bat."

But Señorita Duval was so overcome with grief that she was aware only of her own pain. Besides, her red nose and eyes were concealed behind her handkerchief, so she could no longer see the boy's father. She sobbed aloud: "Then there's his wound, isn't there? I mean that mark on his left temple. It's as if whoever the maniac was who killed him wanted to leave his mark. The poor boy drowned, didn't he? He wasn't killed by the blow to the head, was he?"

"As I already told you, Señorita Duval, we don't know. Until the forensic expert completes his work, we can't be sure of anything. Equally, we don't know too much about certain other objects found at the bottom of the pool. Were they connected to the crime? Were they already there beforehand? Did they belong to the victim or not? And what about his wound? What could those three marks inside the half-crescent on his left temple possibly signify? It's far too soon to know, but my intuition tells me that the mark is somehow linked to the death, even if the official cause remains 'asphyxiation by drowning'. Tell me, Señorita, as well as teaching gym, you're also a dance teacher, aren't you? What kind of dance do you teach? Classical, aerobic, ballroom?"

"Oh, all kinds of dance..."

"Even tap-dancing?" asked Carmen O'Inns.

"Yes, tap as well."

A gym mistress who teaches tap-dancing; a father seemingly completely devoid of emotion; a suspicious mark on the victim's temple... "Isn't it high time I began to introduce the suspects?" wondered Luisa Dávila. Whenever she reached this point in any of her stories, she had to pause to mix herself another drink. It was a ritual, and therefore completely harmless. Whereas in everyday life she only drank wine and then only at mealtimes, she had acquired the habit of confronting any difficulties she encountered in writing her novel with the help of one, two, sometimes even (despite the fact that her methodical mind detested such weakness) three Bloody Marys. An ideal cocktail for anyone who believed not only in symbols but in formulae designed to overcome certain problems. According to the classical model of thriller-writing, it is extremely important to present the suspects in a systematic but rapid manner so as not to break the rhythm of the story, and the easiest way to do this is to use what Luisa called "the Christie Formula". In other words, to make sure that all the characters in the plot approached the detective – here, Carmen O'Inns – one by one and alone, in order to present their version of events. This system fulfils a twin function: on the one hand, to get the suspects to speak, so that the reader can come to know their individual psychologies, and on the other, to provide further clues to help the final resolution of the mystery.

This time, though, not even two (or three) Bloody Marys could convince Luisa to rely on such an old-fashioned device. Or rather, the vodkas helped her shed her fear of experimenting with ingenious alternatives, aimed at making it seem less like a procession of characters, even if that's what it was. It seemed more modern and sophisticated, but even though it was apparently less obvious than classic thrillers, a careful reader could discover the sleight of hand. How could she camouflage such a blatant literary device? Luis Dávila took another sip of her fresh Bloody Mary. "OK, let's see," she told herself. "The best thing would be to let my fingers roam the keyboard, and see what Carmen O'Inns gets up to."

"Aha. So these are the names of Oscar's classmates? OK, all well and good, tell me about each one of them, Señorita Duval. Who were his closest friends? As I understand it, there were two other children at the swimming pool that day without permission, a boy and a girl, who by chance were great friends with Oscar..."

"Surely you can't be thinking that either of those two innocent creatures could be the one... and not even twelve years old, Señorita O'Inns, God's own little cherubs..."

Carmen O'Inns didn't bother to explain to Señorita Duval what she thought of childhood innocence and its cherubic virtues. She was far too sure the dance teacher was among those simple souls who still believed in theories about the noble savage – that old con trick. She herself was secretly convinced that Oscar Beil's death was the product of childhood evil.

"Let's see, Señorita Duval, tell me if I've got it right: which of these two lists is the teachers, and which the pupils? Oh, thank you, that's perfect. You're very efficient. Now that I have both of them, I'd like you to tell me about a few things I've noticed. Let's start with the adults, from the letter A..."

(I can't believe you're going to put the list of names just like that, and in alphabetical order too! Just like Agatha does at the start of her books. You ought to be ashamed of yourself... No, I'll fix it later, for the moment this list is just for my own benefit. Let's see, who could Oscar Beil's murderers be? Let's think.)

She came to a halt. She couldn't come up with anything for now. This had often happened to her before, and she knew it was best not to push things but to give herself time. Besides, who knows – she told herself – perhaps tomorrow, on Elba's first day at school, I'll be lucky enough to meet someone interesting enough to turn into a character. After all, why not? It might come in very handy.

"Your worst defect, my love," the Man of Her Life had said on more than one occasion, "is how unscrupulous you are when it comes to gathering material for your books. Like that mania you have for using friends and acquaintances as your inspiration, without so much as bothering to disguise them; shooting people you know in your books is vulgar and abusive."

That's what he said, but what did he, Enrique Santos, know about literary creation? Zero. Moreover, it was completely wrong to say she used people from real life as her literary material. She used parts of people: "Just so's you understand, darling, we writers don't shoot people: we dismember them, more like Jack the Ripper than Billy the Kid. And just to make myself absolutely clear: we take a head from one person, a heart from another, an expression from a third, so that in the end the person we most resemble is Doctor Frankenstein, because we reassemble all these stolen parts to form a single character. Get it?"

No, Enrique did not get it. He kept on saying she was being obvious as well as utterly ruthless when she set about gathering literary material. To the point that, according to him, although she was so fastidious in other areas of her life, he could imagine her perfectly capable of reading someone's personal correspondence if it came in handy for one of her books.

That was a lie. She'd never read anyone else's correspondence in her entire life. It had never even occurred to her to do so. Anyway, that was enough of going over all this nonsense in her head: it must be the vodka at work; whoever had the daft notion of downing two Bloody Marys in quick succession? She was not going to find an idea in the bottom of her glass. Better go straight to bed.

Luisa shut down her computer. A small drop of liquid remained in the bottom of her glass, so she carried it up to bed with her. Surely it wasn't so late that dawn was already breaking and yet, before she opened her bedroom door, she thought she could see a dim glow at the far end of the corridor, as if the hall mirror were reflecting the first rays of the sun. "Impossible," she told herself, setting the glass down on the bedside table and starting to undress. "Who knows? Tomorrow, when you take Elba to her new school, perhaps one or two of her future classmates (or their parents, why not their parents?) might give you an idea for fresh characters. One of them might even be a potential murderer." She needed at least two children, and maybe also two adults? Yes, that was it: four was a good total number of suspects. She had already included Oscar Beil's father, and Señorita Duval the dance teacher. How about adding some further unpleasant characters such as a school inspector of sinister aspect, a psychologist who cared too much for children, or a dim-witted gardener?

No, no way, that would be to over-complicate the plot: it was one thing to set the readers a challenge, quite another to leave them bewildered. Four suspects were more than enough: two adults and two children.

Her head hurt. The smell of stale vodka reminded her of dead flowers, and it gave her a peculiar glassy-eyed look, as Luisa could see when she looked at herself in the bathroom mirror. Another slight noise, the faint sound of creaking wood in the hall again caught her attention. "Could the caretaker's cat have found a way inside?" she fretted anxiously. That was silly: how would it get in? Anyway, her fear of cats was simply a vestige of the past, when she was a little girl and suffered from asthma. Such stupid fears, brought on by the vodka and the memory of Edgar Allan Poe with his black, treacherous cats. Luisa dismissed the idea with a wave of her hand. "Nobody there, we always hear unfamiliar noises in new flats," she reasoned. "You have to get used to them, like you get used to your shadow, and stop imagining you're seeing ghosts, least of all when you've had a few drinks." Luisa considered Poe and his hallucinations again. She smiled because there was a real apparition right before her eyes. She stared at herself in the mirror – this woman must be her, who else would she be? – just turned fifty-two, her age well-disguised by face creams and make-up by day, but at night, and with three Bloody Marys inside her, things looked very different. How ghastly she appeared, with her dishevelled hair, the dry patches around her lips, and those eyes… "I have to stop this nonsense," she thought, and told herself how lucky she was not to live as a couple: it would be hell to have a husband, lover, partner, whatever, witness such moments of weakness. (So, darling: is weakness an aid to literary creation, as so many people say? Does it help stimulate the imagination and inspiration? Yes and no, it depends. Yes and no? What does that mean? It means that all we can say with total confidence about human behaviour, the most infallible philosophical theory on human nature, is the one the Man of your Life so relishes: what he calls "The Julio Iglesias Theory". According to this, people behave exactly as the song says: "Sometimes yes, sometimes no, sometimes you, sometimes me…")

"That great philosopher and theoretician Julio Iglesias! What am I saying? Only someone like Enrique could come out with anything as crass, and here you are, repeating it. Enough nonsense, Luisa. For God's sake, go to bed."

On this as on every other occasion, Luisa Dávila's collapse was not complete. It only ever lasted the length of time it took her to invent the suspects for her novel, at most one night plus three Bloody Marys every two years. The rest of the time, she was utterly different. Luisa Dávila the super-cool, the paragon; the woman who never smoked, drank or swore; who did yoga and Pilates, counted calories on a calculator, and avoided taxis in order to get more exercise. This ever-so-sensible Luisa found herself insisting how convenient it was for people like her to live alone, because nobody else could possibly be expected to understand her sudden collapses.

It was almost two in the morning when she thought she heard another "new apartment" sort of a noise coming from the hall. Yet again, she couldn't be bothered to go and check it out, she was too tired. "Tomorrow I'll be wrecked," she warned herself. The vodka had left her mouth dry, tasting vaguely of rotten vegetables. Perhaps she should brush her teeth thoroughly, and how about a shower? "N-n-no," she stammered, "straight to bed. That's enough for today. Getting drunk alone is truly pathetic. Makes you think too much. Poe was right: literary creation and alcohol make a dangerous c-c-cocktail, you see everything as melodrama. *And* you see shadows where there aren't any."

The First Day of School

Next morning, Elba had behaved particularly badly, like a little child. She had pretended she couldn't even see her mother.

"I can't, I swear. Look here: my eyes are stuck together and I can't go to school. They'll all laugh at me. You don't want them to laugh at me, do you, Luisa?"

Luisa had tried to put her arms around her daughter's back, in a clumsy attempt to lift her out of the bed, but she was too heavy.

"Come on, we can't be late on day one," she said. Far from obeying, Elba let her head flop back in a highly theatrical manner.

"Shit, I'm so tired."

"You know I don't like you using that kind of language, Elba. That's enough. I'll lose my temper and you don't want that to happen, do you?"

The girl, however, only screwed her eyes up tighter and asked: "If you lose your temper, will you stutter and smell of dead flowers, Luisa?"

"Flowers, what are you talking about? That's enough jokes and I warn you I'm getting fed up with this nonsense about you calling me 'Luisa'. From now on you're to call me 'mummy', at least in front of your new teachers. Come on Elba. Open your eyes and look at me."

She didn't do so until half an hour later when Luisa went back into her bedroom, smart in a sober suit with a pale blue jacket, which she thought was most appropriate to conceal her lack of sleep and best present her in the role of model mother. To Luisa's great relief, she found her daughter sitting on the bed properly kitted out in her new uniform, identical to the one she herself had worn all those years earlier. "Aha – so now you can see me, can you?" she asked, almost amused.

"Yes, of course. When you're dressed as Luisa, and you look like Luisa, I like seeing you," said the girl.

"And whenever do I resemble anything else?" she was about to ask, but didn't. To enter Elba's fantasy world was a risky adventure: who knew what it meant when she kept her eyes tight shut, or told her mother she smelt of dead flowers, and did or didn't resemble Luisa?

A wave of tenderness swept over her as she looked at her daughter. She was still so little, she really was. With her cropped hair and the red-and-grey uniform, she looked so much like herself as a child. Elba was sitting there in the pleated tunic she remembered so well, the bib stretched across her budding, pre-adolescent breasts, peering at her with an expression they also shared, head tilted to one side, as if asking a question or awaiting an answer. Had she been as full of fantasies at Elba's age? Luisa couldn't remember, but didn't think so. She had been shy, even solitary, perhaps due to her asthma, which occasionally kept her in bed and made it difficult to make friends, but she'd never talked to mirrors or cosseted hideous dolls, still less imagined other worlds beyond her own. Given her chosen profession years later, paradoxically she hadn't even got good marks for Spanish composition. "Luisa must pay more attention to her compositions. It's as though she's bored at having to describe what she can see." That or something like it was what her Spanish teacher had written in one of her reports, which Luisa had found by accident during their move, and decided to hang, framed – as a joke – alongside the literary awards she had won. The same teacher had told her: "You've got about as much imagination as a donkey turning a millwheel. You go round and round and never leave the beaten track."

She and Enrique had laughed their heads off at that one. It was at that point that he, seeing Luisa was gathering material for her next book, had sneakily suggested that as far as human behaviour was concerned, the only valid theory was that there can be no theories, and no one can predict how someone will turn out based on their childhood. Whereas she had been bottom in Spanish, he had been the opposite, gaining top marks, and now look where it had got him: a life dedicated to the poetic art of mattress-selling. "Take my advice, sweetheart," he had added with a degree of self-confidence that made Luisa feel jealous and scornful by turns. "If it were possible to predict how adults will turn out on the basis of what they were like as children, there'd be no need for all the psychiatrists, psychologists or any of the rest of the charlatans you've become addicted to. I've told you it before, gorgeous, but I don't mind repeating myself: the only valid theory about human behaviour is Julio Iglesias's: all you can say about people is that sometimes they conform to type, at others not. Or as he puts it: *In life, everything is sometimes yes, sometimes no, sometimes you, sometimes me.* Would you like me to hum it for you?"

"Mummy, Mummy, I'd so *love* to bring her to my new school with me. May I, may I? Tell me I can. I promise I'll look after her."

Elba was a bright child, but she used truly infantile strategies. That was why, even before Luisa saw what it was she so desperately wanted to bring to school, she knew from the unusual use of "mummy" that she ought to refuse.

"Please let me take her, Mummy, *please*. She'll help me explain who I am, and where I come from, to the other new schoolkids."

As she said this, Elba took the doll she had bought at the pound shop from between the sheets. Luisa had so hoped she'd

43

forgotten this ugly replica of herself for ever, with its short thick hair and ragged clothes.

"Now, Elba, I told you yesterday that you're my daughter, and there's nothing more to…"

"OK. But how am I supposed to know when you're lying and when you're telling the truth? Before, when you said I was adopted, or now? Besides, I still don't have a father, do I? You don't know anything about that half of me, do you? For example, yesterday when I begged you to tell me about him, all you could say was that he was much younger than you and that you'd liked his smile. You noticed that, and yet you couldn't even be bothered to learn his last name. You only knew he was an Antonio. The doll isn't so big, she fits in my satchel, besides she's like me – she hasn't got anyone else."

"She's saying all this to punish me," thought Luisa. "My God, how long will this cruel game continue?" Later, as she was helping Elba on with her winter blazer ("Come on, darling, it's better to wear this now the cold weather is beginning") and carefully doing up the buttons the girl (innocently?) had messed up ("look, see how much prettier you look"), Luisa once more avoided catching her eye, admitting to herself she had no right to complain because she alone was to blame. If she had talked to her daughter earlier, if from the outset she had told her the truth concerning her birth, none of this would be happening now: Elba would not be calling her Luisa or pretending not to believe her; she wouldn't be discussing a young man named Antonio, who was far better forgotten; still less would she be comparing herself to such a hideous rag doll. If she had never lied ("Come over here, let me tidy your hair a bit… Look, isn't that much better, sweetheart?") she herself would not be feeling at such a disadvantage as she faced her daughter's sudden whim. Nor would she be listening to herself say: "Please, Elba, you're far too old to take dolls to school." A feeble comeback, without so much as a trace of irony to recommend it. It would have been so much better at least to be able to make a joke of it, but Luisa couldn't even manage that. She didn't joke because she knew – they both knew – that the only reason for Elba's demand was precisely to provoke that rueful smile and hear her say: "Please, Elba…" In fact, the game had been going on for so long, she couldn't really ignore how nearly all her daughter's stubbornness was aimed at winning that rueful smile from her.

"This afternoon, when she gets in from school, I'm going to have a serious talk with Elba. This nonsense has to stop right now," Luisa told herself, as though making a vow. "This very afternoon, I swear it."

"I can bring my doll to school, can't I, Mummy?"

(Are you going to let yourself be browbeaten by a single word? Because that's all "Mummy" is, just a word, Luisa.)

"I promise I'll keep her hidden in my satchel. I probably won't even show her to anyone. Let me take her, please, Mummy."

(A word, my kingdom for a word, my inheritance for a plate of lentils…)

"As you wish, my love."

"I knew you'd let me, Luisa. I love you so much, so very much."

Class 1B

"Where is Class 1B, please?"

"A bit further down on the third corridor. You'll soon see it when you get to the corner."

Luisa had put on her high heels and was the only mother there dressed in a two-piece suit. The others seemed much younger than she was: all wore jeans or other casual wear and to her they were hard to distinguish from the pupils. The fathers looked equally young, although she did see a few men with either bald heads or greying hair. "Bull's-eye for Enrique," she smiled to herself, "I bet, as he says, they are all fathers onto their second or third marriages, who already have one flock of young away at university."

Click-clack, click-clack, the high-heeled shoes tapped along the tiled school floors.

She had to remember to change before she came to collect Elba that afternoon. "No child," she told herself, "likes a mother who's in any way different to the rest." She herself would have been horrified, especially on her first day at school. "Yes, you must remember that, because the worst an adult can do is forget what we most loathed when we were children, and to fall into the same embarrassingly bad habits they made us suffer. To be ashamed of your parents is particularly excruciating." She glanced down at Elba, who seemed happy enough. She'd even held her hand without Luisa asking for it. Just as well, since the corridors were full of parents, children and other visitors, and she didn't want to lose her.

"My goodness," she thought, then said: "Sweetheart, I don't suppose you remembered to bring a hanky with you, did you?" She had just realized that, in the tussle over the doll and their rush to get out, she had forgotten that Elba could have another nosebleed as easily as she had the previous evening. "A hereditary tendency," the doctor had said, but the bleeds always coincided with times of stress and worry, and the first day at school had more than enough of both. Luisa rummaged in her bag and finally found a half-used packet of paper tissues: "Take it, sweetie," she was about to say, when she saw Elba smiling at her. "Don't worry, Mummy. Look, I brought one of your hankies from home." Again, she took Luisa's hand in hers, seeming not to mind that other children her age were walking happily ahead of their young mothers, ignoring any summons: "Monica, don't run so fast." "Manuela, you've forgotten your satchel." "Pablo, come here…"

Luisa strode on down the corridor. She turned the corner as directed, then all of a sudden there was no one around any more, just a long line of closed doors. She looked at the numbers on them, and carried on down the passage, her unsuitably high heels still click-clacking, keeping pace with Elba's silent rubber soles. Luisa recalled her own first day at school, when she'd turned up equally unsuitably dressed. They had reached Spain only just in time for her to start the third term, so for five long days her mother had obliged her to attend school without a uniform and, what was even worse, to wear buttoned shoes while all the rest wore proper lace-ups. "*Click-clack*, time to forget all that, and let's see where Elba's classroom might be. 5A; 5B; 6A… Damn it, it looks as if it can't be down here. Whoever can I ask?"

Luisa had already decided to turn back when she saw a girl of about her daughter's age leaning against one of the doors. "I hope she isn't a new girl, lost like the rest of us." She swiftly rejected the idea as they drew nearer and could see the lazy, sprawling way the girl was propping up the doorpost: one shoulder arched against the wall and one leg akimbo.

"Hello, please can you tell me the way to Class 1B?"

The girl neither moved nor responded, obliging Luisa to ask again, now a little more brusquely.

This time she surveyed Luisa dreamily. She was slight, fair-haired, her features spoilt by an outbreak of adolescent acne. She took so long to reply that Luisa could observe her more closely: to note, for example, that her uniform blouse was badly crumpled, and that her jacket sleeves were too short, as if she had outgrown it. That presumably meant she was no longer new to the school and should know where Elba's classroom was.

"Hey, I asked you a question."

"No idea. I'm new here."

"So where are the rest of the kids your age? And where's the classroom?"

"No idea," the girl said again. At that moment, a bell rang and Luisa thought the best thing would be to retrace her steps to avoid reaching the classroom terribly late. She looked down at Elba once more. She seemed to think all this was hilarious, and let herself be led by the hand until suddenly, as if by magic, classroom 1B was right in front of them. How come Luisa hadn't seen it before? She must have passed right by the door at least twice, once before they went down the empty corridor, and again when they left it. Unbelievable, but at last they were there.

"Come on, Elba, here we are."

The door was closed, as if everybody else had already gone in. Luisa pushed at it with her hand, and the door opened.

As if that gesture were enough to return her to an earlier time and place, her first reaction was a tiny asthmatic wheeze in her throat, just like when she was a child. Then she was hit by a waft of immediately recognizable smells. She could identify the sweet smell of rubber erasers, then the dry odour of chalk, followed by other vaguer ones that resembled plasticine, glue and the unmistakable scent of the wood of the classroom desks with their heavy lids, behind which you could hide from the world, protect yourself and disappear, as if into a welcoming dark womb.

Luisa came to an abrupt halt, looking around her. In fact, none of the things she had imagined were there. No erasers, no glue, and why on earth had she imagined there might be plasticine in a secondary school? Nor was there a traditional blackboard, merely a modern whiteboard, so no possible scent of chalk either. As for the desks, they didn't have lids, just a book rest attached to one side, useless for hiding behind.

The contrast between what she had sensed and what she saw was so strong that Luisa remained rooted to the spot. She and Elba were still in the doorway. "How silly," she told herself. "All morning I've been behaving like an insecure idiot, first with the doll episode, next putting on the wrong outfit, then the hassle finding the classroom, and now here I am, stuck like a dummy with all the kids staring at me." Having such a slow and clumsy mother really would have horrified her as a child. But surely that wasn't her: she was Supermum, otherwise known as Luisa the Supercool. "Come on," she reproached herself. "Just because you once told a lie to your daughter, you don't have to spend the rest of your life doing penance. Snap out of it, otherwise your penance will be worse than your sin, as far as Elba is concerned." Then, speaking aloud, louder than strictly required by the situation, Luisa addressed a female figure on her left.

The woman standing with her back to her had ash-blond hair untidily bunched at the nape of her neck. She had to be a teacher.

"Excuse me," said Luisa, suddenly realizing they weren't the only two adults in the room. It was when the teacher turned to face her that she saw there was also a man at the back, leaning across one of the desks to help a child.

"I'm sorry, I didn't mean to interrupt, I'll wait," said Luisa. But when she saw the woman smiling at her, she continued: "This is my daughter Elba, and I am..."

"You are Luisa Dávila, of course."

At first she thought the teacher must have recognized her from press photos, or one of her book jackets. After all, this was an increasingly frequent occurrence, and she found it not only pleasant but, in this instance, useful: it was no bad thing if Elba's new teacher was also a reader of hers. In response, she began to put on one of her most characteristically literary smiles. It froze when she noticed that the eyes half-seriously and half-mockingly gazing at her were ones that had so often examined her in the past.

At that moment the man who had been leaning over another of the pupils also glanced up at her.

Coincidences

Enrique and Luisa had a habit of meeting mid-morning in a bar near the Bernabeu Stadium. It was a custom they had adopted at the beginning of their relationship, when everything was less stable, while he was still a married man and she hadn't yet decided whether or not she wanted him to be the Man of Her Life. In those circumstances, the noisy bar on Calle Marceliano Santamaría, where nobody had ever recognized Luisa, or asked for her autograph (she consoled herself by putting this down to "too much football in the atmosphere") fulfilled their need for a meeting point in a neighbourhood unfamiliar to either of them, in a remote area of the city where they were unlikely to be under the prying eye of a neighbour or acquaintance. So to the delightful ritual of imbibing an early cocktail was added the no less delicious touch of infidelity. Now, however, that Enrique was separated from his former wife, the Calle Marceliano Santamaría was awkward for the two of them to get to, and they only continued meeting there out of the superstitious fear couples have that a ritual, once broken, might lead to a bigger break-up.

"Do you remember what you said when I told you I wanted to write a thriller set in a school? You asked me if the idea had occurred to me the day I went to enrol Elba, when I went back to my old school after all these years. At the time I said it was nonsense, because the new English High School is in a modern building out in the suburbs, completely different to the old one. Yet when I went into Elba's classroom this morning, I swear it was exactly like stepping back into my own form room all that time ago."

Luisa explained that perhaps the feeling arose from the fact of her arriving late, or for being inappropriately dressed, or because that wretched Classroom 1B smelt of glue and erasers but "what's for sure is that everything combined to make me feel just like a little girl on her first day at school. On top of all that, what should happen but I met up with not one but two old classmates? The most unlikely of coincidences given that, all of a sudden, we three adults not only recognized each other from childhood, but found ourselves in a situation identical to one we had been in so often in the past: two girls (women by now) staring at one another with the boy (man) looking on from his desk beside the window".

"...To cut a long story short, Enrique, the fact is that I met up with two classmates, and not just any classmates, but the two who were most important to me when I was young. Don't you find that extraordinary?"

Enrique replied that no, there was nothing extraordinary in former pupils sending their own children to the same school they had attended. Luisa shook her head impatiently.

"You don't understand, Ri!" (She only called him that in their most intimate moments, but now – for some unknown reason – she needed to feel close to someone.) "Don't you remember, I'm an older mother? You yourself have often told me the chances of Elba having classmates with parents as old as me were very remote."

"But darling, I think we've also said how common it is nowadays for first-time mothers to be as old as forty, and for fathers of grandfatherly age to be on their third marriages. Did you ask them if—"

"She's Elba's teacher, so for now at least I couldn't tell you if she fits into your statistics of early or late motherhood. As for him, I've no idea how often he's been married, but the boy at the desk by the window has to be his son. In any case, he looks a lot like him, despite being fair-haired, whereas he was so—"

"He, she, him… Could I please at least know their names? Another thing: did you ask them if there were more children of ex-alumni in the class? Chances are, you could learn something to surprise you there too."

"Their names are Sofía Márquez and Miguel Gasset and no, I didn't ask them anything, I'm not as inquisitive as you are, Ri. Besides, there was no time: everything I'm saying took place in a classroom full of children who were staring open-mouthed at a scene where I'm afraid the three of us were bawling like babies. A *cringe-making* little interlude, as Elba and her friends would say, fit only to create acute embarrassment when seen from outside. What you need to know is that way back then, Miguel was—"

"Don't tell me: you and Sofi fought over him."

"Don't call her that, she hates being called Sofi…"

"Oh dear, I do apologize: 'She hates being called Sofi…' Do you realize you're still suffering from the 'classroom effect'?"

"What on earth is the 'classroom effect'?"

"I don't know, I've only just invented it, but it sounds like one of your literary devices or one of your psychological theories. Let's just say something like an *emotional flashback* produced when an unexpected encounter takes you back to the past. You enter a classroom and suddenly feel exactly as you did aged eleven or twelve… a former classmate you haven't seen for years turns up and you're bothered by the fact that I call her Sofi… By the way, darling, what was the title of that film where three old friends meet up after many years and remember a crime they committed as adolescents? Wasn't it called something like *Back to School*?"

"Don't be daft, Ri, what on earth are you talking about? Let me tell you what really happened."

When, twenty minutes later, Enrique threatened to leave, Luisa had hardly begun to tell him all she wanted to say. First of all she needed to compare at length how Sofía and Miguel looked now as against her recollection of them as children. Her description was so detailed it took almost half the time they had together.

"I didn't recognize Sofía, how was I to know, Ri, that this woman with thinning hair and hooded grey eyes was the girl I used to dream of becoming? You can't imagine how pretty she once was, with that kind of half-innocent, half-perverse look which only lasts a few years, and usually gets called the 'Lolita look'?"

"Shit, another of those phrases..."

"Sorry, forget the phrases. What I'm trying to say is she had the kind of almost malign beauty that can blossom in early adolescence. It's ephemeral because within a few years either the childish aspects disappear, leaving only the disturbing ones, or else they persist and the child begins to look like a kind of goblin. It may be short-lived, but that kind of disturbing beauty is extremely powerful, and that year, the only one in which all four of us were in the same class..."

"Four, how come four? I thought there were three of you."

"Wait and listen, Ri. As I was saying, that year Sofía had the most amazing gunmetal blue eyes, offset by dark brows and eyelashes. In spite of this, she was naturally blond and not very tall, although she was well-proportioned. A beautiful body, and she had a beautiful smile too. In other words, an arresting beauty made all the more striking by the haughty manner you often see in those who have been worshipped from the cradle onwards. If there's one thing I've learnt from personal experience, it's the huge difference between children who have been adored throughout their lives and those who haven't. Between us mere mortals and those whom the grown-ups pampered and cosseted – either because their parents spoilt them or, as only happens when the child is amazingly beautiful, they are also fussed over by an army of aunts, relatives, friends of the family and even casual acquaintances, who show no mercy when they pay court to them and not to the rest of us. Don't tell me you don't know what I'm talking about, Ri, everybody compares themselves unfavourably to someone else, a boy or girl they remember who got everything and more, simply on account of being so exceptionally beautiful. It may be a cliché to say that this or that boy or girl is bound to develop later into a little tyrant, but what's certain is that they will have an unshakeable self-confidence, so much so that once they've grown up and have lost that aura of beauty, they will still behave as if they had it and – what's more amazing still – they will almost succeed in convincing others of it. There's nothing more attractive than confidence in your own attractiveness."

"What about the man?" Enrique asked, worried that the conversation would last far longer than his morning break.

"There were two of him," replied Luisa, going on to explain: "How can I put this? I don't know where to start. It's a story very like Alexandre Dumas's *The Corsican Brothers*."

"Shit. There you go again with your literature, darling."

"What I'm trying to say is that the idea comes from Dumas's novel, in which he describes the strange relationship between twin brothers, where everything felt by one is experienced by the other. Dumas writes that—"

"Give me a break," Enrique protested, seeing she was about to launch into what seemed to him an unnecessarily literary explanation. "For a writer, your way of explaining things is a bit all over the place, isn't it? Is what you're really getting at simply the fact that Miguel has a twin brother?"

"Had. He no longer has one."

"OK, so he had one. Let's take it from there, but let's see if you can tell me the whole story in ten minutes. I don't belong to a leisured profession like you, and I need to get back to the factory before nightfall."

"Don't get on your high horse, Ri…"

"All right. Start at the beginning, and tell me what happened to the two twins."

Miguel and Antonio

It was three days later that Luisa told Enrique the rest of the story. In fact she still didn't tell him everything because, as she began to relate it, she realized there were some things better kept to herself for the time being, such as the part where she explained the relationship between Miguel, Sofía, herself and the fourth youngster. If Enrique had not had to leave in such a hurry that first morning, she would perhaps have given him a proper description of all she knew but, when she had to cut things short, there had been time to reflect on the usefulness of keeping one or two matters to herself, at least for the moment... "What was the name of that film where three old friends meet up again after a long time, and remember a crime they committed when they were adolescents?" had been Enrique's first question, way back at the start of their conversation. Sometimes Luisa thought he could read her mind, so she had hastily replied, telling him he was talking nonsense. Whatever had occurred forty years earlier wasn't a crime but an accident. It had taken place on a morning in the middle of spring. It's said that, even when it succeeds in erasing the most terrible deeds, memory always leaves traces behind, like Tom Thumb's trail of pebbles showing the path back to somewhere better forgotten. Perhaps that's why Luisa found this morning light with its etched shadows reviving the image of a particular school playground. She had only been attending classes there for a few weeks. It all began with four children playing cops and robbers, although games were forbidden at the far end of the grounds, the least grandiose part of the estate on which the old English High School was situated. The garden here was planted in a strange mixture of styles, somewhere between French and Mediterranean, in which box hedgerows alternated with stone-terraced flower beds. After many years of neglect, it was hard to make out where the line of hedges had once stood, and the old flower beds had been filled in with sand, from which only an occasional stone corner protruded. Beyond the furthest flower bed, by the side of a huge stone urn, there were the vestiges of a grey marble pond, which in former years must have served as home to many exotic varieties of fish, but which the wind and rain had filled only with dead leaves and dirty rainwater.

"Come back, don't go down there, Sofía. You can be expelled for sneaking into that end of the garden!"

"Don't be so stupid! Come on, all of you: Miguel, Antonio and you Luisa, you silly new girl. Come on, last one there's a sissy!"

With all the desire of an interloper desperate to be accepted by the rest, and with a sense of devotion born of fear and envy, Luisa marvelled at the other girl. Sofía stood for a moment, eyes flashing and hair tumbling everywhere. Then she ran off between the flower beds, and perched on the old stone urn beside the pool, balanced on the round rim, pretending to be an acrobat. Sofía jumped down suddenly and, a few seconds later, was standing next to the water, peering into the dirty, shallow pool, which reflected back her features. "Last one down here is a sissy! Catch me if you can!"

They had divided into two teams: Sofía and Antonio were the robbers and Miguel and Luisa the cops. Naturally, it was Sofía who had decided who was with whom, choosing Antonio, who regarded her suspiciously, to be with her. In fact the only difference between the twins was in the way they looked at Sofía: Antonio with unease, Miguel adoringly. In everything else, they were identical: dark chestnut hair, light blue eyes, and a smile that revealed dazzling rows of teeth, the more so because of their slight unevenness. Both of them had crooked incisors, but rather than diminishing their attractiveness, this slight defect only served to make their smiles seem lovelier. Or so thought Luisa, who picked up on every last detail with the insight of someone seeing everything afresh. The boys appeared so similar it was impossible to tell them apart, although on that day of all days, there was one other small detail that distinguished them.

"Hey you, the one with the cut on your forehead! Yes you, Antonio, wait here for me. Miguel, you move over there and be the cop. Let's see if you can catch your brother and me: watch, watch what I'm doing, nobody can run along the edge of the terraces like me!"

It was true. This was what differentiated the two boys that day: Antonio had a cut shaped like a crescent moon close to his left temple. It had happened during gym class, but it wasn't serious, hardly more than a scratch.

"Come on Antonio, you're on my side! Miguel, you're with the new girl. Let's see if you idiots can catch us!"

"None of this is much like a game," thought Luisa, who saw an incredible intensity in the way the other children went about everything. Luisa was new. New not only to the school, but to Spain, which besides smelling of smoke, also had a frightening quality: a strange weight of history, as though even games had a different aim beyond that of mere pleasure. "Get used to it, Luisa, that's how things are going to be from now on," she kept telling herself.

On one occasion she'd even plucked up the courage to mention it to her mother. "Here in Spain, when they're playing games it's as if they're doing something else, though I'm not sure what it is." Her mother had only laughed and said: "No, sweetheart, it's not the change of countries you've noticed, it's the change of growing up. At your age, games begin to turn into something new."

What did that mean? Luisa had no idea what her mother might be referring to, although she was sure she was wrong: it was obvious that her new friends played exactly the same games as all the kids she'd ever met in Buenos Aires, Montevideo or elsewhere. Surely cops and robbers was what they played there too?

"Hey you, Antonio, I'm talking to you. Come up here with me, right here… No, Miguel, not you. You stay over there and only when I say, see if you can catch me. Catch me if you can!"

Sofía had again climbed up onto the stone urn beside the water tank, forcing Antonio to follow her. Her straight fair hair shone so brightly that Luisa looked away in order not to reveal her jealousy, and to refrain from wanting to touch and caress those locks, just as she could see Miguel wanted to do as well. What *was* he doing if not stretching out his hand towards the base of the urn where Sofía and Antonio were balanced?

"Sissy, you're a sissy, and you can't catch me!"

Playfully, as if in jest, Miguel began to push the base of the stone urn towards the water tank.

"Go on!" he shouted. "Leave Antonio up there and come down with me, Sofi!"

"Don't call me Sofi, idiot. What are you up to? Whatever *are* you up to?"

The urn slowly started to topple, and as if in jest, playfully, Sofía and Antonio, Antonio and Sofía, started falling with it. From down below Miguel could only reach out to catch one of them, and of course he chose Sofía, because he was no sissy, and of course he could catch her. "See, I've caught you!" he clasped her close as his brother fell over backwards. It was then that Luisa heard the dull thud of the boy's head against the edge of the tank, nothing more than a soft blow, the sound of an "uh" as his head rolled to stare skywards, and the dirty water in the tank began to lap at his hairline, crowning it with a halo of dead leaves.

There was a frozen moment of silence and terror. Then they all shouted: "It was nothing, nothing!" and the three of them rushed towards the motionless body. "Look," said Sofía's voice, "he's fine. Can't you see? He's got his eyes closed and dead people always have theirs open, I know that for a fact. It was nothing."

"Shut up, Sofi!…"

"I told you not to call me that."

"I said shut up. We'd better go and tell someone—"

"No! It was only a bang. Better that nobody knows we're down here, or we'll be in trouble. As for you, new girl, stop blubbering, you sound as if you're about to drown. If it's asthma, hold it in. I'll pull him out of the water. Everything's just fine."

Sofía put an arm round Antonio's shoulders and tried to lift him. Luisa was once again amazed at how tiny the sounds of a death can be. If the noise of Antonio's fall had been soft and hollow, the one made when Sofía tried to raise him was short and sharp, hardly more than a click. The boy's head, soaking and strewn with leaves, flopped backwards at an improbable angle, like a broken doll. It was a death without a single visible drop of blood. There was no trace of a wound. As if in a sarcastic aside, the only sign of violence on his head among the dead leaves was that tiny crescent-shaped cut he'd got a few days earlier at the gym, now standing out on his pallid skin like a dark question mark.

The Beginning of Term (According to Elba)

Elba looked around at her new classmates and tried to imagine what they could be thinking of Luisa and the other two adults, all talking at once. What must they think of the way they kept interrupting each other, their silly floods of tears? "How much longer," she asked herself, "will they carry on playing the fool? In any case, why are they laughing and crying at the same time?' Elba once again felt her ears burning: there's nothing more ridiculous than adults when they're blubbing, it only provokes the sniggers and nudges which she already suspected her new classmates were indulging in behind her back. She was sure they were in it together, all laughing at her: "Get it over with, please God, get the heck out of here. I hate them, God how I hate her." Then Elba turned to look for someone to confide her embarrassment in, wondering how the other new boy must feel, the son of the man the teacher and her mother were calling "Miguel". At that very moment the man was hugging Luisa for the hundredth time, telling her (how many times had he already told her? Why on earth do grown-ups keep repeating themselves? He must have said the same stupid sentence ten thousand times over): "How pretty, really how amazingly pretty you are now, Luigi, do you remember how we used to call you Luigi? Because you had an impish boy's face and a pudding basin haircut. How you've changed!"

"I suppose that means that I *too* have a Luigi face, whatever that implies," thought Elba grumpily, and instinctively looked for her reflection in a window pane. She couldn't see anything. "Do mirrors only talk to happy children who had other lives, other parents, in some remote part of the planet? My God, don't let the mirrors desert me too," she prayed, looking at herself again in the glass. All she could see was the reflection of a young girl who did indeed have a boyish face, the face of a Luigi.

Ha ha ha, more laughter from the three pathetic adults, and she was stuck there without an escape route, condemned to witness it all, shit, shit, shit. Luisa never liked hearing Elba swear, because her own way of speaking was always so correct, but that was precisely why she felt an overwhelming urge to curse: she was on the point of yelling out the words, because along with her burning ears Elba could feel her eyes starting to prick with tears. It had to be tears, her tears, hell no, shit, so she dug her nails into her palms until they hurt. No and no, I refuse to be the next one to cry.

"What's wrong? What's up, you're trembling..."

One of her classmates was talking to her. Elba looked up. There was something familiar about her face, but Elba was so confused it took her a while to recognize her. She looked like the girl Luisa had stopped in the corridor, and asked the way to Class 1B. That could only have been half an hour ago, but it already seemed like a century.

"Don't worry. The more idiotically adults behave, the better for us, don't you think?"

"But she's my mother..." said Elba, as if revealing a painful secret. Then she realized this was the first time she was using the word "mother" in its true sense.

"Well that blond woman is *my* mother, and on top of that she's our form teacher. Imagine how that feels!"

Now Elba was certain: it was the same girl who, when they asked where Class 1B was, had simply shrugged and said she hadn't the faintest idea, adding that she was a new girl too, when it was perfectly obvious she wasn't. Whatever had made her lie?

"Your mother's the teacher? You must have it easy!" added Elba.

The girl wearily shrugged her shoulders again, like someone so used to answering that kind of accusation she was beyond getting irritated or bored by it.

"Easier on her to take it out on me. You'll see. What's your name?"

"Elba. And you?"

"I'm Avril."

"Like the month April?"

"Yes. But I decided to spare you the joke: the one about April showers, it's spelt with a 'v'. As for you, is it El-ba? It seems like we've both got ridiculous names. Someone once told me that those of us with older mums and dads almost always have names that are supposed to mean something. At least mine's got a meaning. What on earth does Elba mean?"

Elba knew her name was that of an island, because she'd looked it up in books. But she didn't feel like explaining all this to Avril. So she buried herself silently in thought. She thought Avril, despite her strange remarks and the fact that she didn't always seem to tell the truth, could perhaps become her friend. Not just because of the coincidence over their mothers, but because they had other things in common. Looking round her, for example, it was obvious that the two of them were much shorter than most of the girls in the room. And both of them were ugly. Well, perhaps Avril wasn't exactly ugly: without spots on her face, she might even have been pretty. As for herself, if she didn't have such a Luigi face... "What about the boy?" she suddenly thought, because there was a third witness to what was happening, the son of that guy who was clearly their mothers' friend. (Miguel was what they called him, impossible to avoid picking that up, the two of them must have said it a thousand times over: "Miguel, how wonderful, Miguel, what a surprise..." Elba glanced again at the three adults. "Were they never going to leave? What were they waiting for?... Thank goodness, it looked as though they were finally heading for the door, oh no... Don't tell me they're going to spend another half-hour there, one hand on the doorknob, saying goodbye, goodbye again, see you soon!"

"...All right, let's organize our reunion then. Now we've exchanged phone numbers, there's no excuse, is there?" It was the boy's father who was speaking.

"Luigi, why don't you arrange it?" now it was Avril's mother's turn.

"Of course I will," said Luisa, giving them another goodbye kiss.

By now Elba was sneaking a good look at the boy, Miguel's son. She had to admit he was quite good looking, although he was very quiet. She didn't really like boys of her own age, they seemed so childish, still playing cops and robbers and stuff. Besides, most of them weren't interested in girls, more fool them. This one, though, didn't seem too bad. Or rather, he might be all right except for his manner. Why so quiet, so withdrawn? Didn't he have any blood in his veins? Did it upset him to have such a dummy for a father?

"That's it, Miki," the man said, brushing the boy's hair back off his forehead, the way parents do. "Give me a kiss. I'll come and collect you at five o'clock, and if for any reason I can't make it, I'll ask Antonio."

"Oh hell," thought Elba, "now we know the little squirt is called Miki or Miguel, and he's got a brother called Antonio." Elba didn't agree with Avril that their names sounded ludicrous: Miguel and Antonio sounded like normal ones to her, so why then had the two mothers looked startled as soon as they heard them? They stood there staring at the boy as if something about him, or his face, could answer their anxious question.

"What did you say?" This time it was Luisa who spoke.

"Antonio is my son by my first marriage, and Miguel by the fourth: which means to say, four divorces and only two offspring, but despite all the matrimonial ups and downs I've been lucky. The two brothers adore one another."

"Antonio and Miguel..." said Avril's mother. It sounded to Elba as though she were trying to learn the names by heart.

"...As I was saying, they're inseparable," the father added. "That's lucky, given that Miki is... well, you'll get to know him, he's a very delicate child. So," the man concluded, holding out his hands palm upwards, as if explaining something self-evident, "what's important is that there are two Gasset brothers in the world again, just like before, except that Miki is eleven and Tony nearly twenty-eight years old."

This explanation produced a further round of laughter and farewells.

"Bye Elba. I'll be here to collect you at five. Behave yourself, now."

Luisa again. She returned to the room to give her daughter a kiss, and as she bent down whispered in her ear:

"Be careful, my love, that doll you care about so much is about to fall out of your school bag, you'd better put her somewhere else. You don't want to lose her, do you?"

"What is she on about? What on earth is Luisa talking about?"

It genuinely took Elba a while to understand and then, after a few seconds, like someone emerging from a long tunnel, or someone who hasn't heard dolls mentioned in years, she finally realized her mother was talking about that plastic object which so closely resembled her, the thing they had been arguing over that morning, perhaps a century ago.

"Take care of her, you don't want your baby to catch cold, do you?" said her mother with a smile she would doubtless call complicit.

"My *baby*? A *doll* catching *cold*? Whatever is Luisa talking about?" Then, as if it were something dead and gone, like someone throwing away an old and useless object, Elba tugged the doll out of her bag by the hair.

"D'you mean this, Luisa? Take it with you. Better still, throw it in the bin. Do whatever you like with it."

Her mother was on the point of taking it, relieved that at long last she could get rid of such an annoying obsession of her daughter's, when at the last moment Elba stopped her.

"No, I'd better put her away. Don't worry Mummy, you'll never see her again."

"Just as you like, sweetheart," said Luisa, delighted at the thought that her daughter was at last beginning to forget.

Carmen O'Inns's Lullabies

It's no coincidence that Carmen O'Inns has arranged to meet the dead boy's father at the Circulo de Bellas Artes café. Carmen O'Inns is an expert at what she herself calls "The Secret Language of Restaurants". She could have written a book or at least a fascinating study with a title like that, one discussing the best way to choose the perfect place for a romantic rendezvous. It's not that her meeting with Señor Beil was fixed to flirt with him – no, absolutely not, but love's little games can also be applied to professional relationships. Besides, you never know, do you?

"Take note, Isaac Newton," the detective had told her assistant earlier that morning, as she was getting dressed for the appointment (a camel suede coat and grey skirt, as ever worn with Wolford stockings... What to wear for a rendezvous is another topic well worth a book, but time presses).

"Take note, Isaac Newton, one of the basics in life is to know there's a restaurant for every occasion, and a café for every deed under the sun."

"I think your quote from Ecclesiastes runs more like: *To everything there is a season and a time to every purpose under the heaven*," said Isaac Tonñu who, having been brought up a Protestant, knew his Holy Bible by heart. "A time to be born, a time to die, a time to plant—"

"Shut up and listen, Newton, this is important. What would you think of a suitor who chooses a McDonalds as the setting to declare his love? Or a financial adviser who invites you to a restaurant that's as bad as it is expensive, when he's trying to convince you of his investment know-how? People

71

don't pay attention to these basic details in relationships, and they get what they deserve. They choose restaurants because the food is good, or because the decor is pleasant, or because they're fashionable, but very few of us choose them for the one thing that really matters – the message we want to convey to our companion. Would you pass me my bag? The light-brown crocodile skin one."

"And what message does that goldfish bowl at the Círculo de Bellas Artes convey?" asked Newton, who had only been there once in his life, when it had seemed to him noisy and packed with students. In a place like that, two people as worldly and conspicuous as Carmen O'Inns and Señor Beil would be bound to attract unnecessary attention.

"That's exactly why I've chosen it, dimwit: you can only be really sure that nobody will hear you if you go to a really noisy place. In bad novels, detectives meet their clients in dark and lonely dives – just the right kind of place for anyone to listen in if they want to; but if you choose a loud place instead..."

"Yes, I get what you're saying, but when you stand out so much in a place like that, surely you run the risk of being noticed, don't you?"

"Bingo again, Newton: it's important above all that you get noticed, because – take note again – *they need to think you're doing something else*, like flirting with your companion. That way, if at some point you find you need a witness, they'll come forward and say that *they think* they saw you, and not what really happened. Now pass me the powder compact, Othello, I think my nose is a little shiny. What do you think? Will Jaime Beil like me better with my hair up or down?"

Isaac Tonñu had almost learnt not to feel jealous over O'Inns's mania for mixing business with pleasure. In each of her adventures, his colleague flirted with her clients, with the suspects, even with the murderers. She called it "my way of working". He called it something else.

"What you've still not explained is the message you give Señor Beil by meeting him in such an unlikely, bohemian place. What is a man supposed to think when the detective he's hired—"

"His private investigator, if you don't mind, and my compact is telling me that I've got my Wolford tights in a bit of a twist."

"...OK, so when his private investigator decides to meet him in a cultural centre full of students, writers or aspiring painters?..."

Carmen O'Inns sighed. Sometimes she thought Providence had placed Isaac Tonñu in her path not so much to provide her with an assistant in her detective work – after all, it was she who ended up doing almost all of that – but to give her a kind of mental sparring partner to help clarify her ideas (very necessary in her profession: she spent all her time inventing hypotheses, making deductions, investigating, and there was no doubt it was far pleasanter to do all this with a handsome man than with an old-timer smoking a pipe like Maigret, or clutching a violin like Sherlock).

"Think about it, Newton, the explanation is very simple: you need to disconcert your client. No doubt Señor Beil was hoping I would fix a date with him in some hotel bar or other, or else in a discreet bistrot, perhaps in a fashionable restaurant. Somewhere as unexpected as the Circulo wrong-foots the other party, like a football team playing away, and what happens when a team plays away, dear heart?"

"They lose more easily?"

"Precisely... But don't get me wrong, Señor Beil and I are playing in the same team. Even so, the most important thing is to discover how little Oscar died. Did he drown? Was he drowned? If he was, who are our suspects? Lastly, what's the meaning of that crescent with its three red marks on the corpse's left temple? All these mysteries are still to be unravelled, and you know my methods tend to the unorthodox. That's why I need Señor Beil on my side. Even better, to become my accomplice. In other words, I need to convince him to do something he's not going to like one tiny bit."

As expected, Isaac Tonñu asked what that was. So Carmen O'Inns went on:

"I have to convince him – and the sooner the better – to invite Señorita Duval to dinner."

"The tap-dance teacher? The teacher who sent Oscar to look for the stopwatch at the swimming pool on the day he was killed? The one who talks so much and cries all the time? He's not going to want to. I bet he tells you to get me to do it, since I'm your partner. Just my luck, I can see myself comforting Señorita Duval and then, since I'm so practised at drying feminine tears, I'll end up having to go to bed with her to bring her more profound consolation. It's always the same: this job should attract danger money, because dealing with neurotic spinsters like her has catastrophic effects on the libido, O'Inns."

"No and no, ghastly, horrible, disastrous, scrub at least the last two paragraphs," Luisa told herself. "Her partner's character is getting ridiculous. Newton or Tonñu is meant to come from Belize, which means he speaks Spanish like a foreigner. He would never in his life talk about 'danger money' or 'dealing with neurotic spinsters'. The character is out of character: what a disaster!" she lamented. "That means I'll have to rejig all Isaac's dialogue, I can't possibly leave it like that."

Luisa scrolled up and reread the whole chapter, intending to highlight each expression that failed to match Newton's personality. Yet when she reached one passage of dialogue, spoken by Carmen O'Inns rather than Newton, something caught her eye. She paused the cursor and gave a green underline to the phrase:

what's the meaning of that crescent with its three red marks on the corpse's left temple?

She read it again. It was weird. Four weeks earlier, when she had begun the novel, and drafted the first chapter in which Oscar Beil's death in the swimming pool was mentioned, Luisa had decided the boy should have a mark or scar on his forehead. That would introduce a disturbing detail to make the reader uncertain from the very first pages. What could have caused that wound to the victim's forehead? Perhaps a blow? Could it indicate that someone had forced or held him underwater until he died? What does a wound shaped like a crescent with three red dots look like?

When Luisa had first thought of this, she'd been amused to consider where the idea had come from. At that time – she'd written the first chapter a few weeks before Elba had begun school, and so before she had met up with her two former classmates, Sofía and Miguel – what had first come to mind was a novel she had read a couple of years earlier. It was a story about childhood perversion, but she couldn't for the life of her recall who the author was, or the title. She did remember it was related to an old English nursery rhyme, like 'Little Bo Peep' or 'Mary Had a Little Lamb'...

In order not to unconsciously plagiarize the book, Luisa called an old university friend who was an expert in thrillers and B-movies, but he hadn't a clue either. She couldn't remember much of the book beyond its outline: an angelically beautiful young girl, who out of jealousy kills a classmate by bashing him over the head with a pair of tap shoes. She also remembered that when her mother found out the truth, the girl murdered her too.

It was this pair of tap shoes that Luisa was thinking of when she wrote the passage in which Oscar Beil is found floating in the swimming pool. Of course she had no intention of copying the idea of how the people were killed in that novel with the nursery rhyme title. She would find something else, and yet those tap shoes added a disturbing element she could exploit.

Out of all this she hit upon the idea of creating the character of a dance teacher, Señorita Duval, who could give the reader a first clue towards solving the mystery.

Luisa had understood absolutely nothing until now, returning to look at O'Inns's question concerning *what was the significance of this crescent-shaped mark on his left temple?* – how had she not noticed? An idea concealed behind another more innocuous one... In *Little Bo Peep* or *Mary had a Little Lamb*, or what the devil that book about childhood crimes she had read all those years ago was called, a boy had died following a blow to the head. But in the present instance, there had been no crime, only an accident. Luisa suppressed a swift shudder. It was easy for her to see that if she'd been interested in that novel some years earlier, it was because it had so much to do with her own life. "There's no such thing as innocent reading." Who had said that? Luisa couldn't remember that either (she was really having a bad day remembering literary allusions) but whoever it was, it was obvious they knew what they were writing about. If a book draws our attention, it's because it is telling us something we have already lived, or at least something we have already felt, because according to Nietzsche (well at least she'd remembered his name all right): "Nobody can get more than they already know from a book. They lack the ears to hear what they have not deduced from their own lived experience."

Luisa reversed the green underline to black on her computer screen. Then she stood up and took three quick steps towards the door. It was against her rules to break certain rituals or customs, yet her feet had a will of their own. "No, sweetheart," she told herself, "you know it's strictly forbidden to drink when you're writing. You're only allowed one or two Bloody Marys when you have to draw up the list of suspects, and that moment has already passed; the prime suspects in your book have already more or less been introduced. You have Señorita Duval, and Oscar's father, then there are the boy and girl who

76

were the victim's friends, though I still have to give them names and describe what…"

Three, four, five more steps towards the fridge. "Don't do it, you'll be breaking your routine, and only idiots despise routines. Those stupid, boring routines that not only offer us much-needed protection but are indispensable for all writers, whether we're blind or lame. Lame or blind…" How on earth had she been so lame she hadn't realized? How could she have been so blind not to see that at least in part she was rewriting the story of something that had happened forty years earlier in her own childhood?

"Yes, it's true," she told herself, "everybody writes their own story. What else are they supposed to write about? That's not the problem; the problem arises if you don't realize you're doing it. The problem is when you're too blind to see."

Just Like the Good Old Days

Elba had changed a lot for the better since starting at her new school. Apart from one minor argument, there had been no more incidents after her nosebleed and the tussle over the pound-shop doll. Nor had she ever asked again about her unknown father: the argument had been over something very different to Luisa's fears over her daughter. It had concerned the caretaker's cat. Luisa never liked to mention any weakness, but in the end she was forced to explain to Elba that she did not want that black-coated, yellow-eyed cat anywhere near her. This was not merely a whim but directly related to something that had happened when she was young. "You don't know what asthma is, sweetheart, and it's a bit complicated to explain, but when I was little I used to suffer badly from it. It actually made me very fearful and withdrawn. I've got over it now, and it never comes back, but ever since then I've been very careful about certain things, and one of them is cats. You do understand, don't you? I know all children love having pets, but it's not something we can allow ourselves."

From that day on Luisa never again saw the cursed cat prowling outside their door, and Elba never mentioned it. Luisa knew she played with the animal when she went downstairs, but there was nothing she could do about that. Apart from this, Elba had become far more obedient and docile. For example, Luisa was delighted when she came home after school: the two of them had tea, and then went off to their rooms like diligent students; she was busy writing about the adventures of Carmen O'Inns, Señor Beil and Señorita Duval, while Elba did her homework.

Elba had become inseparable from one of her classmates: none other than Sofía Márquez's daughter. She invited her home on as many afternoons as possible. "I should have recognized her as soon as I saw her," thought Luisa, "the minute I saw her standing there in the corridor leaning against the wall, with her blond hair drawn up in a ponytail just like her mother used to wear it. Perhaps I did recognize her without noticing it, and that's why I approached her."

Luisa liked to go and stand in the doorway to her daughter's bedroom and watch them for minutes on end. The two girls usually sat over by the window, very upright with their heads to one side as they concentrated on their work. Luisa had the impression it was she and Sofía sitting there, as if by some magic she had returned to her own childhood. All of a sudden, the gap between past and present vanished, and Avril became Sofía, Elba turned into Luisa. The fact was, the two young girls looked very similar to their mothers: Elba with her black hair cut short like a boy's, Avril as slender and pretty as her mother used to be, even if for the moment her beauty was somewhat spoilt by her adolescent acne. If she had not had those spots, Avril's face would have been a perfect copy of Sofía's: her gaze was exactly the same as her mother's, and so was the slightly cruel smile on her lips. The first time Luisa noticed how alike the two were she was taken aback, but she immediately decided not to attach any importance to it. "There's nothing strange," she told herself, "in the fact that two girls look like their mothers. Besides, it's not strictly true. Elba's manner for example is completely different from mine: she's not only much more self-confident, but more intelligent too. As for Avril, who knows? She doesn't seem to be like Sofía was at that age. She's not as stunning of course, and she seems more introverted, but perhaps I'm simply imagining things. Girls of their age don't really take after their mothers or fathers, they're far closer to other girls, and especially to their best friends. Just look at the two of them: they're starting to dress the same, they laugh in exactly the same way, and of course they use the same expressions when they speak. They're each as excruciating as the other, I can hardly tell them apart on the phone! Yes," she thought, laughing to herself, "it's just as well they don't actually look like one another at all, because otherwise, my dear, some day soon you'd have a real problem knowing which one is Elba and which one is Avril. Everybody knows that teenage girls are all clones."

At the same time, Luisa was making progress with her novel. Her current favourite candidate as the murderer of little Oscar Beil was Señorita Duval, the dance teacher. It seemed to her a pretty good idea to present the reader with a red herring, leading them to believe at first (this was after all a novel about childhood evil) that the murderer was a child, only later revealing that the mystery lay not in the youngsters' childhood, but in the teacher's own past. However, it was still too early to make a final decision about her. For example, she first needed to make more out of Oscar's two friends: she had not properly drawn their characters yet. All at once, Luisa decided that to make them more real she would base them on her former school friends Sofía and Miguel. She would even give them the same names. To avoid any later complications, when the novel was ready for publication, she would go back and change them. For now though, she needed to see them in action, to study what possibilities they offered. So naturally, she had to give them both good reasons for wanting to kill Oscar. "Let's see, what could they be?"

While she was searching for the most disturbing reason that could lead a child to commit murder, Luisa kept a close watch on what was happening around her. Three weeks after term began, Elba seemed to have matured rapidly. She might still be somewhat childish for her age, but already there was something adult about her gestures and movements. Avril too, despite her acne, remained more of a child than an adolescent, even though all the signs were that they had both entered that highly disconcerting growth spurt when changes take place with almost obscene speed. Luisa couldn't help looking at them like rare exotic flowers, undergoing subtle daily alterations: first a light down appearing on an upper lip, next their nipples pushing out against their lycra tops. To Luisa, the girls' sexual explosion was so disturbing – the more so since her own daughter was involved – that their own indifference amazed her. It was almost as if they had nothing to do with the revolutionary shifts taking place in their bodies. Had she been so unconcerned at her developing breasts, at the down on her upper lip? She was certain she hadn't. Luisa remembered many secret sessions alone in the bathroom observing her bodily changes. She also remembered having gone to school wearing a woollen jacket in the middle of June, in order to conceal the hint of her growing breasts, still so small they didn't require the redemptive support of a bra. Luisa could clearly recall that period of sexual limbo in which she was no longer a girl nor yet a woman, along with the surprise she felt at discovering a perspiration stain under her armpit, where she as yet had only a few straggling hairs, or the whiff of an unfamiliarly acrid smell which seemed to permeate her whole body. Luisa remembered that whole explosive period as one of shock and fear, yet neither Elba nor Avril seemed to experience either emotion in the least. It was as though both of them were indifferent to the changes: they neither hid them nor showed them off. They simply went on as before, with their alternate routines of study and games.

Games: now there was a real change. Perhaps because Luisa was aware of how imperceptibly these games changed in the confusing years of puberty – how for example cops and robbers could turn into a far less innocent game without the rules or even its name changing at all – she could spot the telltale signs in the girls' attitude. Although their beloved dolls had finally been consigned to the back of the wardrobe (even the hideous one that Elba had claimed so much resembled her and which Luisa never saw again), she thought she could detect how certain of their pastimes, such as dressing up, dancing in front of the mirror or singing, together with all the other activities they so enjoyed, had changed at least in one respect: all of them were now accompanied by the maximum amount of chit-chat and excited whispers.

In addition, the two girls were capable of spending hours alone in Elba's room, just sitting on the bed talking. Then, after the time came for Avril to return home, only a few minutes went by before they were phoning each other to continue their apparently interminable dialogue. They also got into the habit of writing one another endless emails. Elba often used to print them out and store them in a file on which she had written: "SECRET: KEEP OUT", and which lay open and challenging on her top bookshelf like a banner proclaiming "Freedom". Occasionally, since Elba had got into the bad habit of using her mother's high resolution printer rather than her own, she would leave behind one or two of the sheets intended for her private folder, and Luisa had been tempted to glance at them, if only out of literary curiosity. After all, her two child characters, now baptized Sofía and Miguel, were about the same age as Elba and Avril, so it would have been very useful to know precisely what language the girls used when no one else was around. However, unable to break her own rules, Luisa had not dared read another person's correspondence. Instead, she simply observed them growing up day by day, and confirmed their almost physical need to tell each other everything, to continually confess what they had done to one another, to the extent that they hardly had time for any other games and activities. A couple of weeks earlier, when she had returned from one of her trips, she brought them each a gift they had desperately wanted: a mobile phone. Just as in earlier generations the purchase of long trousers for a boy, or of a pair of girl's shoes with just the hint of a high heel, had been the symbol of incipient adulthood, now that moment ("much earlier than when I was young," Luisa thought to herself, "much earlier") seemed to be the purchase of a mobile. Luisa warned her daughter that her tariff only allowed her a fixed number of calls per month, and that if she exceeded that, it would come out of her allowance. Even so, this did nothing to deter her. Elba had always been disciplined in her spending, but she now appeared happy to pay any extra expense simply in order *to speak*. To call Avril every night, to send her an infinite number of text messages, to offer a running commentary on even the minutest activity and on every thought.

"Well I suppose that most clearly marks the end of childhood," Luisa said to herself resignedly. "Little girls play, adolescents talk and confide in one another."

Despite such a close friendship between their two girls, Luisa had not seen Sofía Márquez since the first day of term. They had managed to speak on the phone a couple of times, to congratulate one another on what great friends their daughters had become, but the conversation always ended with a "let's make sure we meet up soon" – a promise which was never fulfilled. Elba had adapted very well to the new school. Her marks were good, and this meant there was no real need for Luisa to pursue a meeting with Sofía which neither really wanted to take place. "Just like the characters in the film I told you about, *Back to School* or whatever it was called," said Enrique one day when he asked her whether she had seen her former classmates again, and she had replied "No". "The outcome of the film was far too obvious, but it did have one truly unsettling psychological aspect. As far as I can remember, those children who committed the murder together—" "That's enough, Ri. I've told you a thousand times that it wasn't—" Luisa interrupted him. Whereupon he ("with all the sensitivity of a charging rhinoceros," thought Luisa) went on: "I know, my love, but where's your sense of humour?" ("Typical man, to confuse a sense of humour with an utter lack of tact," thought Luisa). "OK, I know that in your case there was no murder. But from what you've told me, there was an accident leading to the death of a boy. Believe me, that's why the three of you don't really want to meet up. However, it seems to me it would be far healthier to talk about it in the open. Horror stories are like infected boils," ("Hurrah for the poet, full marks to the amateur psychoanalyst," thought Luisa). "They're just like a big pimple, squeeze hard and all the pus bursts out."

Luisa always rejected his advice with a "Don't talk nonsense, Ri". After all, it might have been true that the novel she was writing did have some points in common with the incident in her childhood, there was no need to give it too much weight. Because, as she also told herself more and more frequently, all the obsessions and dark sides of childhood could provide a useful source for her literary purposes, but, once she had closed her computer, she also had to forget this unhealthy rummaging in her past if she didn't want to become one of the many dotty writers who already existed. Besides, if she had "forgotten" to ring Sofía and Miguel and organize the reunion, it was not out of a secret doubt, still less fear, but simply because of what all of us attribute to a general kind of excuse like a "lack of time" or simply the inertia of daily life taking over, and postponing anything that wasn't urgent, immediately rewarding or offering the promise of future pleasure.

That was why, since the idea of meeting up again failed to fit this list, Luisa was more than surprised to wake up one night dreaming of Miguel. There were no images from the past in her dream: Miguel as the boy she had known didn't figure. Miguel as a man, however, did put in an appearance, accompanied by a moist and unfamiliarly pleasurable sensation. Luisa tried not to move, not even to see the time, because she recalled from past experience (oh so distant!) that delicious dreams of this sort are by nature fragile and evaporate at the first intrusion of external reality. She curled up again and almost at once Miguel's body appeared next to hers, as if he were asleep with his back turned to her. She ran two fingers up the full length of his naked legs to the point where she could feel the gentle beginnings of a growth of hair. Her fingers continued to the coccyx, then on up the spine where the vertebrae formed a perfect ladder, helping her hands up to his shapely shoulders and the nape of his neck. Luisa, who felt a strong desire to turn his head round to kiss him, was suddenly terrified: all too often, dreams are either treacherous or cruel or both together, and it was possible that, if she forced him to turn around, she could be confronted by an old, withered face or, worse still, a childlike one, covered in blood. "With a cut on his forehead, the mark close to his temple," said a cautionary, wakeful voice that had somehow slipped into her dreams. "Don't pull him round, Luisa, leave him as he is, caress just his back, not his face, follow the same path back down his spine if you wish, with kisses this time, if you prefer. Best not to tempt fate. Beware of dreams, only fools and adolescents would have the nerve to turn a strange body round and look it in the face. Dreams are like the curse of siren songs: they urge us on to marvellous adventures, only to plunge us back into nightmares. You'll see – the dead child's scar, Antonio's mark, will appear on the forehead of his adult brother, Miguel. Be very careful."

Yet, as if she really were a fool or an adolescent or both, Luisa decided to continue. She had already caressed that perfect back and needed to caress the other side of him too. "Don't do it!" her watchful voice again called out, but the voice of her dream whispered: "Go on, go on," and proved to be the stronger one. Her hands were already cradling Miguel's head to pull him around, and to her infinite relief she discovered there was no reason to be afraid. It was not the child Antonio's face looking back at her, but the adult Miguel. His smooth forehead showed no sign of the blow that had disfigured his brother, there were no signs of death at all. Quite the opposite: he was alive and warm, and now the sleeping man's lips parted in a smile, so she thought she glimpsed that slight unevenness in his incisors she had loved so much as a girl. The sensation lasted no more than a second, for that same mouth was already seeking out hers in an endless kiss.

Hours later, beneath the hot water of the power shower, already reviving the sensation of those caresses, Luisa relived all the tender moments she had dreamt of. She struggled to remember how many years it had been since dreams had offered her a night of love; many, far too many. "Now I'm going to be thinking about that man like a silly schoolgirl," she thought, "and probably this very morning or some other night I'll find myself trying to retrace the paths my fingers tracked on a body I hardly know." Luisa let the water caress her a while longer and then, imitating the slow sweep of her finger on Miguel's skin, she stroked her own neck, pausing here and there, and the deception was so pleasurable she closed her eyes for a few seconds, reopening them like someone expecting to witness another miracle, then paused to see the distance her fingers had covered. It was now she saw, on the inside of her left arm, only a few centimetres from her shoulder, a red, round, almost semi-circular mark. After she had emerged from the shower and dried herself, she looked down again, expecting it to have vanished, but it was still there, as stubborn as the memory of adolescent love. "It's a kiss," she told herself, "it's as though last night someone kissed me passionately, and gave me what the English call a 'love bite'. Oh, what nonsense you're talking, Luisita, you must have scratched yourself: you're going nuts, you really are. All these stupid ideas you get, at your age. Come on, get dressed, enough of that rubbish." And – like someone who wanted to make a clean break with an embarrassing situation – Luisa took some foundation fluid out of her make-up purse, and rubbed two dabs onto the red patch. That was all it took to conceal the mark.

Yet several days later, when the semicircle on her arm no longer needed covering up, and her dreams had reverted to their normal, boring routine, without the faintest hint of arousal, Luisa rummaged in her handbag, in among the pieces of paper, post-its and business cards she kept in her old diary, trying to find Miguel Gasset's mobile phone number. It didn't take her long to unearth what she was looking for: a leaf torn from a school notebook where she herself had written down Miguel and Sofía's numbers on Elba's first day at school. She had done it so rapidly, or so carelessly, that the two names were so close to each other that it was impossible to decipher which one went with what number. "Scatty as ever," she told herself. "Now you'll probably call Sofía imagining you're ringing Miguel. And if Sofía is like I remember her, she'll laugh out loud at my confusion, and start circulating her own rumours. Of course," she told herself, "I could ring both of them without saying who I was calling..." But after she'd already begun dialling the first number, she suddenly thought that no, it was far better and more natural to meet Miguel the first time by using the pretext of the dinner she had been delegated to organize but had never got around to. "Why do you want to meet him anyway? I don't know, no particular reason, just to see how he is now, as an adult. But then I'd also like to see how Sofía is, call it *literary curiosity*, or *professional curiosity*, if you prefer. Fine, the next week I have to be in Frankfurt to give readings at the book fair, but when I get back I'll invite Sofía and Miguel around for dinner one evening, so it can be just the three of us. (Are you sure it's only *professional curiosity*? What else could it be?) Anyway," she told herself convincingly, "Enrique's right: what could be more natural than old friends meeting over dinner because they'd decided to get together after forty years?"

Avril and Sofía

Elba: my mums off nxt wk. wll gt hr 2 cll u so I cn stay there. kool huh?'

    Avril: At my hse?

    Elba: Yes.ok?

    (No reply from Avril).

    Elba: OK!!?

    (No reply).

    Elba: Sht, gl OK?? Ok???

    (No reply).

The special telephone ritual the girls performed was always the same. Every evening after dinner, they talked to each other for as long as possible, but always on the landline so as not to waste their mobile credit. Early in the morning, they might send each other a text message before school, but once they were there, their mobiles sat quietly, switched off and silent, only to spring back to life after class, with further txts to arrange 2 mt.

    Elba: am i styng with u or nt?

    (No reply from Avril).

    Elba: U crazy or wot? I snt U 5 txts.

    (Still no reply, then two text messages later):

    Elba: Dsnt mtter, my mum ll cll yrs 2 invte me + thts it.

Usually the girls would meet in Elba's flat rather than at Avril's, but that week there was a change of scene. Whenever Luisa needed to make a journey, she used to ask the housekeeper to come and stay with Elba. The woman had no children and, although her husband protested, she always managed to get her way. This time, however, her husband had a perfect excuse for saying no. "An acute case of colic, Luisa, you should see him. I don't dare leave him on his own, but if you like, you can bring Elba over to my place, and she can sleep in the living room." Luisa was considering taking her up on the offer, but Elba had other plans. She wanted to stay with her friend, just as Avril had so often done with her. What could be more normal? So why on earth was her mother so against it?

"Well, because things don't work like that, sweetheart, believe you me. You can't just turn up at someone's house without even having been invited. Avril didn't suggest this, did she? You have to understand that some people don't open their homes to others that easily."

"Oh come on, Mummy, you can arrange it. You've known her mother since you were kids, haven't you? Give her a ring, pleeease, Mummy, do."

Elba had changed a lot in recent weeks. Not just physically: she was very affectionate, cloyingly so, but Luisa was well aware of the reason why her daughter used that word *Muuummy* like that, and refused to budge. She also knew that if a girl, in this case Avril, hadn't even suggested that Elba stay at her place, it was because she and not her mother wanted to avoid the visit. Quite why this should be so was harder to understand. Kids' stuff, she guessed.

All the same, as the time for her trip drew nearer and Elba persisted in wanting to stay with Avril, Luisa finally gave in. After all, she had been considering ringing Sofía anyway, to organize their reunion with Miguel, and if she – or her daughter – really didn't want Elba to sleep over there, they could tell her fairly and squarely, in which case she would no longer have to hear all her daughter's pleas or whines of *Muummy*.

Contrary to her expectations, Sofía was delighted at her suggestions, both that the three friends should have dinner together when Luisa got back from Frankfurt, and also that Elba should stay with them. "I like your daughter a lot," Sofía had said. "I get on especially well with her. It'll be like when you and I were small, won't it Luigi? I used to love going over to your place, and having you come over to mine. In those days, if you remember, we had very similar apartments, in fact we used to live in the same neighbourhood, near where you've moved now. Now I'm afraid it won't be the same, 'cause I'm what they call one of the New Poor, whereas you're going from strength to strength."

There was no note of envy in her voice, more one of condescension. For a moment Luisa imagined her former classmate exactly as she had been all those years ago. Whereas physically she was unrecognizable, her voice still had that old sound, the same attractive lisp that Luisa had endlessly attempted to copy as a young girl.

"Yes, Luigi, so you see. What goes around comes around: now I belong to the select club of the New Poor, whereas you're going places, and I couldn't be more pleased for you."

"True," thought Luisa, her friend hadn't changed a bit. To judge from the tone of her voice, she was just as free of envy as in her childhood, because Sofía – or at least the Sofía she had known – might have had a thousand defects, but that was not one of them. This was quite logical: why would the girl who had it all – money, beauty, a sense of humour to boot – fall prey to the green-eyed monster?

"Now she's lost the lot," thought Luisa, still on the telephone, although she had to admit that in their conversation Sofía had shown she could still laugh at herself.

"So you can warn Elbita not to expect any great luxury. Just to give you an idea: Avril's bedroom is more or less the size of the broom cupboard back at the family home on Calle Alfonso XII. Do you remember when you first came round and I shut you in it? How silly of me, you were such a little mite back in those days, and now look how things have changed. As for me... Or rather, you've become what I ought to have been, given what

91

everyone was predicting back then. Who would have thought it, eh Luigi?"

Luisa hung up with a sense of elation she'd never felt before. She was in the front hall, standing in front of the smaller mirror. Then, as she'd so often seen Elba do, she turned back to look at herself in the larger one, as if she too was expecting to spot a ghost. Instead of a phantom, the result of a reflection from one mirror into another, she saw the shadow of the little girl she had once been, dark and skinny, her hair cropped like a boy, and a face that was neither ugly nor pretty. It was no effort to recall Sofía at that time, her exact opposite, and then, effortlessly, to superimpose one image onto the other to produce a new appearance that looked disconcertingly like her own now. "How odd," she thought. "As if Luigi the Silly, Luigi the Prude, Luigi the Asthmatic, who had always wanted to be Sofía, had finally succeeded and was taking revenge. *Yes* – after all, what is success, if not the greatest and most subtle of all forms of revenge?"

The Further Investigations of Carmen O'Inns

"To sum up, Newton, where are we? Who are the dramatis personae of our story? And who are the main suspects?"

"Well, let's see, O'Inns. On the one hand we have the tap-dance teacher Señorita Duval, a source of concern because she's hiding a shady past in which another accidental death occurred, in circumstances remarkably similar to Oscar's. Then we have Sofía and Miguel, the dead boy's chums. As yet we don't know too much about them, except that they were close to him when the accident happened."

"Is there anyone else you're worried about?"

"For now, we shouldn't leave anyone off the list. Not even Señor Beil, Oscar's father, whom you've asked to check out the tap-dance teacher, and who seems very taken with his role as a possible detective."

"Far too taken with it," Isaac Newton thought to himself, allowing his fingers to stray down Carmen's neck, slowly stroking it as if searching for some trace or mark left by other fingers that might have intruded there a few hours earlier.

"There are a handful of other suspects we shouldn't rule out," O'Inns's assistant went on, "indeed everyone on the school payroll, including cleaners, teachers, the cook and her kitchen boy…"

"Anyone else, my love?"

Isaac Newton continued to let his fingers slide further down her throat but stopped at her collarbone, deliberately avoiding the temptation to go any further. He knew that was precisely what she wanted, because Carmen O'Inns missed no chance to tell him how much she liked him stroking her body's erogenous zones. But he wasn't going to do so, no way! Playing on someone's desires was a delicate balancing act, one they both indulged in the full knowledge of when it was best to cast aside all the rules. For now, though, he ran his fingers down her arm and said: "We still have one more suspect."

"Child or adult?" said O'Inns, breathing out heavily.

"Very adult. I mean…"

Newton's fingertips slowed gradually on their delightful journey, until they came to a halt. One of his expert fingertips had encountered a slight irregularity on the inside of her left arm: what could it be? Newton looked down to inspect it, saying: "According to my investigations, it's someone with a very dark past. I still have a couple more people to talk to, but…"

But… what was that on her arm?

"Carry on, Newton, don't stop. What were you saying?"

"I was just saying that among his possessions I've unearthed a *bilongo*. Do you know what that is?"

"I'm a Cuban, remember. Of course I know what it is. A *bilongo* is what, in Cuban witchcraft, they call a fetish spell. They come in many different kinds, but they usually contain flies, hairs and other disgusting substances. Apparently they're used for…"

Newton wasn't listening. Newton couldn't care less how erudite Carmen O'Inns could wax on the subject of Cuban *santería*, since he had just discovered a red semicircle on the soft, inside skin of the detective's arm.

"*Aue!*" he exclaimed, a Belizean invocation of the same master spirits, "*Aue Sofylo!*" It was obvious that only a short while earlier, someone had been tracing the same path down Carmen's body and here was the irrefutable evidence in the form of a love bite. "*Yes indeed, a bloody fucking love bite!*" Newton swore indignantly to himself. "Who else could have done it but Señor Beil, bloody fucking Señor Beil, amateur detective and potential murder suspect? Fine," thought Newton, "so that's how O'Inns obtains her information, is it? By sleeping with suspects? Of course, she can do what she likes with her body, but don't let her come begging to me for sex after all that. Enough... No more... That does it!"

Newton closely examined her inside arm again, to confirm his diagnosis. He did it so gently and she took it as a caress, sighing even more deeply...

"Ah..."

"Yes, clear as daylight," Isaac Newton told himself, making a point of moving away from O'Inns and her embraces. "Another man has been there ahead of me. What else could the mark be? How ironic it should so resemble the one on Oscar Beil's corpse, and the mark on his left temple."

It was then, as she finished page 96 of her *Adventures of Carmen O'Inns*, that Luisa realized all the remaining sheets in the pile were not typed in Baskerville Old Face but Times New Roman, which she never used. "For God's sake, don't tell me Elba's at it again," she grimaced. She'd already told her a thousand times not to borrow her printer: that was why she'd bought her a smaller one of her own. Yet here was the proof, no two ways about it, that Elba had disobeyed her yet again. All these sheets in another typeface must have been left by Elba. Who else? Her daughter never took the trouble to reload the paper tray, so that whenever Luisa pressed *Print* the machine ejected quantities of Elba's stuff mixed in with the manuscript of her novel. "Now," thought Luisa, "instead of 97 onwards of Carmen O'Inns's adventures, I've got pages of nonsense from Elba or perhaps Avril, since the two of them are always corresponding as intensely as if they were lovers, one living in Madrid and the other in Havana. Not satisfied with mailing one another, they insist on printing out and keeping the emails. So Elba has a folder full of bits of paper, with 'SECRET: KEEP OUT' written in red on the cover – as if I were going to read anyone else's correspondence. I'll have to have a serious chat with her, I've had it up to here and that's enough of her teenage crap. Enough of her taking stuff that isn't hers, enough of wearing my clothes and, now, using my printer."

It was true, Luisa would never have read those printouts in Times New Roman mixed in with her novel, were it not for the very first line:

Topic: The Story of Sofía and Antonio 2. Read it then we'll talk. XX Avr.

Love

Some years earlier, when Avril Márquez was much younger and wanted to prevent something from happening, she would sit on the edge of the bed, screwing up her eyes, and wish with all her might that a huge catastrophe would come along: any fire, flood or earthquake that could disrupt the normal course of events, and so avoid her having to attend the dentist, or take her Grammar exam. She knew the spell worked. Not literally, because she hadn't actually managed to make a cataclysm occur, but something must have had an effect on the heavens, because whenever the dreaded moment came, it never turned out to be as fateful as she had feared. Her mother always said she should be cautious with what she wished for, because fortune had a bad habit of granting everything, only in unexpected ways. "The worst of it is, sometimes it can take years to get what you desire, and by then you no longer desire it. At others, it comes at too high a cost; then again, it can come in return for you sacrificing something that matters much more to you. So you have to be extremely careful what you wish for, lest it becomes reality."

Perhaps her mother was right this time, and in a few years destiny would bring what she so wanted, but Avril couldn't wait that long. So she preferred another method, knowing that praying for an earthquake didn't alter the proper course of events, but did slightly shift things around. It was as if the telluric powers of natural phenomena (her geography textbook was full of these words and Avril loved the sound of them) could produce a faint tremor, a minimal modification of events, so that they no longer occurred in the terrifying way she had feared. So, despite having wished with all her might for Elba not to come and stay while her mother was abroad, Avril was sure that something vaguely like an earthquake would guarantee that Elba wouldn't remember a thing of what she had seen there. Not the shabby state of the furniture, nor the gloom of the bedroom where the three silver picture frames were displayed, still less the smell of boiled cabbage rising from the inner courtyard. No, fortune smiled on Avril and always awarded her a consolation prize in place of a longed-for earthquake. A tiny tremor which she was certain would erase anything Elba might think about the economic straits she and her mother found themselves in. That substitute earthquake so desired by Avril, even without knowing what shape it would take, turned out to be love.

Elba and Avril had often chatted about how silly this word that everyone else used so frequently actually sounded. To them, at least up until recently, "love" was a stupid expression, even in the way you had to purse your lips to say it. Then there was the way people in love looked stupid, and how creepy love songs were, how ridiculous their billing and cooing, how pathetic their expressions. Until then, the girls and their friends had avoided mentioning the word, preferring to say things like "I like him"; "I'm all for him"; even "I'm going out with him" – even if "going out" meant no more than walking round and round the school playground together. Love was a taboo word, only soppy girls used it. So how come such a strange term could come and cause an earthquake in their lives?

When Avril thought of the five days Elba had spent at her place against her wishes, the first thing she recalled was a phone call her mother took the night before she had arrived.

"...Of course, Avril will be delighted to go, I'm sure of it, she's crazy about birthday parties. We'll be coming with Elba – you know, Luisa's daughter – who'll be spending a few days with us..."

"…Yes, I know you spoke to her, she called me too, for the three of us to hook up next week. For us three to get together again, after all these years, fantastic… a great idea."

"…Getting back to the birthday party, what present should I bring your son? I'd like to bring something special, for old time's sake, Miguel."

Avril had become increasingly annoyed as she listened to this scrap of conversation. An invitation to a birthday party didn't seem like the kind of earthquake she so desperately desired when she shut her eyes. As for the boy, what boy were they talking about? She couldn't mean that new kid, Miki Gasset, could she? The son of her mother's former schoolmate? Neither she nor Elba were interested in the birthdays of little squirts from their own year, still less a shrimp like him, so quiet they'd hardly exchanged two words. He was a real oddball, always on his own.

"Perfect. Do give me the address… From half-past five to eight o'clock, is it?"

("Five-thirty until eight," Avril thought to herself in disgust. "The time when only shrimps hold parties.")

"The corner of Alfonso XII and Montalbán? I don't believe it. Didn't you know I once lived in the same street when I was a kid, how strangely things can turn out… In those days I was…"

("In those days my mother was like them, like all rich people," thought Avril, unable to suppress a shudder when she saw her mother seated on the bed, never finishing a single sentence, the way she always did when she was upset, and running her thumbnail down a groove in the bedhead as she spoke. "One day I'll be like my mother," she thought, "just like Sofía.")

"…Of course, now I know that, it'll make it much easier to bring them. I guess you don't happen to live on the fourth floor, do you?… You do? Incred… incre… how strangely things…

It'll be like going home, after so many... like going back in time. Big kiss, José Antonio, I mean Ant... I mean of course Mig... a big kiss anyway."

Avril didn't know which of the two bits of information was more intriguing: the fact the party she had just been invited to would take place at her mother's old apartment, or the man's name she had half-heard her mother mention. It was typical of Sofía to leave her words unfinished, whenever she was surprised, but Avril could have sworn she almost said the name *José Antonio*. Avril had been going into Sofía's room to ask for some shampoo when she discovered her on the phone, and had come to a halt in the doorway, pausing there quietly as if awaiting further revelations.

"What's the matter, Avril? What do you want?"

"Who're you talking to, Ma?"

"To Miki Gasset's father. He's inviting you and Elba to Miki's birthday party this Friday..."

"What were you saying about returning to your old home? And which Antonio did you mean? Tell me."

"Antonio? There isn't an Antonio and you shouldn't be listening to other people's conversations, because that's the best way to get everything mixed up."

Her mother had stood up and was smoothing down her skirt. She raised her hand to her head to push back a lock of hair that had slipped out of her slide and was falling in her eyes. Then she crossed in front of the wardrobe, where the half-open door offered her a mirror image, but she didn't pause to check her hairstyle. In Sofía's flat, mirrors were an aid to the most basic daily rituals: cleaning your teeth in the bathroom, checking your clothes were straight before leaving the bedroom; apart from this, no one ever looked in them. "Why?" She wouldn't hesitate to explain to anyone who asked: "It's a bit too much like looking into the past, so it's stupid to do it if you're not going to like what you see."

"I also heard you say the Gasset family live in your old apartment, Ma. I'm sure I heard that."

"That's enough, sweetheart. I was only confirming the boy's address and the time we were invited. Isn't it great? We've got a plan in place for when Elba comes, so you won't have to worry about your friend getting bored to death while she's here. You know how much you like parties!"

Avril, who had in fact never liked birthday parties, as her mother knew very well, said: "Yes, Ma… brilliant idea… I'm really thrilled," because she thought this might be the only occasion she'd get to visit her old family home and see how things might have turned out if her mother's life hadn't taken so many twists and turns.

"The chance to retrace my steps into the past is so tempting," she thought, "so, who knows? It might just be the first sign that somewhere or other a secret earthquake is about to happen."

True to their habit of sharing everything, that same afternoon Avril sent Elba an email saying how she had just discovered that Miki Gasset, the quiet boy nobody paid any attention to, lived in the apartment that had once belonged to her family, adding that they would both get to see it at his birthday party on Friday. She told her, without making a big deal of it, that Sofía had called Miki's father either "Antonio" or "José Antonio", despite the fact that she knew perfectly well he was called Miguel, just like his shrimp of a son.

Elba had replied at once, so excited that she left no spaces between the words: "Don't be silly, don't you realize that's the real secret? Those two have known each other since they were kids, right? 'Jose Antonio' just happens to be the name we heard before. Don't you know my father's also called Antonio? Of course mine, according to my mother, is far younger than she is, so they can't possibly be the same person. Whereas yours… who knows? How really lucky you are, Avril, now you'll know once and for all where you come from and who you are."

It was pointless telling Elba her fantasy made no sense, that she was simply imagining it, and that she remembered perfectly well having heard that Miki's father was called Miguel, yes, Miguel, absolutely, nothing to do with José Antonio, still less Antonio on its own. Avril herself would confirm as much that Friday in the Shrimp's apartment and, if she had told the story of her mother's confusion over the names, it was only to show Elba how agitated her mother had become on learning that the Gasset family were living in her old home. Of course it was something that must have awakened old memories in her mother, and no doubt this was the reason she had muddled up the names. So many intriguing secrets! Avril finished her email with: "…hopefully I'll discover a bit more on the day of the party. Who knows? Isn't it brilliant to be able to spy on the past, Elba? And to learn how things would have been if they hadn't all got so mixed up?"

But Elba didn't understand, nor had she ever understood how Avril could be so fascinated by the mysteries of a distant past while there were so many more close at hand, like the one surrounding the name "Antonio". Nor did she understand how her friend could be so blind and so trusting: "They're deceiving you, Avril, it'll be the same for you as it was with me and my mother. Adults only explain things by halves, and they always lie to us."

It was no use her friend trying to explain that she didn't think Sofía was lying to her, that she had told her when she was a little girl that she had no father and that, if they had to choose between mysteries, she was much more intrigued by a different one – that of her mother's world before life began to turn somersaults. "Come on Elba, it's not worth getting into such a state about it, there must be thousands, perhaps millions, of children in the world who know nothing about their real parents, but they don't let that stop them loving the ones they are with. Stop harping on about it. Forget it! There's no point going round and round in circles, or feeling different because you don't have a father. I don't have one either, and so what? Anyway, some secrets are best left untouched, because most likely they are unhappy or very ugly, or both. You yourself say that girls who give themselves airs are the biggest idiots. On the other hand, what happens when you know, when you're really and truly sure that *yes*, there really was once a past much happier than the present, eh, Elba?"

Elba hadn't even bothered to read the last part of Avril's email. For some time now, she had let her fingers fly over the keyboard, writing one sentence after the next, without commas, full stops, or any punctuation: "howluckyyouare Avri idsolike to beyou, nowyoullbe able tofindoutwhat your past waslike goingback to your mothers house, andthatway youll discover oyur future too. Kidswith Fathers" (Elba had written the word in the plural and with a capital letter) "youneverthink aobut it ofcourse, but thoseofus whodont cant seeinto the future, because weve nowhere to seeourselves in. Everyonein the family isamirror. Haventyoualways thought ofitlike that? Father mothergrandparents unclesandaunts are mirrors, whether bigsmall, exaggerated, deceiving, dirty, rearview mirrors, Snow White's mirror mirror on the wall, or a fairground hall of mirrors: who cares? Some ugliersome prettier but in each and every one of them youre there, howeverlittle attention you pay them. Whereas we orphansdont have anyone to seeourselves in, so we haveto look for ourselvesinsomeone, someone who…"

Elba went on tapping so hurriedly she kept on joining up the words, until finally Avril got tired of trying to decipher the email and closed down her computer. Elba could think what she liked, even that Antonio could be the person they had heard about, or someone else like Elba's own father even, if you allowed your imagination to run away with you… When she got a bee in her bonnet, it was impossible to get her to change her mind. "She'll get over it tomorrow," thought Avril, "when she realizes that there's no Antonio in that apartment."

Antonio and Another Love

"Oh my God, I'm going to die!"

"What are you talking about, Elba?"

"Feel how my heart's thumping, Avri."

"I told you, don't call me Avri…"

"Sorry, but put your hand here, will you? I think I'm about to die."

"Don't talk nonsense. Come on and finish cleaning your teeth. Let's get to bed. You're raving. What about the performance you put on this afternoon?"

"What are you talking about? What happened was perfectly normal. All I did was fall in love…"

"Fall in love? Don't be silly, Elba, you're still only eleven."

"Yes, I fell in love, so what? You were the one to put on a performance, and what a pathetic one it was…"

Usually, other than in anything related to the past, Elba and Avril saw everything through the single, astonished lens of their shared adolescence: they wept at the same films; sang along to the same songs; laughed in unison; were amazed at the same things; used identical catchphrases to express happiness or sadness. They viewed the world in such harmony that they were as surprised as anyone else at their differences that evening. Because, as soon as the door to Miki Gasset's flat swung open at 5.30 on the dot, Elba and Avril saw two very distinct places. Although the people they saw might have been the same, they perceived them in a very different light. For example, before they'd even properly gone inside, Avril had been unaware of who opened the door, because she was in such a hurry to look right and left to take in everything she could see. By contrast,

Elba could not take her eyes off the person who had come to the door, and she only had eyes for him, not only for the next few hours but for ever thereafter.

"What are you doing? What are you talking about? Are you crazy, Elba?" Avril asked her when they were back at her mother's flat a few hours later. She was annoyed to see how her friend kept spinning in circles clutching her pillow, staring at herself in the small mirror on the bedroom dressing table without really seeing herself, and not taking in anything in the room around her: neither the damp patches on the wall nor the shabby furniture.

"You're off your head, Elba, come down from the clouds. He'll never notice you exist, so don't get your hopes up. He could be your father, you're nothing more than a baby to him, just a friend of his brother the Shrimp. He—"

"He, he, are you too scared to mention his name? He's called Tony—"

"Scared? Don't be such an idiot, Elba. Scared of what?"

There was no reply because Elba was still going round in circles, hugging the pillow, without noticing her feet were entangled in the fraying carpet and repeating over and over her new word – "Tony" – as if it were a spell – "Tony" – as if no one had ever said it before, standing on tiptoe to make herself taller, raising her arms to wrap them around Tony's invisible neck. Tony was tall, grown up, nothing like his brother the birthday boy, the silly, silent Shrimp whom Elba hadn't spared a glance at the whole afternoon because she had been so busy gazing at Tony as he took photos of the party, or organized the treasure hunt, or got them all together to sing 'Happy Birthday' to the poor little squirt. That was why Elba was now twirling round and round with her pillow, repeating his name over and over, feeling so very grown up and oblivious to everything else.

"What rubbish, Elba, that has to be enough!"

Avril had never seen her friend so distracted, so unaware of her surroundings. Of course, she wasn't in the least bothered about what Elba might think of life in general, or of birthdays in particular. She wasn't even concerned what she might think about the state of the furniture or the flat. If Elba had fallen in love, so had she, but the objects of their devotion were entirely different. Avril was equally unable to see anything more than the reason for her elation, love which embellishes everything, which paints pockmarked walls unsullied pink, makes even old furniture look brand new. As a result, that night the two girls fell asleep, each cherishing a dream. Elba's dream was called "Tony Gasset". He was very tall and had big hands. He smiled in a very special way that offered a glimpse of slightly and deliciously uneven teeth. He was almost twenty-eight years old – twenty-eight marvellous, adult, bewitching years that made him so handsome and yet so inaccessible to any young girl of eleven. Anyone, that is, except for Elba, who – as she told Avril – was already busy planning a whole series of strategies in order to meet him by chance, to talk to him, to become a part of his life, even if that meant she first had to make friends with his brother, that poor and invisible Miki Gasset, the Shrimp nobody noticed. Elba knew that for the moment this was only a dream, but she thought that in the not-too-distant future it might become reality, for although Avril had never told her about the telluric power of desire, she had her own way of making her dreams come true. If this involved chasing after them, giving them a helping hand, somehow getting them within her grasp, that's what she'd do the very next morning, or so she promised herself.

The object of Avril's desire, on the other hand, was not made of flesh and blood but rather of the escapist fabric of dreams themselves, elusive and so simultaneously real that the moment she walked into the apartment which had once belonged to her family, Avril knew she was on home territory. Everything was so eerily familiar that she felt she could instantly find her way around and discover, as if on a strange treasure hunt, evidence of each and every detail she had so patiently and perseveringly collected regarding her mother's childhood.

Avril waited for the guests to gather around the birthday cake in the dining room, then set off to explore. First she went through the swing door leading from the dining room to the kitchen. Everyone there was so busy preparing sandwiches and snacks, saying "What's happening with the colas?" and "Who's going to pour out the Fanta lemonade?" that no one noticed a little girl had sneaked in and was now sidling along with her back to the wall towards the far door leading into the adults' private rooms. Luckily she picked correctly, as Avril soon found herself in a corridor which widened out to reveal four exits.

Avril attempted to guess as if blindfolded: which doorway could lead to her mother's old bedroom? Which led to her grandfather's bedroom, that she had visualized as immense? The problem was that everything in this flat was twice the size of hers, especially the doors, rising up like towers with a coloured fanlight across the top of each one, through which daylight still streamed brightly. Or was that truly daylight? Who knew, since anything could happen in such a place, however unlikely or astonishing? As she walked down the corridor, Avril did not dare touch anything she saw. She clasped her hands behind her back, just as her mother said she had been told to do when a child: in the way well-educated children were supposed to behave, *you can look but not touch*, keep your hands to yourself and your eyes wide open. Look, keep looking, Avril!

Her eyes roamed across the ceilings, down the doors and along the stucco mouldings. Everything else she saw – in other words, the furniture, the many paintings, the soft furnishings and the plants – didn't really interest her, because they belonged to a life that wasn't hers, but that of the Shrimp's family. The same couldn't be said of the wooden floorboards, or the impossibly high ceilings, which had known distant times, and witnessed the comings and goings of her own family's footsteps, doubtless gentle and well-bred, which Avril was now determined to emulate. Which could possibly be her mother's old bedroom? The one with the en suite dressing room? No, it must be further on.

Still with her hands clasped behind her back, trying to tread as lightly as possible so that no creaking floorboard could betray her presence, Avril advanced down the corridor. Could it be this door? Or perhaps that white one at the end? She paused before this one out of a sense of intuition: it was slightly smaller than the others, although it resembled them in every other respect, especially the ornate lock with its huge keyhole. Avril had only seen keyholes like that in films, but how fortunate that it was an old-fashioned and not a modern lock, otherwise she would never have been able to attempt what she was about to do now, bending over and staring through it. *Be careful, Avril, don't let anyone catch you.* She peeped through just for a second, then quickly straightened up. She was prepared for any encounter in this world of giants, for example an irritated father demanding: "What are you doing here? Come back and join the party!" or for a woman, someone's mum or auntie, to pretend to be surprised at this lost child: "Come on, sweetie, I'll take you to the bathroom. That was what you were looking for, wasn't it?" Yes, Avril was ready to face a maid, chauffeur, cook or any other giant lurking in this castle. The one thing she had not expected was to see her own mother through the keyhole.

It was impossible. She must have been mistaken: Avril was about to bend down again to the keyhole when a sound at the far end of the corridor, where the party was being celebrated, brought her up short. "Please don't let them come," she prayed, "please don't let them find me now. Give me just one more minute, please…" Avril wanted to shut her eyes and clench her fists once more, and to wish for the salvation of another earthquake. Anything – earthquake or cataclysm – that would let her look again, just once, through the keyhole into the room where she had seen her mother. No, it hadn't been either a dream or a nightmare, but possibly one of those strange flashbacks, like you see in films, that had allowed her for a split second to glimpse how Sofía had lived years earlier, her mother in the spoilt child's bedroom of her youth. Sofía, at almost the same age Avril was now, exactly as she looked in the photo they had at home. This unknown Sofía, who knew all about a death which everyone else regarded as an accident, when one boy killed another, and who still hoped one day to bring the guilty party to justice.

There were so many shadows that Avril had imagined she saw in the briefest glimpse through the keyhole, one stolen moment before she was startled by the noise from the far end of the corridor. But it must all have been in her mind, or else a cruel joke played by this gigantic house, because just as suddenly the noise vanished and all was quiet again. Then Avril opened the door and saw that in this room – once painted yellow and now apparently occupied by a boy rather than a girl, if the clothes strewn around were any indication – there was nothing but silence. Avril wanted to get away as quickly as possible, to forget what she was seeing and remember only what she'd imagined she'd seen through the keyhole a few seconds earlier, but it was impossible. The spell was broken and she didn't dare move. Also, as if it were a symbol of profanity or some other illicit incursion, Avril saw – on top of one of the table tops in this alien space – a silver frame very similar to the three she'd already seen in the living room at home, stuffed with recollections of time gone by. Avril took a couple of steps towards this memorial to a former life, then saw that, unlike those at home, which contained only one photo apiece, here there were several together, all of the same person. They were all pictures of the Shrimp: skiing with his elder brother; swimming in a pool; or with his father; plus one in particular which immediately caught Avril's attention, of him on his own. "It's impossible," she thought, because it showed Miki sitting by a hearth in the library surrounded by Christmas decorations, and seemed to her to make a mockery of a photo she knew so well: that of her mother forty years earlier. It was a sick joke, a theft – so, to break the spell, so that this nosy kid (staring out at her from a photo where she should have been, in a flat that should have been hers) would stop smiling, Avril had no option but to take her hands away from behind her back. "*You can look but not touch* – but I *can* touch, stupid Shrimp, you'll see!"

Almost without realizing it, she had done it: the heavy frame clattered to the floor; the glass front shattered... "Let them hear me! What do I care? It doesn't matter to me." As she heard the murmur of voices approaching down the corridor ("What was that?" "Who's in there?" "Would you like me to see what's going on, Señor Gasset?" "It sounded as if something got broken in there.") Avril thought that any telling-off or punishment would be all the same to her. ("Whatever happened, child?" "Nothing, Señora, I couldn't find the bathroom, so I came in here, where it was all dark... and it fell over, the glass smashed, but I didn't mean to do it.") As she bent down to pretend to help, Avril suddenly thought it was lucky there were several photos in the frame; lucky too that the woman who had come to see what had happened was from the catering company, and not a family member, so wouldn't notice too much. ("Here, Señora, don't worry. I won't touch the glass, but let me help you. Here are all the photos, all of them, I'm so sorry...") Nobody would realize one was missing. Avril, whose hands had long since been withdrawn from behind her back, had decided she would keep the photo showing the Shrimp by the hearth. Her first idea was to tear it up as soon as she got out of there, but as she was on her way back to the party, escorted by the grumbling caterer ("Come on, kid, enough of this nonsense..." "You're right. I'm very sorry, Señora, I won't do it again"), a much better idea slowly formed in her mind. It was clear the photo was hers now. Hers to do with as she liked. It so happened that she could work wonders with photographs on her computer – like by swapping the faces. She would replace the Shrimp's face with her own, so that from then on it would be she who was seated by the roaring fireside, just as it was meant to be, before this wretched life took on all its fateful twists and turns.

The Reunion of Three Old Friends

"No way," Luisa told herself, annoyed. "When a conversation starts out this pedestrian, how the hell is it going to become interesting?" Then, glancing again at Sofía and Miguel seated at the dining table in her apartment, she couldn't help adding: "Perhaps I was wrong to arrange this for just the three of us. I should have invited Enrique as well. After all, he's someone who can get anybody talking, even a ghost at a banquet."

They were finally holding the long-promised reunion, yet conversation had been stilted from the outset, perhaps because the invisible presence that hung over their meeting was the shade of Antonio. At least that's how it seemed to Luisa. Both her guests had arrived early and alone, informally dressed. In jeans and a green tweed jacket, Miguel had that air of studied casualness which demands hours in front of a mirror, and is best noticed in the smallest details: a silk Paisley handkerchief just protruding from his breast pocket; pink socks that would have been insufferable on any other man... For her part, Sofía had probably not made too much of an effort for the occasion, since she looked exactly as Luisa remembered from Elba's first day at school: thin, fair hair scraped back in a bun on the nape of her neck; a grey wool dress which did nothing to hide those shapeless lumps women acquire around the time of the menopause. After they had both politely admired the apartment (Sofía's comment was: "Great place, Luigi, the view over the Retiro Park is to die for, you're sooo lucky"; similarly, from Miguel: "...What have you got here? Photos by Porcarelli and Michael Malka, I'm crazy about signed portraits, one day I'll invite you back to see my collection"), they had seemed determined to make *small talk*, which Carmen O'Inns would doubtless have dismissed as *idle chit-chat*: "You know what I mean, Newton, the kind of meaningless babble that's a pandemic nowadays. Why does *nobody* talk about what really matters? What's wrong with us?"

So the first forty-five minutes of the dinner that had been planned to bring them together after so long did little more than confirm what Luisa already knew about her old friends. It added a few fresh details: Miguel, for example, had been married and separated no less than four times, and even now he was in the midst of a messy divorce. ("We've been fighting every which way to obtain custody over Miki, short of coming to blows. I lost custody of Tony from my first marriage, and I swore the same thing wouldn't happen again.") He also told them that for the moment he lived with neither of his two children, except at weekends, but that Tony and Miguel – despite their twenty-year age gap, and the fact they were very different characters – were inseparable. He also explained something about his job ("I'm a lawyer, I work in commercial law. Not much glamour, but it's well-paid") and his hobbies ("I love collecting things, a bit of everything: furniture, paintings, old photos, especially by Lewis Carroll. I'm fascinated by his beautiful and perverse little girls: don't you find the age between childhood and adolescence deeply disturbing, and so ambiguous?"). This was the sole allusion Miguel made to childhood, but – to judge by the ease with which he went on to discuss the past, even including the accident that had happened to his brother, witnessed by the three of them – it seemed to Luisa there was little left of the shy boy who had lived in the shadow of his brilliant brother. On the contrary, Miguel was one of those men it was impossible to ignore. Probably Enrique Santos would have instantly dismissed him as a pretentious sort, even a snob, but then what did Enrique Santos know about men?

As for Sofía, Luisa hadn't learnt much that was new about her, except that once she'd reached a certain age she'd had her one daughter *in extremis* (that was her expression): "I expect I was the same as you, Luigi. Avril was born just before mother nature pensioned me off, so tell me: did you have to go and find someone to father Elba in the sales? Or, worse still, like I did, in the bargain basement?"

Luisa had let the comment pass with a laughing aside: "Well, perhaps something like that. I went on a 'mating trip' and yes, it was to the Isle of Elba." She realized at once that this was the first time since her conversation in the kitchen with Elba some weeks earlier that she had told the truth about her daughter's origins. But she didn't need to add anything further on a topic she'd never liked to expand on, because the mention of mothers *in extremis* had led her guests to comment that nowadays the world is full of fathers and mothers the age of grandparents: old people like them raising adolescent children. This led the conversation in a completely impersonal direction. Miguel and Sofía started to talk about other former classmates, and what they knew of their lives, which wasn't much, and the talk became so boring that Luisa suddenly found herself wondering not about what she had just heard, but about other much more revealing details of Sofía's life she had read, as written by Avril and sent to Elba by email.

There, Luisa found a lot from their shared past it was worthwhile reflecting on: such as how strange it was that an accident and its repercussions could have such different results in the adult life of each of those who witnessed it. Different and unpredictable, she added, because if her intuition was correct, the Miguel at table with them currently recounting old, inconsequential stories about his school days seemed to have completely got over his brother's death. Nothing in his attitude, apart from bestowing his dead brother's name upon his eldest son, indicated that the incident still weighed on him. Even this repetition of the name did not so much prolong the memory, but rather contributed to erasing it completely, thought Luisa, because the best way to forget a dead person is to substitute a living one in their place: stealing their name helps kill them off once and for all. This appeared to have happened in the case of the first Antonio Gasset. She herself had found another way of coping with the memory: she had completely forgotten about it. Wasn't it odd that until a few days earlier, when she realized the details of her new novel were very similar to those of the childhood accident, she had never once thought about what had happened in that school garden, and couldn't even remember the face of the dead boy with the mark on his temple? To forget is the best way to exorcise a ghost, and the most obvious, so that was what she had done. Sofía on the other hand, as far as Luisa could tell from the emails, was still obsessed with Antonio's death, to the extent that she had fallen for a man with an almost identical name – or so Avril's messages suggested. "Fine, let's say it's true," Luisa thought, glancing across at Sofía to see if she could spot any secret inkling, any sign that the past still weighed on her, "let's say it was a silly excuse, a simple justification for why someone falls in love with an obviously unsuitable person." Even so, from what Luisa had read, there was a much more disturbing detail, one that clearly showed how the same event could affect the three of them so differently. This was the fact that the way they remembered it was completely different too. According to what Avril had written, Sofía thought it hadn't been an accident, but that Miguel had let his brother die. But that wasn't true at all, at least it wasn't the way Luisa herself recalled what had happened, when she had finally allowed herself to think about it.

Luisa surveyed both of them at the dinner table, trying to discover from their gestures and their faces some clue as to their thoughts or emotions. What could Sofía be feeling now that she was back with someone she considered responsible for another person's death? Here we are, the three protagonists of that far-off tragedy, making small talk, thought Luisa, observing the way the other two moved their hands, and trying to discover from the tiniest inflections in their voices, or from something in their expression, the telltale signs of suspicion, hatred, doubt, bitterness, rancour or perhaps even love. She could not detect a thing – no sudden catch in their voices, not the slightest indication of hidden thoughts reflected on their faces, nothing: the sad fact was that in this way too, reality was unlike novels or films, where every gesture had a meaning, and every attitude betrayed a secret. If only it were so simple, and those who were guilty in the real world cast sly looks at one another, had foreheads filmed with perspiration, or stammered as they spoke. But it was not true that one could read a person's thoughts on their face, completely untrue. Perhaps in the dim and distant past the face had been the mirror of the soul. For too long now, however, thought Luisa, every gesture had been tamed, every facial expression was willed, every laugh was forced, every teardrop a pious lie. A person's face is no longer a mirror, but the mask we have created to defend ourselves: for centuries now, we have all been mere characters in that eternal masked ball or *commedia dell'arte* known as life. Isn't this a fact? And sometimes we put on one mask, and at others wear a different one, whichever is most suitable: Harlequin's smiling face, Pierrot's tearful one or Colombina's face of innocence; and the others too: thoughtful Pulcinella, foolish Pantalone…We are all perfectly aware that these are nothing more than masks, but we all fool ourselves into thinking that the cardboard smile conceals a sincere emotion, that a tearful mask is a sign of true suffering, even though we know from our own experience that nobody allows any more of their emotions to appear than they wish to show. "All right," thought Luisa, almost going so far as to say it aloud, as if she herself had just put on another mask, "all the same, it's perfectly possible to read other people's faces.

If it weren't, not just literature, but also psychology, sociology and even philosophy would be pointless, and even though it may not be as easy as novels suggest to guess what others are thinking, there has to be some way of intuiting it, because we do it all the time."

Luisa studied Sofía, whose features had obviously not been distorted by any plastic surgery. She concentrated not on her eyes, but on the fact that the corners of her mouth drooped as though pulled down long ago by the weight of some secret suffering. Also the way her grey-blue eyes, whose lively sparkle she had so envied in her childhood, were now half-hidden under hooded eyelids that spoke of surrender. It was only her perfect teeth, which incongruously seemed untouched by the years, that seemed odd, like a true note in the midst of an otherwise off-key tune. Yet Sofía showed them so frequently when she smiled that it was easy to be fooled, because when she did so, and spoke in that voice of hers that sounded so similar to her adolescent one, she cast such a spell that all at once Luisa had the impression she was once again in the presence of that stunningly beautiful, self-confident girl: *Come on Antonio, Miguel and you too, you silly new girl, yes you, Luisa... see if you can catch me, come on, the last one's a sissy!* Luisa concluded that the mask Sofía was wearing now was that of herself as a child. Perhaps that was why it was so hard to detect any sign of pain or doubt in her: when she spoke, and above all when she smiled, Sofía once more became the child she had once been. It was an amazing and very effective device.

What about Miguel? Luisa had observed him while they were having their aperitifs, and again more closely during their candlelit dinner. What mask was he wearing tonight? Pantalone? Harlequin? Or his own childhood face, like Sofía? It was hard to tell: Miguel looked like one of those men whose smile was so fixed, so perfect, that you didn't ask yourself what they were feeling, but what toothpaste they used. At that very moment, he was saying: "This wine is fabulous, Luigi, and so is everything else. I'm really impressed with what you've organized here, I always knew you'd go far." That's a lie, thought Luisa, neither you nor Sofía had any idea how we would end up: not a soul could have predicted it. Who would have thought that the winners would be losers, and vice versa? None of us, not even me, because we all tend to think that childhood is a foretaste of what adult life will be. We love to read signs, predictions, oracles and prophecies into it. Yet it seems as though they all obey the unshakeable Julio Iglesias law: sometimes they come true, sometimes they don't. And in this case they obviously hadn't.

Luisa scanned Miguel's face again. It was true: despite his constant smile, there was a moment when it seemed that, like Sofía, he too was hiding behind a mask that was his own face as a young boy. Or even – what came down to the same thing – behind the face of his twin brother Antonio. Remembering her daughter Elba's obsession with mirrors, Luisa thought how odd it must be for someone who had lost their identical twin, every time they saw their reflection, to have the image of the dead person staring out at them throughout their entire life and until the day they died. A dead person who was never quite dead. Then again, perhaps it was the complete opposite that happened, perhaps a twin brother is even more dead than others who don't have an exact copy in the land of the living, because when the latter die they live on in the memory of those who remember them, fixed in time, for ever young and innocent. Poor Antonio Gasset though had suffered not simply one, but three deaths. Not only had he died, but now his place had been taken by a boy who had the same name, while at the same time he would not live on in his loved ones' imagination as eternally young. He had an exact copy in the adult world of the living, which meant that now he was nothing, not even a memory, nothing more than a shadow in a mirror. Luisa recalled her dream, when she had seen an adult Miguel Gasset lying naked in bed beside her. She remembered how terrified she had been of turning him round and finding that he had his dead brother's face. But in her dream, that had not happened. When she had finally succeeded in overcoming her fear and looking him in the face, she discovered the sleeping man's features were not those of the dead boy's but those of the adult, strikingly handsome, Miguel Gasset. So there you are, sweetheart, Luisa told herself, even dreams fit into Julio Iglesias's implacable law: sometimes they can be cruel, sometimes not. By the way, wouldn't you perhaps like that so unexpected dream of yours to come true? Wasn't that the real reason you organized this oh-so-boring dinner party? Tell the truth now: you didn't do it so you could come face to face with your past, did you? No, you wanted to see Miguel again. Go on, admit it, you think he's gorgeous, despite looking like a Ralph Lauren advert in those pink socks, and despite the fact that, if Sofía is to be believed, he allowed his brother to die. So tell me, wouldn't you like to?...

Sex at Fifty

It sometimes happens that dreams become reality, even when you are not sure are good or bad. When we are least expecting it, we wake up one night to find ourselves next to the body we once dreamt of. That word "dream" is deceptive too, because its closest synonym is "desire", yet it is all too obvious that most of what we dream about is neither desirable nor acceptable, and in this case was at the very least a complication. All this was going through Luisa's mind several hours after that crushingly tedious dinner as she stared at the back of Miguel Gasset, who was curled up facing the wall on the far side of her bed. Since she couldn't sleep and was in a philosophical mood, she observed that one of the chief differences between men and women is, as everyone knows, that after sex men sleep like logs, whereas women lie wide awake, eyes wide open, and with a tendency to go over and over things in their minds.

Luisa glanced again at Miguel's back. She wasn't thinking how unexpected and rapid everything had been, but was more concerned to note what most interested her about this kind of precipitous lovemaking. For example, the fact that the bodies of those who embark on a sexual adventure (even if they have made love together before in their dreams) fulfil a long-standing premise: in sleep, they want to be alone. That was why it came as no surprise to Luisa to see her body and Miguel Gasset's each in its own corner, like two boxers at the end of the first round in the ring. In the morning, the bell would sound, and they would have to square up to each other again, but for now they could rest on their stools in the corner, be rubbed with liniment, and reflect on the punches thrown and taken.

The second thing that went through Luisa's mind was the same old doubt. The one about waking up next to a new lover, someone she hardly knew, when she had not really planned for it to happen. She usually programmed everything, especially when it came to love affairs – don't forget, you're fifty-two now, sweetheart, it's high time you thought a little more about the consequences of your impulses, because to go "wherever your heart takes you" might be fine written in some New Age pamphlet, but as a way of life it's a disaster. "*Your head*, Luisita, you need to use your head, that organ so often maligned as far as emotions are concerned, your head, not the heart and still less those other parts located somewhere between the thighs. My God, this time you didn't even have the excuse of drinking so much as one Bloody Mary. All you had was wine. How on earth did things come to this? How did you end up in bed with a dream on your first night? You, Supercool Luisa, who knew only too well that love in these times of AIDS had to obey all three of the rules you ignored right from the start. Rule Number One: going to bed with someone simply because Sofía left early and the two of you stayed on talking, and then one thing led to another... (And I'm sorry, but to claim that he is not exactly a stranger and that besides, the situation had been predicted in a dream is not only a stupid excuse, it makes things worse: does that mean that all the absurdities one dreams about are meant to be put into practice?) Rule Number Two: embarking on a new relationship when – after all that anguish, all those emotional failures (don't forget that, sweetheart, remember all those catastrophes) – you have finally settled into a comfortable and perfectly satisfactory monogamy. And Rule Number Three, the worst of all, the real gut-wrencher: not having a single miserable condom in the flat."

From her corner, Luisa ran her eye over exactly the same path she had taken in her dreams along Miguel Gasset's body, evaluating every inch. That's another consequence of this kind of fling, she told herself: at the same time as you are lamenting having broken all the rules, you also judge the prize you've won, and not always entirely favourably. However, despite her doubts, what she saw this time did not displease her. Quite the contrary in fact: Miguel was an attractive man. Apart from that, he looked younger than his years, which by their time of life could only be a blessing. One of the most difficult things to bear in having sexual adventures after forty was the lack of aesthetic enjoyment. If love at fifty was a shipwreck, or "an emergency situation", as she herself had dubbed it a few months earlier when she chose Enrique Santos as the Man of Her Life, then sex at forty – never mind fifty! – was a challenge to anyone's good taste, a terrorist attack on the aesthetic principle.

Aestheticism – Luisa reflected, in the moments of peace offered by insomnia and the clear-sightedness of post-coital content – "the attitude of persons who place beauty above other values such as morality, or social and political commitment..." according to the dictionary. Fine, understood, and it's perhaps not a very valid life philosophy, but in bed next to a body we don't yet love, who on earth wouldn't be an aesthete? That was why sex with strangers after the age of fifty was so risky. Not simply for plain prophylactic reasons, but because without affection added to the mix, our own physical deterioration (not to mention the other person's) becomes increasingly obvious.

So Luisa gazed at Miguel's back in much the same way as she had in her dream weeks earlier. It looked so young and beautiful she felt a similar desire to run her fingers up his spine like a perfect stepladder. Her eyes (only her eyes) reached his shoulder blades, the back of his neck, and then his face, the keeper of who knew what secrets. This time, however, as she thought of his face and its secrets, Luisa was not afraid that if she turned him round she would see the face of the young Antonio with its livid death mark. No, what worried her now was something else: the possibility that another spell might be broken, the one produced by admiring the back of a mature body rather than its front. Because while it was undoubtedly true that when sleeping faces relax, they gave away their owner's worst secrets – their bitterness, envy or egotism – it was also true that, however much we all pretend it is not the case, a face inexorably also betrayed that person's age. Bodies though, or at least some fortunate ones, can lie brazenly, as Miguel's did now. To Luisa, it looked ten or even as much as twenty years younger, and thank God for that, because for a bit of hanky-panky (which was how Isaac Newton would probably have described this bedtime romp if she had been Carmen O'Inns and not Luisa Dávila) you need to be seriously drunk, and to have made sure there is a bottle by the bedside so that you could carry on the same way the next morning. Otherwise the fact of waking up beside a strange, ageing body could seriously upset your emotional balance, let alone your libido. Luisa knew this from personal experience, because before Enrique (who was seven years younger than her) came along to put an end to a lengthy period of serial monogamy, Luisa had often woken up alongside other bodies who were the same age as her or older. Bodies which looked perfectly acceptable when dressed for a romantic dinner, but which later in bed, and above all in the harsh light of dawn, turned into disgustingly flabby (or what was almost worse, shrivelled) carcasses, into bald or wispy heads that all too often lay sweating on the pillow. Limp, scrawny bodies of all shapes and sizes, from waists two yards wide to skinny, mummified remains. Then there were the drooping chests or ones with breasts as big as women, the creased backsides, varicose veins, bad breath in all its varieties (and all this without even touching on other details which were literally lethal to the libido)… All of which had led Luisa to conclude that if her regard for the owners of any of these bodies managed to survive a night of sex, it must be a sure sign love was involved.

It had been precisely this thought that had led to her getting together with Enrique Santos. Although he wasn't as physically repulsive as some she had known, he was no George Clooney either; and yet, from the first time they had gone to bed together she had discovered that, far from being repelled by his ample stomach, she loved to bury herself in its gentle, downy pillow. His whole body reminded her of a teddy bear. She soon concluded that if she liked his flab rolls so much, she must also really like him: love at fifty might be a desperate affair, and sex a risky adventure, but just occasionally, in among all the wreckage, you find an unexpected footprint in the shifting sands of your subconscious that tells you that at last you're on the right track to find a partner. If that's the case, it's better to follow the footprint and surrender to the person who left it. Even if that person is not the blond, handsome Robinson Crusoe, but Man Friday.

So Luisa, who had learnt to love Enrique's rotund form, was suspicious of her feelings towards Miguel Gasset. Something about him disturbed her – quite apart from the obvious fact that he was onto his fourth divorce and clearly liked women far too much. She looked over at his clothes on the bedside chair and was amused at the contrast with hers. Luisa was proud of the fact that she could tell people's characters from tiny details. What did her own clothes, thrown off just before they had sex, say about her? They were strewn about the floor, wherever Miguel had stripped her of them. Her skirt and blouse were in the middle of the floor ("You're fantastic, I've been wanting to undo your blouse all night, let me do it"). Her stockings lay crumpled in a corner, and her tanga had come to rest on one of the bed corners ("you're beautiful, so beautiful, kiss me, you fool"), a sign of their final rushed struggle. Her clothes, then, were easy to read, but what about his? Luisa looked again. Miguel's trousers lay carefully folded on the chair. On them lay his shirt, also perfectly folded, and on top of that was his tweed jacket, with the Paisley handkerchief still sticking out of the pocket as it had done all evening. His shoes were on the floor as if ready for inspection: two cones of light-brown suede with the pink socks poking out of the ends like raspberry ice cream. Where were his briefs? "Oh my," thought Luisa, "it's all so neat and tidy, he must be the ideal man." Even so, she had a troubling presentiment. "Beware of men who are too tidy" – she could remember her mother warning her – "the tidiest man I ever knew was found years later to have buried the body of his niece in the garden". Luisa had never paid much attention to the things her mother told her – mothers always try to warn their daughters of future dangers, as she herself did with Elba, but the truth was that now, as she lay awake alongside Miguel's disturbingly youthful body and could see his neatly folded clothing on the chair, she was worried. What did she really know about him? Nothing, despite being acquainted for more than forty years. The problem was that when you had known someone since childhood, you tended to think they were close to you in their tastes and interests. That they understood your way of life and shared your values, simply because once upon a time you knew them in the magical world of childhood. But surely that was misleading, simply another mirage produced by the shipwreck of being in your fifties? What really happened that distant afternoon? What if Sofía's version of it were true, and Miguel had let his brother die? "In that case, sweetheart, you're in bed with somebody who has got the death of a young boy on his conscience. What do you make of that?" Luisa made two things of it ("and please let them be the last, that's enough of going over everything in your mind, what you need now is to get some sleep, or tomorrow you won't be able to write a single blasted line"). First, her present situation was very similar to that of her ineffable character Carmen O'Inns: they were both sleeping with two men at the same time, one of them sensible, convenient, comfortably domestic; the other possibly inconvenient, dangerous even, and in the best of cases simply an unknown quantity. Second, no doubt an offshoot of the first, concerned something Sofía Márquez had said as she had left after dinner. Something Luisa should have paid more attention to. What was it she had said, exactly? The three of them were saying goodbye at the front door. As a foretaste of what was soon to follow, Miguel's hand had stayed on Luisa's waist three or four times longer than was socially acceptable. Before she finally left, Sofía had stood for a long while by the door, as if she hadn't wanted to go before she got something off her chest. She looked at the two of them with that radiant smile of hers that almost recreated the illusion of her adolescent beauty, and said: "I'm pleased that the two of you are going to carry on chatting for a while on your own. It seems to me you've got a lot to talk over." Thinking she knew what her friend was referring to, Luisa moved away from Miguel's encircling hand and tried to defuse the situation by asking Sofía straight out what she thought the two of them had to talk about. To her surprise, Sofía's reply had nothing to do with her or Miguel, or his hovering hand. "About your children," said Sofía, the smile fading from her face. "I mean Elba, Miki and possibly Antonio as well. Ever since Miki's birthday I've seen the three of them together when school gets out. It seems as though they make, or are about to make, an odd threesome. It's strange, because whereas in the past it was Miguel, Antonio and me who were inseparable, now I reckon they could be headed in the same direction." As she finished, the shining smile that was the only surviving trace of her young days returned to her face. What happened next between Luisa and Miguel Gasset, namely the seduction, surrender, sex, doubts about Robinson Crusoe and so on, had prevented Luisa thinking any further about what Sofía had said, but now, while she was pondering on how little she really knew concerning her former schoolmate, and how you tend to feel you know people merely because you shared your childhood with them, her friend's words came back to haunt her. So too did what she had said next. Miguel had just given her a goodbye peck on the cheek ("Bye, Sofi – I'm sorry, I mean Sofía – let's meet up again soon") and Luisa had been studying their faces carefully to see if their physical proximity could offer her some clue, some suggestion that their ritual smiles and farewells were trying to hide. ("Thanks for coming, Sofía, I'll give you a call soon"… "No, thank *you*, Luigi, it was a fantastic dinner, give Elba a kiss from me. I'm sorry she was already asleep when we arrived, you know how much I like her.") It was not until the very last moment, when there seemed to be absolutely nothing more to say between them, that Sofía had turned back in the doorway and added: "And what about Avril? Have you thought that if your children form a group like Miguel, Antonio and I once did, who is Avril going to be?" Naturally, the other two had no reply to this, or to any of the other odd remarks Sofía had made about their children. Even the fact that she should bring them up now, just as she was leaving and after a dinner that had carefully avoided any personal matters, seemed to Luisa completely misplaced. Sofía was talking about things that *might* happen, but what did that matter? "I guess that for those who believe that the parents' past is unfortunate enough to be repeated in their children's present," Sofía had said, "it would make sense if, seeing that your children are like Miguel, Antonio and me, Avril were to play your role, Luigi – the outsider, the interloper. Life's like that; it repeats itself, but people's positions change. It's always playing games. I'm not sure, it's too early to say what's going on with those three, I've only seen them talking together on afternoons when Tony has been to collect his brother, but if I were you I'd keep a close eye on them. Especially you, Luisa, watch out for Elbita, you know how impressionable girls her age are, and you know how much I care for her."

It was then that Sofía had added something which Luisa, in her corner of the ring with all this racing through her mind, only now recalled: "Look, Luigi, I'm not one to make speeches, but there's something I do believe: we all think we know our children. We think that because they are our flesh and blood, nothing about them can be truly odd, incomprehensible or abnormal, and yet a child is always a perfect stranger. Worse than that: a child is someone who speaks with a voice like ours, who looks like us and even laughs like us, and yet they are not us. We have no idea what they are feeling or what their hidden motives are. A father or mother is the worst judge of their own child. Not just because love makes us blind, and all that clichéd nonsense, but more importantly because there's a fundamental error of judgment: we take it for granted that a child is like us, or at worst like their father, uncle or grandfather... but the truth is that the character traits of two people mingled together do not produce an exact copy, but an entirely new and almost always alien being: a perfect stranger."

Well, it had been a speech in the end, but Luisa could not see why Sofía had launched into it then and there. Miguel and she had exchanged enquiring glances, and Sofía had not elaborated on it. Instead, she smiled, picked up her bag, and once she had finally got out of the door, the other two had more urgent matters to attend to, because seduction has its own demands, and doesn't exactly lend itself to reflection. They dismissed what Sofía had said with a shrug of the shoulders, and a brief "Well, that's Sofía being Sofía".

Afterwards came a final drink, the first kiss, then "why don't you turn the music up a bit?", "let me help you undo that", "close your eyes", "part your lips", and what with these and all the other whispered encouragements with which love – or sex – at fifty (and at least in the first giddy moments there is not much to distinguish between them) Luisa somehow no longer thought about her friend.

Now however, it was these parting words that were keeping her awake: "We know nothing about those we are closest to, and we are unaware of even the most obvious things about our children." This sounded like a phrase Carmen O'Inns might have used, and of course it was perfect for the novel Luisa was writing, so she would probably include it. But she had to be careful, because perhaps in the morning it would seem complete rubbish, and all the fears that were assailing her now would appear equally groundless. "That's what is so good and yet so bad about sleepless nights like this: you think so much that appears convincing at the time, but most of it can't bear the light of day."

"We'll see in the morning," she told herself, realizing it was going to be hard for her to write a single line after so little sleep. "I'm going to feel like death warmed up. I'll have to do some serious reading if I'm not to think I've wasted a whole day. After all, why not? There's nothing like reading when so much is going on in your life. Too much, if you ask me."

Dress Rehearsals

Luisa's life did not get any less crowded. The month of October turned into November, and to her surprise, just as she had seen the friendship between Elba and Avril begin and blossom, she now thought she could see it cooling off. In fact, it was not so much a cooling as an adjustment, a falling-off in intensity. Elba no longer mentioned Avril all the time, they didn't spend every hour of the day and night sprawled on their beds talking, it even seemed they were speaking less on the phone. "What's wrong, my love, have you fallen out with your friend? Why doesn't Avril come round so often any more?" When her daughter heard this, she'd simply smile and say: "We talk on Messenger and write each other mails. Besides, my exams are coming up and I've got a lot to revise. I thought you'd be pleased that I'm growing up, Mummy."

That word "mummy" was no longer such a difficult one between Luisa and Elba. Even though her daughter still occasionally called her by her Christian name, she also used "mummy" without this seeming a way of flattering or trying to wheedle something out of her. On the contrary, it had become more of a habit, a way of showing she was more adult. Which she was. It was obvious from the way she dressed. ("Why do pre-adolescent girls all dress like Julia Roberts in *Pretty Woman*?" Luisa wondered when she saw her going out to buy something in a local shop. "Why are they looking for trouble from the moment they're born?") It was also obvious from many other small details, which Luisa observed with the tolerant resignation of a poacher turned gamekeeper. Recently, for example, Elba would spend hours shut in the bathroom or in her bedroom, talking on the phone or looking out of the window staring at God knew what. "What are you looking at, Elba? Who are you hoping to see in the street?" "No one, Mummy. I was talking to one of the boys from my class."

A few days earlier, although she had never gone in for extra-curricular activities, Elba asked her mother to enrol her in a local gym. The fact that there she would be mixing with adults as well as other teenagers also added to Luisa's belief that she was growing up fast. She thought this whenever she saw Elba leaving the flat after she had done her homework, with her gym things in a big bag and her school skirt hitched up round her waist to make it look like a miniskirt, and with her hair (surely that had grown a lot recently too?) scraped up at the back of her neck in a casual way that reminded her of Avril, and therefore of Sofía too. "Don't worry if I'm back a bit late, Mummy. Sometimes I like to stay and chat with the others; but I promise I'll be back soon, before eight in any case."

Apart from this daily outing, which lasted only an hour and a half, or two hours at the most, Elba was spending a lot more time at home. Most of this was at her computer (chatting or sending mails to Avril, Luisa imagined) but still she seemed more settled, more a creature of habit. From school to home, from home to her computer, from the computer to the gym, and from the gym to lengthy sessions in the bathroom with her music on full blast, dancing or striking poses. Also apparently kissing mirrors while wearing lipstick, as red smears on the big bathroom mirror appeared to confirm.

Mirrors. Those tried and trusted companions in Elba's life. But here too, her relationship had changed. When they had moved into their new home, Luisa had been worried at her daughter's odd habit of spending so much time peering at herself in the larger of the two mirrors out in the hall. Now however, Elba seemed to have so completely forgotten its existence she didn't even pause when she passed by. Other mirrors had become her accomplices: the one in the lift when she went out to the gym, for example, or the one in her bedroom. This was opposite the window, so that Elba could see her reflection looking thoughtful and languid, framed by the glass as she stared endlessly out at the street. But her absolute favourite, the one she spent hours dancing and preening herself in front of, was the one in the bathroom. "Come on out, sweetheart, it's time for dinner." After a few seemingly endless minutes, Elba would appear, fixing her hair, black smudges around her eyes, lipstick still all over her mouth, breathing heavily and with a broad smile on her face. "Dress rehearsals," Luisa chuckled to herself, "she's at the stage of trying out clothes and make-up. Let's just hope there's still a while to go before she gets to boys."

"Or perhaps she's already started with them too, and I just haven't realized," Luisa wondered one day when she saw the bathroom sessions growing longer and more secretive. "Perhaps I ought to try to find out what those girls are really up to, to have a look in that famous file marked 'SECRET: KEEP OUT'."

She thought about it, but did nothing. The last of Avril's mails she had read were from a couple of weeks earlier, two or three days after Miki Gasset's birthday party. This was around the time that the three old friends had met up again after so many years, and it had given Luisa the sensation that she was prying into someone else's life. After all, it wasn't even her own daughter's life she was spying on, but her best friend's: all the mails in the file seemed to have come from Avril. The last one she had read was telling Elba how she had discovered that the apartment where the Gassets were now living had belonged to Sofía before her life had taken so many different turns. She also wrote about how she had explored the whole flat, and how in one room she had stumbled on a photo of the Shrimp (that was the name she gave to Miguel's son: "that silly, nosy Shrimp, we hate him, don't we, Elba? He's such a geek"). Avril wrote about a photo of him that she had taken as a souvenir. "It's incredible, Elba, I discovered that little squirt in a photo taken in exactly the same spot as one of my mother years ago. You know the one I mean, you saw it at my place. It shows my mum at more or less the same age as us now. Both photos were taken in exactly the same spot, by the hearth in the living room of the apartment. Worse still, they're both taken at Christmas. You can tell from the decorations. Incredible, isn't it? That's why I took the photo. Do you know what I did with it, Elba? I deleted the Shrimp's face and put mine there instead. No one can tell. You must see it! It's looks just as though it's me beside the chimney, and not him. I'll send it you when I've got it perfect. Do you think I'm crazy, Elba? Do you think I'm obsessed with the past like my mother says? Tell me what you think, please, you haven't written in ages. What are you up to?"

This intrusion into someone else's life produced two very different reactions in Luisa: first, she was surprised at what Avril had done (and was even more astounded that the apartment she had also known as a girl should now belong to Miguel), and second, she decided not to pry into anyone's life ever again. "That's enough spying," she told herself. "The vampire feeding off the blood of others is going into hibernation right now. You've more than enough information you need for your novel thanks to Avril's mails. You've no need for any more voyeurism."

So the first part of November went by, about ten or twelve days since the meal when the three former schoolmates had met up again. Days when Luisa's own life had demanded more attention than her daughter's. If Elba's life had become one of routine, and apparently almost solitary, hers by contrast had turned into a complicated chess game, or worse still one long juggling act where she had to keep several balls in the air at the same time: her creative problems which prevented her from making any progress with her novel; her research into evil; the Man of Her Life; putting the finishing touches to her new home;

trying to make sure Elba was not left out of the equation. And to top it all, a new element to juggle with: Miguel Gasset.

Ever since their first lovemaking session, they had decided – or rather Luisa had decided, and Miguel did not seem to have any objection – that until they had a clearer idea of where things were going, the most sensible thing would be to see each other more or less infrequently, and always very discreetly. They had met no more than four or five times, and each meeting consisted of a hasty drink in a bar, followed by an hour or two in a hotel room, whose main attraction was the fact that they did not bump into anyone in the corridors. They said a great deal to each other, but these were mostly sweet, passionate nothings rather than anything about their lives. Their bodies did the talking, with the result that they never, for example, commented on what Sofía had said just before leaving, that time the three of them had met up again. Why should they? Luisa was increasingly convinced that her friend had been talking nonsense. "You need to talk about your children, and see what's happening with them." That didn't seem relevant now that Elba hardly ever left the apartment, and she herself was so busy organizing her timetable in order to keep two relationships of equal intensity going at the same time. From her first meeting with Miguel, Luisa realized her two lovers were so different that they seemed to complement each other rather than cancelling one another out, to the point where she wondered if she didn't need one to be able to love the other. She could count the number of times she had been to bed with Miguel on one hand, but even so it was clear that whereas he was the passionate sort, Enrique made her feel more secure; where he was mysterious, Enrique was strong and reliable. They were sophistication versus common sense; delightful uncertainty against settled commitment. What else? Poetry and prose, night and day, sun and the – oh! so necessary – rain... "How complicated love can be," thought Luisa the fourth time she saw Miguel and had to make up some excuse to give Enrique, "how complicated and how inconsiderate! Why was it always the same? Either you couldn't find a decent prospect in a thousand miles, or you found yourself overbooked, with the added twist that if neither of them on their own was perfect (who is?), the two of them together made the ideal man. So then: who do you give up on? Which one do you choose? What the devil do you do? Well, sweetheart," she continued with a laugh, "you do exactly what men themselves have been doing since the world began: you don't choose. Men are very clear about it. None of them gets into a state because they're playing a double game – and they're quite right. Why choose just one life when you can have two? Who was it who said that men are by nature polygamous while we women are serially monogamous? All of us are polygamous, the only thing you have to do right from the start is make sure there's a safe distance between your affairs, so that you aren't leaping from one bed to another and making love to two different people every half-hour. That way at least we women are different: we like a certain rhythm to our infidelities."

What Luisa had to do to ensure her plan worked was for the Man of Her Life, the "official" one, never to find out about her double life. Not him or anybody else: not Elba, and of course not Sofía either. Miguel needed to be kept in the dark as well, because real betrayal is not so much cheating on somebody, but making them look a fool.

Carmen O'Inns was also making progress in her two love affairs. She didn't have to bother about keeping her bed-hopping a secret because Newton wasn't exactly the Man of Her Life; he wasn't even her Man Friday. All the same, she tried to keep her passionate nights with Señor Beil from him. Since Luisa could not think of any way of advancing the plot of her novel, she decided to add a few torrid scenes between O'Inns and Señor Beil by adapting a few details from her lovemaking with Miguel. Like him, Señor Beil did not say much. He dressed immaculately, and even wore pink socks. She also wrote that he didn't say a word about the affair to anyone outside the four walls of the hotel room where they met, and with regard to his intimate sexual performances, she had him practising tantric sex (would you believe it?) just like Miguel Gasset claimed he could. OK, fine, all this stuff about love within four walls was entertaining enough, but what about the plot? Luisa reproached herself, after devoting four pages to O'Inns's sexual acrobatics and Señor Beil's tantric prowess. "Be careful, make sure the tension is still there, otherwise that's your thriller down the plughole. Remember what Enrique always says: action and more action, and to hell with any background details. Let's see. What comes next? It's never taken you so long to set a novel on the right track before. What the devil is happening to you?"

Luisa resolved to concentrate more on her writing and less on her real or imaginary acrobatic lovemaking, but try as she might, nothing came of it. The only clearly defined character in her novel seemed to be the tap-dance teacher, that elderly spinster in whose past a death very similar to Oscar's had occurred. "OK, let's see where that takes us: let's definitely make it a story about child assassins where the guilty party turns out to be not a child but an adult who commits the murder for reasons buried in their past. Would it be plausible for somebody to kill in order to gain revenge for another murder that took place thirty or forty years earlier? Of course it would: I don't need to look any further than Sofía, the real Sofía Márquez, do I? According to Avril's mails, like Señorita Duval, she sees what happened in the past differently to the rest of us. She thinks Miguel was the one responsible for his brother's death. Yes, sweetheart," Luisa told herself, suppressing the crazy urge to have a Bloody Mary that always grabbed her when she started thinking about her literary suspects, "but as far as I can tell, Sofía has not killed anyone to have her revenge on a childhood memory. Is it really plausible for somebody to kill from a motive like that? You would need to be pretty disturbed to murder a child just to settle an account with the past, wouldn't you?"

So, while the dance teacher Señorita Duval began to look like the prime suspect as the murderer in her novel, Luisa went on living her double life. This proved complicated, until she succeeded in adding a new element to the double life of her professional and personal duties: infidelity. As soon as she had done so, however – and it only took a couple of days – she felt relieved, and had none of the sense of panic that usually gripped her. How strange these things are, because once you get used to infidelity – thought Luisa as she called Elba from the hotel lift ("Have dinner on your own, darling, I'm stuck in a dreadful traffic jam") – once you get used to it (and the fact is this happens very quickly) you find it benefits not just you but all those around you. "Because infidelity," Luisa laughed to herself, "is inevitably accompanied by guilt, and that has the merit of making those who are unfaithful much more generous with others, more understanding and far more tolerant. Really, it's amazing how generous infidelity can be." She could see it everywhere and with everyone. With Elba for example. ("Don't worry, my love, if you haven't finished your maths today, you can do it tomorrow. What do you think of this skirt I bought you? And this? Try it on as well.") And thanks to being unfaithful, she was much more generous and understanding with Enrique too. ("You can't come today? It doesn't matter, my sweet, I understand completely, let's talk tomorrow. Take care.")

On other occasions, however, Luisa saw things differently. She saw what she was doing not so much as being unfaithful as untidy. "Infidelity when you're married is one thing, because everybody needs a bit of fresh air once in a while, but to betray someone you've staked everything on quite recently is different. It's like buying another two bars of chocolate when you've got a box already started."

It was one evening, when she was on her way to her fourth tryst with Miguel, that she almost ran the boy over. She was just coming out of her garage and the first thing she saw was the porter's cat. She just had time to think: "You nasty animal, I haven't seen you for a while," and was so taken up with her feelings about the cat she didn't notice that close behind it a boy was running across the garage exit. In her headlights, his eyes glowed almost as brightly as the cat's. A split second later, and she would have run him over. Luckily though, she managed to brake in time, but even so, the boy fell to the ground, staring up at the sky.

She leapt out of the car and ran up to him.

"My God! Are you all right?"

He had a small cut on his knee and was crying. For some strange reason, Luisa wondered if he hadn't been crying before the accident: his face was wet and grimy. The cut on his leg was fresh, however, because it began to bleed. Fortunately it did not look serious. The important thing now was to make sure he could stand, and had no other injuries. ("Here, look, it was nothing. Wait, I'll wipe your face a bit and help you pick up your things. Would you like me to take you home? Where do you live?") It was only after she had helped the boy to his feet that Luisa recognized him. This took her much longer than it should have done, but the circumstances didn't help. In fact, she had only seen Mikki Gasset once, that first day at school, and in a few photos his father had shown her hurriedly: in hotel rooms it wasn't parental love they talked about, but another sort.

"You're Miki, aren't you? You gave me a real shock. Are you sure you aren't hurt? Let's call your father, you live near here on Alfonso XII, don't you?"

She didn't ask him what he had been doing running out of her apartment block, because at that moment Elba appeared, and there were more urgent matters to think of. Instead what came out was:

"What luck you're here, Elba. Come on, help Miki collect up his things. We need to call his father to tell him what's happened."

It looked as though Elba was arriving home after a gym session, because she was wearing her school skirt (raised even higher above the knee than usual, the silly girl) and a garish green lycra top that didn't even cover her midriff. "For heaven's sake, Elba, where are you going dressed like that?" Luisa was going to say, but she didn't get to ask that question either, because her daughter was already bending over Miki to help him.

"Stand up, Miki, it'll be all right. You look as though you've seen a ghost. Come on, don't be such a crybaby!" Then, turning to her mother: "Don't worry, Mummy, he isn't hurt, it's only a scratch."

After that, Elba fished her mobile out of her backpack and rang Miki's house. She asked to speak to "Señor Gasset on behalf of Luisa Dávila", and when he replied, said: "Just a second, I'll put my mother on." She sounded so adult that Luisa stared at her without saying a word, but thinking to herself that young teenagers were not so much like Julia Roberts in *Pretty Woman* as Irma la Douce in all her glory. For goodness' sake, all her daughter needed were a suspender belt and fishnet stockings and she'd look like a real streetwalker. "I have to pay closer attention to what she wears when she leaves home," thought Luisa, "even if it's only to go to the gym next door."

A few minutes later, by which time the boy's cut had stopped bleeding, Miki, Elba and her mother rang the bell at the Gassets' apartment, and Luisa stepped inside Sofía's old home forty years after the first time she had been there. Now it belonged to Miguel: what an odd way to discover where her lover lived! She wondered what would attract her attention when she crossed the threshold. Finding out what the home territory of someone she had recently spent several afternoons of lovemaking with looked like? Or the differences between past and present?

"Come in, Luisa, come in," said Miguel, giving her a peck on the cheek. When he bent down to give his son a big hug, Luisa, remembering what she had read in Avril's emails, decided to do as she had done: she let her gaze wander to right and left, inspecting everything to see what stirred in her memory. She soon stopped, however: this didn't seem the moment for nostalgia.

For his part, Miguel stood up again and turned towards her with a smile that was hard to classify, a mixture of despondency and wry humour.

"Some days it really would be better to stay in bed," he said. He was carrying a phone in his hand, and held it up to Luisa.

"What do you—"

"When Elba called a while ago to tell me about the accident, I had just finished talking to my lawyer. Apparently, the judge has decided I'm not to have custody of Miki. He is to go and live with my ex. So you can imagine how I feel: first that, and now this. But I'm sorry, do come in." He fell silent, and when he spoke again there was no trace of humour in his voice: "There's something in all this I don't understand. What was Miki doing coming out of your apartment, Luisa?"

That was the last time Luisa Dávila saw the boy. Scarcely two days later, Miki Gasset was found dead at the foot of his school's main staircase. The small cut he had received when Luisa almost ran him down went unnoticed. It was another, much heavier blow which had caused his death. Apparently he had asked permission to go to the infirmary because he had a sore throat. He had rolled all the way down the stairs. Nobody was with him. He was a lonely sort who few of the others paid much attention to. He fell onto his back, and apparently broke his neck.

Part Two

The Vigil

When I think of the night following Miki's accident, all I can remember are faces. The sense of unreality that any death brings is even stronger when the dead person is someone who in the natural order of things was not meant to die. It may also be that this sense of unreality is the only slight compensation for someone who has lost a child: I can't be sure, because fortunately I have never had that experience. What I do know is how I felt when I heard the news: "It could have been my own daughter." I repeated this to myself time and again throughout those night hours, giving a thousand thanks to a God I had not prayed to in years: thank you my God for taking Miki and not Elba, his child and not mine: a gratuitous, mean-spirited and banal sense of relief. What can I say in my defence? Whenever disaster strikes close to us, we always feel that "there but for the grace of God go I".

As I said, it was the faces I remembered from that night. Those of the adults and of the children. We were all there: Miguel, Sofía, Elba, Avril and that boy who was new to me – Tony Gasset, Miguel's eldest son. I should of course count him as an adult, because he hasn't been a child for years. I reckon he must be almost thirty. Miki's mother was there too, but some charitable soul took her home. She was given a sedative. Deaths involving separated couples are very different in many ways, although at this moment I could not describe exactly what they are. I do recall how long that night was when we sat vigil over Miki's body. Vigils without prayers are sad. The muttered rosaries of the past may have been irritating and even fake in their emotions, but at least they helped pass the long hours.

145

There were no prayers for Miki, and nobody wore mourning: who wears black these days? As a result, our everyday clothes looked even more out of place, and clashed with the expressions on the faces I studied so closely that night.

I can remember observing them one by one. The first person I looked at was Sofía: I was surprised, because this was the first time I had seen her cry. We never imagine that strong people can have weaknesses, and when they do succumb, we find it inexcusable. She put her arms round Miguel in a way that made me wonder because, as far as I knew, she did not feel very close to him. On the contrary, she was suspicious of him because of what had happened in our childhood. Although, I asked myself almost at once, what did I really know about either of them? Nothing. So much has been happening recently it feels like years since we met up again, despite the fact that the dinner in my apartment was only a few weeks ago. When everything is changing, it's as though time almost stands still, and yet a couple of weeks is no time at all in which to get to know someone. That's why I know so little about either Miguel or Sofía's lives. In fact, all I know about Sofía is what I've read in Avril's mails.

Sofía on the other hand behaved as if she knew everything about me. It may be my imagination, but I could swear she even knew about my incipient relationship with Miguel. I have no proof of this, but the thought came to mind when I recalled her saying: "you two should pay more attention to your children". That was what she said that first night, as if she already knew what was going to happen a few minutes later between Miguel and me.

That's why I say she knows me, whereas she has always been a mystery to me. What did she mean? And what did she see concerning the children that had escaped my attention? I didn't even know if the three of them were friends or hated each other, as Avril's emails seemed to suggest: "You hate the Shrimp as much as I do, don't you, Elba? Both of us hate him." That's what the long mail she sent Elba after the birthday party said, although I know we shouldn't pay too much attention to what children write. They use that word "hate" far too easily: "I hate your face" they say, or "teacher hates me", or "I hate spinach". We shouldn't put too much on it. The same is true of the lies they tell: I remembered Avril lying when she said she had no idea where classroom 1B was, for example. Does that make her a habitual liar? If she were an adult, that might be the case, but she's only a child, so it's not that important.

Be that as it may, and thinking about Elba and Avril and what their relationship to the dead boy might have been, perhaps I ought to have asked Sofía what she meant by that warning she had given us. After all, she is (or was) teacher to all three of them, and so knew them all well, including my own daughter. Perhaps far better than me, if we give any credence to her extraordinary thesis that parents are the ones who know the least about their own children. Besides, Sofía always says she has a soft spot for Elba, and affection always means we pay close attention to someone.

Elba also cried that night. She looked very pretty. It was no moment to be thinking how pretty somebody was or wasn't, but that is another strange effect of death: those left alive seem even fuller of life. Poor little Miki Gasset seemed even more dead when compared to my daughter. That evening Elba was in her school uniform, but worn properly, without rolling the skirt up to make a mini out if it. This made her seem even more childlike. Ever since we arrived, as if she was somehow trying to make up for the absence of his brother, she stayed close to the second Antonio – or rather, to Tony Gasset – who I was meeting for the first time. What was he like? I suppose that if I hadn't been so busy trying to be of use to his father ("Are you all right? What can I do to help? Is there anything you need?") I would have paid more attention to this new character in our story. Why shouldn't I do so now? There was nothing to stop me. Vigils without prayers go on and on, so that the only way to fill in time is by thinking, describing, interpreting.

So: the boy did not look much like his father. Or rather, he was like the Miguel I remembered from our childhood, and that person was very different from today's Miguel. Almost unrecognizably so. Family likenesses are so odd: it's weird how a child can look nothing like a parent but be exactly like the memory we have of him, or better still, be identical to a boy who disappeared years ago. Tony was an exact copy of the previous Antonio. Yes, I know. At some point soon I'm going to have to stop and think about the blindingly obvious similarity between the accident that happened in my childhood and the way the boy we are going to bury in a few hours died. But death has what I call a photographic effect: it's as though reality were frozen at the moment it happened. Normally, we all spend our time remembering the past or imagining the future. But death freezes things, so that for a few hours at least we live entirely in the present. That was what I was doing then. I was completely absorbed in studying everyone around me. Studying Tony's face, for example, and watching how my little Elba was trying to console him. The two of them standing there next to the coffin. Elba brought him a drink and several times tried to whisper something in his ear. He did not look at her once. He did not move away from the coffin, and could only stare down at his brother's face. I didn't know how often he glanced at him throughout that long night. It's very common for us to stare at the body of someone we love time and again. It's as though we want to make sure that it is in fact them, or perhaps we simply want to remember their features so that we won't forget them: although that's not something I could ever do. If Elba were to die (my God, that superstitious fear again, how stupid of me, nothing is going to happen to my girl, absolutely nothing), if that were to happen, I'm sure I would avoid looking at her lifeless body. A dead body can never remind us of the person who has left us. It's as if, once the soul has departed, nothing about the body corresponds to the living person. I don't know who it was who said that the dead are nothing like the person they were when they were alive, but only resemble other dead people, but they were right. After a few hours, a cadaver is simply another cadaver. And who wants to perpetuate the image of someone so remote from us?

I looked at Elba once more. She had just put her slender arm – in the red school blazer – round Tony's shoulder, as if she really did want to protect him. As far as I could tell, they hardly knew each other; they might only have met a couple of times after school, as well of course as at Miki's birthday party, and yet there she was, trying to offer him protection. That's women for you: we always want to be where we think we're most needed. They made a lovely picture, I told myself, with him so tall and her so small and childlike. My daughter was not yet twelve (and Miki will never have another birthday, just like his uncle Antonio, that other boy who will always be a boy...) Come on Luisa, what did you promise yourself? You said you weren't going to think about that first accident or link the two deaths, you're not Carmen O'Inns with all her theories and speculation, now's really not the moment. Tomorrow after we've buried him there'll be time enough to think about all that. It's still a few weeks before my daughter reaches twelve, although tonight the uniform made her look much younger. The boy was good looking: Tony I mean. Forget any similarities with the past, forget the dead; just concentrate on observing him as you would do in less tragic circumstances. Yet even if I could do so, I don't think I could ever be completely impartial, because of a tiny fault in his teeth – his top incisors were slightly crooked. Strange how our tastes depend on what we liked as a child. Ever since my schooldays I've had a thing about men with teeth like that. It's what I notice first when I meet someone; in fact, Elba's father had a similar defect. How simple it all is when you start to analyse it. It's elementary, my dear Freud, attraction is based on tiny things like these.

I wondered whether Elba found the boy as attractive as I did, and for the same reason. I remembered that when I told her about her father I mentioned this detail, but I doubt whether she took it in. Anyway, whether or not she likes irregular teeth, she must have found him attractive. After all, my daughter was reaching the age when girls started to look at men. Yes, real men, not eleven-year-old shrimps like the ones Avril described in her mails: "the stupid Shrimp", "that silent, wet little dwarf", "that silly Miki…" My God, what am I saying? That's another of death's disconcerting effects: it makes us irreverent. Who hasn't had an inconvenient, tasteless or frankly evil thought when faced with a dead body laid out in front of us? It doesn't matter what our relationship with the dead person might have been, we always find ourselves thinking something inappropriate about them. Death somehow makes us suffer either because it affects us too much, or too little. Either out of love for the deceased, or compassion; and if not compassion, then a sense of guilt.

What about Avril? She was also there, although she was the only one who didn't cry. I definitely don't like that girl. I'm glad Sofía has a soft spot for my daughter, but there's no way I feel the same about hers. Not because her friendship with Elba is so close (or at least seemed to be, until a few days ago) that it's hard to tell where one ends and the other begins. Nor is it anything to do with her character, which basically I know nothing about (it's incredible how girls of that age can be such clones of one another). No, what worried me is what I've learnt about her through her emails, especially the one in which she talked about a photo of Miki she stole from the apartment we were holding the vigil in.

Only a few hours ago, something like that would have seemed unimportant. A bit of nonsense, a silly prank. But I'm afraid that death changes everything, and this is another of its absurd effects: whereas it can make important things seem insignificant, it can also blow up small things, childish pranks for example, and give them a very different meaning. That was why I found Avril so disconcerting. I know, I know, I'm judging her entirely by the emails she's sent to Elba. And how can we judge anyone, and especially a young girl, by the rubbish they send to their friends? Desires, secrets, the most unlikely wishes – and their pet hates, of course. Adolescents' conversations and confessions are always made up of these disparate elements. So stop looking at the poor girl like that; stop imagining all those wild notions.

I could not stop myself though. I studied her for quite some time. Sofía and Miguel were talking to each other in a corner (as teacher and father of a pupil, I guess: or was there something more? No, absolutely not), talking as people who had shared a death in the past and were now faced with another very similar one. Elba in the meanwhile was looking at Tony, Tony only had eyes for his dead brother, and I was watching Avril. Like Elba, she was wearing her school uniform, because immediately after Miki's death, and without waiting for the police investigation (there was no reason she should have – Miki had been on his own when he died) or for the body to be removed (or precisely to protect them from that), Sofía had taken the girls to her apartment first, and then later brought them here. I was in favour of sparing them such an arduous night – where was the sense in two young people of their age taking part in a vigil for someone like this? Sofía insisted however: "That's enough of this ridiculous modern idea of wrapping kids up in cotton wool," she said. "They shouldn't be kept in some everlasting Disneyland where they have no contact with pain or death. Don't you see? That way the only knowledge they have of it comes from TV news or from films, and that's a disaster. Today's kids have breakfast staring at corpses outside some police station in Iraq; they have tea killing Martians on their PlayStations, and eat supper zapping between reality crime shows and that stupid Terminator thing. They end up without the slightest notion what is fiction and what reality. Of course, everything becomes fiction, so that the corpses in the news seem just as real or unreal to them as the ones in their video games. Can you really not see it? We're creating little monsters, dammit."

Sofía dixit. She always did like to sit in judgment. And when it came to children, she always sounded like a psychology manual, with a few added embellishments of her own. I disagree with her completely; besides, no one could ever accuse me of wrapping Elba up "in cotton wool", quite the opposite. Ever since the mistake I made by not telling her the truth about how she was born, I never hide anything from her. The other evening for example, on one of the few occasions we had dinner together, I told her a lot of things about my life that parents normally never tell their children. About my asthma and how vulnerable it made me feel, and the great impact it had on my childhood, so much so that even today (although it's been years since I last had an attack) I always carry an inhaler in my bag. Some people think you shouldn't reveal any of your weaknesses to your children, but I think I was right to do so. I also talked about the ambivalent relationship (a strange mixture of fear and admiration) that I have with Sofía. I didn't say anything about Miguel however, apart from telling her about the death of his brother and everything that had happened on that distant afternoon. This was the part that most interested Elba. She listened very closely, and asked hundreds of questions: "How did he fall, Mummy? It didn't seem as though anybody had pushed him, did it? What does 'a broken neck' mean? You don't mind if I tell Avril all this, do you? It's such a fascinating story. Explain to me again how it happened: did he fall backwards, like this?"

I answered each and every one of her questions, so nobody can accuse me of being a coward or of protecting my daughter from harsh reality. But it's one thing to share an ancient, unpleasant memory, and quite another to bring your daughter into direct contact with death. That's what I told Sofía, but she insisted and, as usual, she won. As far as I'm concerned at least, Sofía always wins. So there the three children were, just like we were forty years ago at the vigil for Antonio, in days when it goes without saying we were not wrapped in cotton wool, and Disneyland didn't even exist.

What I remember now about that far-off night were the prayers, the murmuring and the strict mourning clothes everyone wore. Yet there were few tears. I can remember Miguel's face as if it were yesterday – identical to Tony's now, but wide-eyed and completely dry, because in those days real men didn't cry, and those who were growing up to be men didn't do so either. "Men don't show their feelings. Only women cry, so be a man, come on, restrain yourself, show you're a real male…" Yes, that's how it used to be. Now though, Miguel hadn't stopped sobbing all night. A silent, bitterly painful way of crying that touched me deeply and which I was unable to comfort (he wouldn't allow me to) because at no moment did he turn to me. He seemed to prefer Sofía's company. That's yet another disconcerting effect of death. New lovers don't make good shoulders to cry on. People find more comfort from a friend or relative, or even an old acquaintance they don't have any particular affection for, like Sofía. Why should that be? Who knows, although I do have my own theory: when a love affair begins, it's too much concerned with the pleasures of the flesh, which give rise to very intense but much less solid emotions than what we call "compassion". Yet it's precisely compassion rather than passion, or desire, and much less lust that's needed when we feel so much pain. At least I'd like to believe that was why my efforts to comfort Miguel were not welcome. Although I can think of a further reason for his unexpected rejection of me. It may be that any comforting gesture from a recent lover (in this case, me) seems much more profane in these circumstances. Because, after all, the consoling hands are following the same paths they took only a few hours earlier, when the world had yet to crumble, when "love" meant "desire" rather than "son", that terrible word that Miguel repeated ten, a hundred, a thousand times or more with his head on Sofía's shoulder, crying his eyes out in a way he would never have done at his brother's death, because back then real men did not cry. Even if it must be a good thing for men to cry, it was heartbreaking to see all that despair in his eyes, to see how he had fallen apart, especially as he was usually so correct and reserved. Then there was the trickle of saliva I saw drip from his mouth onto Sofía's grey woollen suit, the same one she wore on the evening the three of us had dinner together, the one that does little to hide all the bulges of her menopause. A welcoming, maternal sort of dress, one that immediately offers comfort. Not like mine, which was perfect for what we were doing a few hours ago, the last time we met in the hotel: "let me undo the zip, my love, yes, that's right, like that..." but might appear obscene in this context. It's obscene, indecent, unforgivable to seek comfort where a short while earlier you were looking only for pleasure. What about Sofía in all this? Did she still feel that strange resentment towards Miguel that Avril wrote of in her emails? Could that be true? What if it were the exact opposite, and there were something between the two of them? How would I know? When it comes to that, I don't know much about Avril either: a strange girl playing strange games. When I think about it, possibly there's a lot about Elba herself I don't know. There she was at the far end of the room, trying to comfort the elder brother who had the same name as his uncle, who died in such similar circumstances. (What did happen this time around? How did Miki fall? Was it an accident? Was there really nobody with him? How could no one see anything in a school full of children, teachers?... Could it be possible?...) Not now Luisa – I told myself sternly – tomorrow. Tomorrow you can have your doubts about two boys, uncle and nephew, who both died of a similar blow to the head, at more or less the same age. Oh come on, we've agreed you're not going to behave like Carmen O'Inns, haven't we? Not tonight, at least. Death commands respect. Death freezes time like a photograph, so be content with taking a good look round you and don't try and be so smart, trying to find more parallels than there are between the two accidents. After all, there weren't many other similarities. Miki was alone when he died. Everyone says he was a shy, lonely boy, whereas Antonio was by far the stronger and more attractive of the two brothers. So he was the opposite of this poor boy whom nobody thought worth paying much attention to when he was alive: the Shrimp who adored his elder brother, the little boy over whom Miguel and his ex were fighting for custody.

Did nobody really see anything? Were there no witnesses? I couldn't help asking myself those two questions again, but almost immediately answered myself by saying that it really didn't matter, because that was no guarantee anyone knew what had happened. There were three of us present when the first death occurred, and yet we all saw completely different things: to me, it was an accident, Sofía saw a deliberate murder; and Miguel – what did he see? When he talked about the incident that night in my apartment, which was the only time we ever mentioned the past, he spoke as if the accident had not affected him that deeply, and of course he shed no tears the night we sat vigil over his brother – I remembered that distinctly. Yet he had lost a brother, and for a brother one can feel all sorts of things – love of course, but also hate, admiration or envy, you can feel close or distant – a whole range of emotions, anything but indifference. That's the only feeling there is no room for – so what did Miguel really feel? What did he see?

Impressions, suggestions, attempts to interpret people's attitudes – or, what amounts to the same thing, vain attempts to read their minds, I told myself, giving up again. Isn't it true that in life everything is speculation or wishful thinking, because in fact nobody knows anything about other people? That is why some argue that a person – you, me, anyone – is not a well-defined object, but is simply what other people see and believe him or her to be. This, by the way, is the reason why most writers prefer to tell stories in the first person, because that is the way we see life: from the unique, subjective eye of our own point of view. Yet it seems to me that there are thousands of points of view, and there is no reason why ours should be better or closer to the truth. And even if there are thousands of points of view, that doesn't necessarily mean that one of them *has* to be right. It may well be that they are all wrong, and the truth is hiding somewhere else. That is the reason why bad novelists – and some good ones too (the ones who don't care what is fashionable) – still prefer to tell their stories in the third person. That's because above and beyond any point of view or interpretation that each individual might make of a fact, there are the facts themselves. And these deserve to be set before the reader without the distortion implied in having to see everything through the subjective eye of a single narrator.

That's quite enough of that. The night is already long enough as it is, so I'm going to stop describing what I see – or what I think I see: reality, points of view, truths or lies... Literature is one thing, life is another, and in life, only the most arrogant or the stupidest think things are really as they see them. That's enough of playing detectives. Yet here's another of death's weird effects: it's precisely when we are brought face to face with it that we need an explanation for everything happening around us. We try desperately to understand, when in reality it is only irrelevant details that can be explained. The important things have no direct explanation, or if they have, there are so many of them that it's the same as saying there are none.

I try to stop myself thinking about it. To forget the trace of saliva on Sofía's dress when it should be on mine. To forget that I'm worried about Avril and her desire to know what things would have been like if life had not taken so many twists and turns. To forget as well that my daughter changes hour by hour, and sometimes seems like a grown-up young woman, and at others like a little girl. A little girl who is trying her utmost to comfort Tony after the death of his brother. Her attitude seems so feminine, so protective. To forget all this, and to remember instead that tomorrow I will probably be unable to silence the crazy Carmen O'Inns I have inside me, and will be doing all I can to discover what really happened. Despite the fact that I'm aware now, and hopefully will still be aware tomorrow, that it doesn't matter what I think I can see, what I sense or deduce from the attitudes of the other mourners. However much we persist in trying to work out what is going on by studying the people around us, reality has nothing to do with what we believe or suspect. Reality is an omniscient narrator who couldn't give a damn about what I believe, sense, suspect or deduce.

"Leave me alone, Elba. Let go of me, for goodness' sake!"

I might have fallen asleep for a moment, because I have no idea how and when these words became mixed up with what I was thinking. Although dawn cannot have been far off, the room was still in darkness, and I tried to make out where the voice was coming from.

All at once at the far side of the room I saw Tony struggling free of Elba and moving to the side of the coffin, where he began to sob once more.

"Now I'm the only one you've got," she said. He replied:

"That's enough, Elba. Enough."

My daughter didn't move: she removed her hand without saying a another word. She slowly turned her face in my direction, and in the first light of day I could make out her expression. She seemed quite calm, showing no sign that Tony's outburst had upset her in any way. I was the one who felt angry, and thought: he has no right! However terrible he feels, he has no right to talk like that to a young girl who is only trying to show her support. Then, as I was about to intervene, I heard Tony's voice once more:

"Leave me alone, d'you hear? What have you done? What have you done, Elba?"

Like someone turning in on themselves, I saw him move closer to the coffin by the wall, leaving my daughter behind. She stood for a second without reacting. A shadow falling across her face prevented me from seeing her eyes, but I could make out her lips. She half-opened them as she stretched out her hand towards Tony's arm. He shook her off again. That was when Elba started to bleed. The blood came pouring out of her nose, in such quantities it was as if she were choking on it. She was still staring straight at Tony. "I'm all you've got," she struggled to say again, but the bleeding was so intense that by the time I had reached her side to help her, to say, "Come on, Elba, let's go, my love," and try to separate her from Tony ("What are you doing? Leave my daughter alone, can't you see she was only trying to help?") it was coursing down her blouse and staining her skirt. Elba stood there without moving, a desolate but impassive look on her face, like a wounded animal.

"For heaven's sake, Elba!" I said. She tried once again to clutch at Tony's arm, but as she did so, for perhaps the first time that whole night he turned and looked straight at her, horrified at the way my poor daughter's blood was dripping onto the face of his dead brother.

Non-Filter Cigarettes

"Fine, sweetheart, let's say I'm more than happy to help you, but before we start digging let's make sure we're straight on a few things. I'm *not* Isaac Newton – in other words, I'm *not* a black... I'm *not* your detective assistant and/or your inseminator. And on behalf of the dwindling, battered (and bewildered) heterosexual male collective of which I am a part, I hope I'm not your erotic refuge either. So let me have another cigarette and we can talk about all this more calmly."

I watched Enrique light yet another Ducado, and as I turned to reach him an ashtray, calculated that he must have beaten the world record for the amount of political incorrectness that could fit into a single sentence. But that's the Man of My Life for you: take him or leave him, and I couldn't leave him, especially not now, after all that had happened in the past few days. So instead of taking him to task, all I said was:

"Oh come on, darling, anyone would think that..."

If life had a rewind button and we could go back twenty or thirty minutes to see how our conversation began, it would be obvious that from the outside, or rather from the viewpoint of a reader of my novels, the scene was very similar to one of Carmen O'Inns and Isaac Newton's erotic-cum-professional encounters. The decor, however, was slightly different. We were not in Newton's fabulous postmodern penthouse, the one with panoramic views over the Royal Palace. We were in Enrique Santos's apartment. (One of these days I really must decide whether or not to change the description of Newton's place: "postmodern penthouse" is probably a little too much. Then again, what do details like that matter when since the death of young Miki I've found it impossible to write a single line of my novel, and suspect I might not start again for some time to come). Back in reality, I have to say that Enrique's apartment is the opposite of a postmodern penthouse: the decor is far from Zen, and he thinks feng shui is a Chinese takeaway. To my distress, Enrique likes to think his home has taste. "Castilian style" he calls it: heavy panelled wooden furniture, cupboards with wrought-iron hinges, chests of drawers of all shapes and sizes. In short, Spanish Remorse at its most horrendous. "What's the point of earning so much," I had tried to argue when I still thought it was possible to change him, "if you're stuck with the sort of taste that went out with the Ark?" Not only did Enrique laugh at the idea, but the next time I went to his apartment, even before the first kiss, my eyeballs were seared by the sight of a new carved wooden cabinet installed on its own stand in the hall. Enrique was obviously trying to provoke me, but that's the way he is: take him or leave him… And as I was saying, there was no way I could leave him, not now, not after all that had happened in the past few weeks, when my life seemed to have imploded and to have room only for people related in some way or other to my childhood. Except for Enrique, my Man Friday, as I've called him more than once for very different and not very charitable reasons. Now however, on the island my life seemed to have become, I needed Mr Friday more than ever. That was also why, after the funeral at which Enrique had the opportunity to meet all the people involved in my past, I had decided to confide to him the many aspects of it that were bothering me. To do so I chose one of our rituals: Friday night, which we always spend at his place, because Enrique is a man of habit and this was one of our sacrosanct habits. Even so, after I had arrived I couldn't find a proper way to begin, so we ended up in bed without even having broached the subject.

If we rewind a bit further, let's say half an hour before Enrique said the sentence that figures at the start of this chapter and which seemed to me such a monument to political incorrectness, we would be found together in bed, with me holding his hand like a little girl and Enrique about to light his second Ducado as he said:

"OK, so tell me what's so terrible that it's frightened my little girl like this?"

"I don't know what makes you think I'm so frightened," I replied, trying my best to seem less on edge than I felt, not only to try to fool Enrique, but myself as well. The fact was, I didn't succeed either way: it was almost impossible to fool Enrique.

"Sweetheart, when a woman trembles from head to foot *long before* making love to you," he said, "either she is overwhelmed at the mere sight of you (hardly likely in this case, because I think we are what's known as 'an established couple') or she is scared to death for other reasons, and needs your arms around her for something other than pleasure. So don't try to pull the wool over my eyes, and tell me what's wrong."

I smiled, and spent a few seconds watching how the ash on the tip of Enrique's cigarette kept growing dangerously. Enrique is one of those people who always seem to be balancing the ash unbelievably – now it's going to fall, now it isn't – in a way that's as captivating as it is irritating. It's impossible not to stare.

"I don't really know where to start," I said. "Basically it's only an intuition, or even worse, a superstition. Have you ever found life repeating a situation exactly the same as one you lived in the past? In other words, the past is reproduced almost exactly, so you inevitably think that something terrible, perverse or even criminal has happened a second time?"

"You'll have to explain that nonsense, balderdash – or whatever you clever people call such confused reasoning – a bit better to someone as slow as me. You see, sweetheart, those who say that everything is catching except for beauty are wrong: having a girlfriend who's a writer doesn't make you a cryptographer, so start again, and this time talk in words of less than three syllables, please."

I had to laugh, and while he was busy rearranging the pillows, could not help but be amazed yet again at the difference between my two lovers. Three or four meetings in a hotel room is hardly enough time to form an opinion about someone with as shady a past as Miguel Gasset. Especially as since the death of his son we haven't seen each other again on our own. Even so, the two couldn't be more different: the sophisticated Miguel, and Enrique the exact opposite. The one, cultured to his fingertips; the other perhaps not as uncouth as he tries to make out. Miguel so impeccable always, so elegant, and Enrique:

"For God's sake, Enrique! Your clean sheets! Couldn't you just once put the ash in the ashtray?"

Ah well, after all he is the Man of My Life, and however much I tried to build up one and criticize the other, the truth was I could only bear Miguel's extreme sophistication thanks to the counterbalance of Enrique's lack of it. The same was true of Miguel's obsessive neatness and Enrique's untidiness. And anyway, why did I call one of them "the Man of My Life", and the other simply "Miguel"? That was beyond me, as was the fact that it would never have occurred to me to tell Miguel what I was happy to tell Enrique. Why? Who knows: some things are best left unanalysed.

"All right, sweetie pie, now would you like to explain to me all that guff you were talking about just now? I know you women love a post-coital chat, and are happy to discuss everything under the sun, whereas we poor macho men only want to lie there and snore, but even so, don't you think you're taking it a bit far? Besides, what you seem to want to talk about is hardly post-coital chat, is it? Come on, my love, tell me properly what's wrong: I hate to see you this way."

It was only then that I told him everything that had happened since my re-encounter with Miguel and Sofía (well, not *exactly* everything). First of all I explained how strange it had been to realize that each of us present when Antonio died had such a different recollection of it, to the extent that Sofía (and here I had to confess to reading Avril's emails) thought Miguel was responsible for his brother's death. I then said what an extraordinary coincidence it was that Sofía's former apartment now belonged to Miguel, and told him about Miki's birthday party, which I hadn't been to, but which I knew so much about thanks to the girls' emails. I also explained how Avril wrote in one of them about all those there that day: Sofía, Miguel, the three children and Tony. "He's just like the first Antonio, and not just because of the name. Ri, you can't imagine the effect it had on me when I saw him for the first time at the vigil. It's incredible, there are so many coincidences in everything around me it's scary, I can hardly believe it." I hesitated awhile, then also told him how – again, according to what Avril wrote in her emails – neither of the girls seemed to like Miki Gasset much. "Just imagine, they called him the Shrimp. How cruel can you get? But you know what kids are like. I only ever saw him a couple of times, but I can tell you he was a frail, insignificant sort of boy: how can I put it? He was one of those who seem to go through life walking on tiptoe, without making any noise, or – apparently at least – causing anyone any trouble. Poor little boy!"

I remember I also talked about Avril and her obsession with her own past. About how she had managed to sneak into the rooms at the back of the Gasset family's apartment during the birthday party. I went on about how she had tried to discover which had been her mother's bedroom "before life took so many twists and turns". I mentioned the silver frame and the photos in it, including the one Avril had found showing Miki next to the hearth in the living room, with Christmas decorations in the background. "Just think – according to Avril, he was in the exact same position as Sofía had been in another photo taken at Christmas, in the same apartment! Isn't that absolutely incredible, Ri? A photo taken in the same spot and at the same time of year! I tell you, I'm really scared: all these coincidences don't seem possible, but wait, I haven't told you the worst about the story of that photo, just listen!" I told him exactly what Avril had done with the photo: "She edited it on her computer, Ri! She put her face in place of the boy's… Yes, I know you're going to say it's only a prank, but surely you must agree that now the boy is dead there's something really macabre about it."

At this point, I paused to wait for Enrique's reaction. All the while I had been talking, I was worried he might make some sarcastic comment about the fact that I, Luisa the Supercool, the Superperfect, had been reading the girls' emails. The fact that he said nothing encouraged me to tell him everything I had found out about Sofía in the same way: what I'd learnt about the wrong choices she had made in love, and how she had justified them by saying that she was paying for a childhood sin. What sin would that be, asked Enrique? And I shrugged my shoulders and took the opportunity to snuggle up even more closely to his warm, inviting body.

"I'm not sure; maybe she didn't mean anything really important; maybe it was simply a manner of speaking. That's the worst thing about everything I'm telling you: what exactly is the truth, and what's simply different people's opinions? Avril wrote that Sofía fell in love with Avril's father merely because he reminded her of someone from her childhood, 'someone who had been snatched from her'. But listen, because here is where it really begins to sound like something out of a nineteenth-century novel: she also wrote that Sofía was hoping that one day life would give her the chance to settle scores with the person who had done this. And that person is obviously Miguel Gasset, since she's convinced he let his brother die."

I paused once more. I was afraid that all these melodramatic details might make Enrique laugh, or come out with one of his down-to-earth comments like: "Sweetheart, everything you're talking about makes it sound like a Mexican vendetta, a real soap opera." I quickly decided it would be better if I were the one to lighten things up a bit:

"As you can see," I said, "it could be that nothing of what I've been telling is true. Avril wrote that perhaps Sofía had been making it all up to justify having fallen in love with someone so obviously unworthy of her as José Antonio. By the way, what do you think about the coincidence over their names? That makes three Antonios so far in this story…"

"Darling, I can't believe what I'm hearing: are you really taking everything you read in those mails to heart?"

"No, of course not… Well, only some of it, the things I think might be most useful for my novel. But I've got the feeling that we still haven't got to the bottom of Sofía Márquez."

"Now listen to me," said Enrique, shifting uncomfortably in the bed, while I was secretly praying that he was reacting not to what I had been saying but simply out of the proverbial male distaste for any post-coital discussion, "your problem, sweetheart, your only problem, is that you get carried away by literature."

"OK, but what about all the things I've been telling you about – the coincidences, the chance occurrences? Don't you see—"

"Luisa, you're the one who doesn't see. If as it appears you're trying to link everything to poor Miki's death, just wait a moment and let me deal with all your fears one by one, all the 'terrible coincidences' as you call them, linking past and present. Where would you like me to start? With the fact that the Antonio of your childhood looks like his nephew Tony? Fine, let's start with that. If, as we know, his father Miguel and Antonio were twin brothers, don't you think it's quite likely that uncle and nephew would look like each other? Let's look at another coincidence. What about the strange fact that your friend Miguel Gasset lives in an apartment that once belonged to Sofía?" At this point, Enrique paused to light another cigarette, and as if to signal the class divide between us, snapped off the filter beforehand. "You rich people," he said, "the ones who've had dough since you were born, are great ones for endogamy, not to say incest in all its fifty-seven varieties, including the property one. You marry each other, you do business with each other, and you naturally buy places from each other. You can test it out: pick up the phone book and see who Miguel Gasset's neighbours are: I bet you anything you like you know them all. And as for the photo of Miki by the hearth and the fact that there's one of Sofía taken forty years earlier in the same spot, and with Christmas decorations to boot: it's not even worth wasting a second on. Everybody (everybody with a nice hearth, that is) has had their Christmas picture taken alongside it at some point or other. It's typical of the sort of thing your lot do. And finally, the most ridiculous coincidence of all: the name of Antonio recurring in Sofía and Miguel's lives. Do I really need to tell you that Antonio is one of the commonest names in the Spanish language? How many Antonios do you know? Even Elba's mystery father was called that, wasn't he? As for me, I've got an uncle called Juan Antonio, my cousin Toño, not to mention my grandfather... If you'd said we were talking about Nepomuceno or Casimiro you might have a point, but *Antonio?...*"

"All right, I accept that, but what about Avril putting her face in Miki's photo? I admit it's not exactly a coincidence, but you have to admit that at the very least it's a macabre kind of game."

"What can you have been reading to give it so much importance?" said Enrique, laughing. *"How Psychopaths are Born? Early Warning Signs of Infantile Criminal Tendencies?* I bet in the past few months you've read all the books Amazon has to offer about crime and criminality, haven't you? Please, just forget what all those weighty tomes say and use a bit of common sense. If you intrude or spy on anybody's life it's bound to be full of holes, of craziness, of small betrayals. Isn't yours?"

"He knows I'm seeing Miguel, I'm sure of it," I thought with a start, but fortunately I immediately managed to recover my composure. I would have had to be very stupid to leave any traces of an affair that had only been going on for a few weeks. The thing is, I'm terrified of Enrique, he can see things as sharply as a laser beam.

"You're quite right," I laughed, and then, since the best way to divert attention from one failing is to bring up another one, I went on: "You're absolutely right, my love. My sinful life would never pass the whiter than white test. What I did was very wrong: I mean reading emails that were nothing to do with me. I promise I'll never do it again. I'm truly sorry, I…"

"Sweetheart, I haven't even mentioned that particular sin, have I? We all know that literature excuses everything," said Enrique, and I couldn't for the life of me tell whether he was being serious or not. "And as for what we have been talking about, all I was trying to do was to show that with a bit of common sense everything in this life can be seen to have a perfectly reasonable explanation. What happened to Miki is very sad and regrettable, but as you can see there's no need for you to rush off in a panic and call for Hercule Poirot."

However, as far as the other coincidences were concerned, and the fact that many of the accidents seemed to have so much in common with the novel I'm writing, I didn't find Enrique's explanations entirely convincing. So I took advantage of him referring to Poirot to ask him, half-seriously and half-joking:

"Now you come to mention it, that was precisely what I wanted you to do, Ri…"

"Precisely what?"

"Precisely for you to be my own Hercule Poirot. No, don't look at me like that. It's not what you would call another of my literary extravagances: all I want to know for sure is what happened that day. After all, the accident took place at Elba's school, and that's enough to leave any mother scared, isn't it?"

"What do you want me to do then?"

"I remember that when I enrolled Elba, you told me you knew somebody who worked there, although I can't remember exactly who."

"The caretaker, my precious, the fetcher and carrier at your elegant school. We grew up together."

"And couldn't you ask him?..."

"Aha! So Señora Dávila would like to meet my childhood companion, my friend from before the time when 'life took so many twists and turns'. I'm honoured."

"Yes, well all right, not exactly, but... don't confuse me again with your diatribes about social class. I don't want to talk to him: all I want you to do is ask how Miki Gasset's accident happened. According to the school – and Miguel and Sofía seem to agree – the boy was on his own at that moment at the top of the stairs. He fell backwards, and broke his neck. But how can it be possible for the school to be full of children and teachers, and yet nobody see a thing? Besides, something else worries me: Miki was not your average young boy. For example, let me tell you a little story that made a big impression on me. Kids of that age like to collect stickers, don't they? And logically enough, they all collect the same ones, so they can swap them in the breaks. Usually it's footballers, makes of cars and so on. Miki was unusual even there. He was a loner nobody paid much attention to, apart from his elder brother, whom he adored. Well, when they removed his body after his death and were dressing him for the vigil, somebody found a whole stash of stickers in his pocket. But they weren't modern ones – they were old, and had belonged to his brother. This might seem like nothing to you, but it was a terrible moment. We all burst into tears again. It was like a symbol of what his life had been. Just imagine, all those old-fashioned pictures of animals, strange reptiles, chameleons, salamanders, cobras, all in a handful of faded stickers. He had no friends, and spent his time playing with something that belonged to his brother. Did I tell you Tony is a biologist?"

"No, but I don't see why that's relevant. Look, this is real life, not one of your novels. We're not investigating a crime, so stop searching for suspicious clues wherever you look."

"Please, Enrique…"

"All right, sweetheart, if you're really so worried I'll be your Hercule Poirot for a day and ask my friend Peñuelas if everything really did happen the way the official version says it did. But let's get one thing clear: I'm not your Isaac Newton."

It was then that Enrique pronounced the sentence beginning… I'm not your black man, your detective or your inseminator, etc., that had seemed to me a world record for political incorrectness. Enrique's always someone who before he does you a favour has to rub it in. "But at least he does you the favour," I said to myself with a smile, confident I could rely on him. "Most people do the exact opposite. They promise you the world, then nothing happens." I turned towards him to give him a kiss and found myself confronted with the ash from the umpteenth Ducado, which like all the previous ones was teetering dangerously on the tip of his cigarette. But once again, I didn't say a word: that's the way Enrique is…

"So tell me, what exactly would Señora O'Inns like to know?"

"I've already told you. I want to be reassured it was nothing more than an accident. The previous time, the accident that happened when I was a child…"

"Yes, sweetheart, I get it. I take the trouble to dismantle one by one all the coincidences between past and present that you were so scared about, and yet that First Lady of Crime brain of yours can't help rooting out dark, suspicious deeds all over the place. What is it you're thinking but don't want to tell me straight out? Let me guess: what's the literary term when something that happens in a person's life is repeated in the life of a child of theirs? Destiny? A curse? Symmetry? That's what you're worried about, isn't it? That damned symmetry. So what would reassure you? Proving that there's no possibility of anyone acting suspiciously? In other words, correct me if I'm wrong, but what you want to be able to rule out is any question that Avril, Sofía or Miguel Gasset might have been near the fatal staircase that day, because, as you already know from having spied on somebody else's emails—"

"Enrique, please, I... I was only looking for information for my novel."

"All right, let me rephrase it... as you already know from having *consulted* somebody else's emails, both Avril and Sofía (and Miguel Gasset, by the way) have each got the odd skeleton or two in their closets."

"What rubbish! What are you talking about? What's Miguel got to do with all this?"

"Now that you've taken me on as a detective, you might at least have the courtesy to listen to what my little grey cells tell me. You see, my love, if we think like Hercule Poirot, there are reasons why all *three* of them could be suspects. Avril was jealous of the Shrimp, wasn't she? She wanted to be in his place. Apparently, Sofía spent her life seeking revenge from someone who stole the person she loved from her. And finally, our highly sophisticated and elegant Miguel Gasset let his brother die. Don't look at me like that. If we're to be detectives, then it's plain that your two childhood friends and also that charming young girl by the name of Avril have childhood psychological problems that would be the envy of Freddy Krueger. And of course, according to the theory nowadays, a troubled child inevitably leads to a psychopathic adult. Which leads me to conclude that perhaps Avril, or Sofía, or why not, that Miguel of yours—"

"That's enough, Enrique! What do you know about Miguel?"

"Only what you've told me about him, sweetheart. Well, that and another fact that the delectable Señorita O'Inns would love, one I worked out all by myself with my little grey cells. Miguel Gasset is in the process of divorcing his *fourth* wife, isn't he? And according to what you yourself told me, two days before Miki died, in other words the afternoon you saw the boy coming out of your building and almost ran him over, Miguel heard that the courts were denying him custody of his youngest, just as they had done long ago with his eldest. Am I right? Fine. And have you any idea how many children died last year alone at the hands of fathers or mothers who killed them just to get at their ex-partners?"

"But that's nonsense! Completely idiotic! Now you're just being ridiculous!"

"OK, calm down," said Enrique. "I was simply trying to show you that once you start looking for suspicious motives, you, me and the man in the corner shop could all be murderers. You've just fallen into your own trap, my love: there's nothing easier than to pull together true facts from all over the place and end up with one huge lie. To give you another example: imagine for a moment that your daughter Elba, who doesn't have a father—"

"Stop right there. What you said before about Sofía and Avril might have some truth to it, and I've even come to a similar conclusion myself in the past few hours, but what you say about Miguel, apart from being in very bad taste, is the silliest, most outlandish thing I've ever heard…"

"No it isn't, Luisa. Somebody who kills once is quite capable of doing it a second time. You're so well-read, you must know what the ancient stoics said: 'Like virginity, innocence can only be lost *once*'. So if the first Antonio's death was no accident, perhaps this one—"

"Enrique, that's enough. It's not funny. The first Antonio's death was an accident: I saw it with my own eyes. And as regards the accident the other day, all I'm trying to do is make sure that my daughter's school is a safe place, or if they are lying to me. That's all."

"That's *all*? So you're not worried about any coincidences or those damned symmetries, you're simply concerned about safety at school?"

"That's right. I'm only concerned with Elba's safety. Are you going to talk to your friend Peñuelas or not?"

A Fortnight Later: Black Humour Is No Good for Literature (or Sex Either)

"Enrique mobile" flashed onto the screen of my Nokia. I had no need to read it, because as soon as I heard the theme tune from *The Pink Panther* I knew who it was. I have a different ring tone for all my "loved ones". Elba's is *The Little Mermaid*, Sofía's is the Nokia tone, and I know it's Miguel when I hear *Toreador*. My short sightedness makes them a necessity: can anybody over fifty read the name on a tiny mobile screen?

Now what on earth do I do? I thought to myself. Shall I answer or not? At that very moment I was in the hotel lift on my way up to Miguel's apartment. It was the first time since the start of our romance that we were going to meet there and not in a hotel. It was also the first time we were finally going to see each other alone after all the sad events that had taken place. So it was a very delicate, sensitive moment, and there was *The Pink Panther* getting in the way.

"What to do?" I asked myself. "It's Inspector Clouseau himself reporting back," I joked half-heartedly. "What on earth should I do?"

I could of course have switched my mobile off and called Enrique once I got home again. The fact was, I'd been expecting him to ring for hours. That midday, after lots of delays and hesitation, Enrique had finally had lunch with his friend Peñuelas, the school caretaker. Yet ever since, in that irritating way of his, he had kept his phone switched off until the moment I was about to meet Miguel. "I'm so sorry, Ri," I had told him the day before, during one of our traditional Friday nights, "but I won't be able to see you until the day after tomorrow. The thing is, my Brazilian translator is in town, and I have to have dinner with him. Paulo is fantastic, he's a wonderful translator, but he's also one of those irredeemable night owls who you can never finish with early. All I hope is that we don't drink too many caipirinhas: the last time we worked together I had to leave the car parked where it was and take a taxi home. A big kiss, and please don't forget: call me as soon as you hear anything from your friend Peñuelas. Yes, yes, any time during the day: I'm supposed to meet Paulo at ten in the evening, so after that I won't be able to speak." Now it was half-past ten, and Enrique was calling me anyway. Typical. I decided to at least offer myself a momentary truce: I pressed the "end call" button so that if he wanted to, Enrique would have to call again, and I would have time to think. Fortunately there were still two more floors before I reached Miguel's apartment (thank heavens for these slow, old-fashioned lifts...) but there goes the Pink Panther again. Come on, Luisa, make up your mind, and quickly.

"Is he deliberately calling at this time of night to check up on me? To see if I was lying about the translator?" All of a sudden, I was in a panic. No, that was nonsense. What if Enrique's insistent calls meant he'd discovered something important about the accident? Something that couldn't wait until the next day? What could his friend Peñuelas have told him? Could it be there was a witness, someone who had seen what had happened?

The lift stopped at Miguel's floor. In a few seconds someone would open the apartment door, just as a few minutes earlier, somebody whose voice I didn't recognize had opened the front door for me. Just a few more bars of Henry Mancini's tune, then it would switch to "answering message". Do I respond... or not? If I don't, I'll be nervous the whole night thinking something important happened that I should know about. But if I do answer, he'll hear something in my voice. Miguel will probably notice something, and Enrique is bound to: there's no fooling him, not even on the phone, he's got such a sensitive radar about these things. Make your mind up, Luisa…

"Yeees, Enrique?" (That's it, *the die is cast*, now you'll have to pretend as best you can, sweetheart.)

"Poirot here."

"Hello Ri, that's very funny, but I can hardly hear you, there's almost no reception."

Thank God the apartment door hasn't opened yet, I said to myself. That gives me a couple more seconds to practise my skills as a faker, to adjust my tone of voice.

"Yeees, I can hear you much better now, but I can't really talk right now. Is it really important? I'm just about to meet my translator."

At the far end of the line, Enrique began a lengthy explanation about how he had finally met up with his old friend Peñuelas, where they went to eat, and what aperitif they had before the meal… I felt like screaming for him to get a move on, but didn't dare say anything (remember Enrique's radar for this kind of thing).

"Yes, fine, but what did your Peñuelas actually say? Anything we didn't already know?"

I could hear the bolts on the apartment door sliding back. I hope it's a maid or someone who has come to the door, I thought, that'll give me a few more precious minutes to talk to Enrique. But Murphy's Law always wins, and I found myself smiling straight at Miguel in person. All I could do was to mouth a silent "Hello" and then an equally silent "Sorry, it'll only take a minute", with my hand over the phone. Then, clutching it tight in one hand, I grimaced and pointed my finger in a (I hope) convincing way at the mobile, as if to say to Miguel: "It's nothing, just someone insisting on giving me some information, I'll be right with you", adding to this kiss and an inaudible "I'm sorry, darling", and almost cursing (and I'm someone who never swears) because the situation was becoming truly grotesque.

"…Yes, I can hear you better now, tell me what it is, but hurry up, before the reception goes again."

Enrique told me that part of what the school had said to me about Miki's death was true, but part wasn't. It was true that the boy had fallen backwards. "Peñuelas told me there were more than twenty steps between the first and ground floors," he explained. "But even so, it was really bad luck. If he hadn't fallen backwards, nothing would have happened to the poor kid."

"…Fine, fine," I said, interrupting him. "And the part that wasn't?"

"The part that wasn't what, sweetheart? Tell your translator to wait a minute. This is no way to talk on the phone, you sound like a switchboard operator."

"The part that wasn't true, I mean. What does the caretaker think?" (See, Miguel? I pointed my lying finger at the mobile once more, see? We're talking about caretakers, it's not a personal conversation; I'll be with you right away, darling.)

"You could use his name, couldn't you? He's called José Peñuelas. But then you rich people…"

At that moment, Miguel had moved away to hang my jacket up in one of the bedrooms or in the guest wardrobe. I breathed a sigh of relief and thought: "Thank the Lord and all the saints," because that meant I would have a couple more minutes' respite, and with a bit of luck as much as three or four minutes to finish my conversation with Enrique. What was that I could hear from the living room? Brahms? Oh, that's nice music… Miguel is always the one for these little touches, perhaps Brahms will help me calm down a bit.

"Never mind that, just tell me what Peñuelas has to say…"

The Lord and his saints must have answered my call, because this time Enrique's explanation was quite succinct, so that I learnt a good deal before Miguel came back. I already knew some of it: the reason why Miki wasn't in class for example – he had asked permission to see the school matron. Something else I knew was that the incident occurred during the last morning class – that was why there was no one on the main staircase, as they were all in their classrooms. "...Although just imagine, that day the staircase wasn't as empty as usual; for one reason or another several people were there more or less at the time of the accident. Shall I tell you now, sweetheart, or save it till we meet tomorrow at home? It'd be better then, wouldn't it? Even though it's Sunday," Enrique went on, "we could pretend it's a Friday and play at detectives in bed for a while, couldn't we?"

At that point I, Luisa the Supercool, the superduperperfect one, the one who never swears, mentally let loose a string of curses. While Enrique was fantasizing about us being in bed together, Miguel was heading back towards me, arms outstretched in a way that, if I know anything at all about men, meant he was going to hug me and then beyond any shadow of a doubt was going to plant a kiss on my neck while I was still talking on my mobile. For God's sake, why do men *always* get romantic when they see us women doing something else? While we're talking on the phone is classic, and if we're talking to somebody important, it's supermegaclassic.

I'd better hang up, I thought, but then I stopped myself with the thought that it might be megaclassic for a man to start nibbling your ear while you're on the phone, but that in this case it wouldn't happen. "Miguel is still mourning his dead son, which of course means that the last thing he'll feel like is erotic foreplay. What ridiculous ideas you get," I said to myself, "and anyway it's a relief that's how it is, because I hate the idea of leaping from one bed to another. I don't want to swear undying love to two men in twenty-four hours. No thanks. As I always say, there has to be a rhythm to infidelity, a certain pause... Hang on, what's going on now?..." My theory was in ruins, because I may know men, but perhaps not quite as well as I thought, because what I was afraid of was already happening: Miguel was slowly, gently kissing me all up one side of my neck. "Shi-it," I couldn't help exclaiming (under my breath, of course), me, the superduper etc., Miguel nibbling up and down, and there I was pretending it had nothing to do with me. A scene worthy of the crummiest Blake Edwards, or more like his Spanish counterpart, the fat slob Torrente, because there I was receiving alarming news about something I was really concerned about; one of my men (who had lost a son less than a month earlier, for crying out loud: who can plumb the depths of the human heart?) was kissing and licking my neck and shoulder, while my other lover was determinedly filling my ear with:

"...so you can see that Poirot never sleeps, my love. Let me just say that you were right: this is beginning to seem more and more like one of your Carmen O'Inns's fantasies. You know what? At least four people you know very well *could have been* near that main staircase around the time that the boy died."

"What?..." (Careful, Luisa, keep cool). "What d'you mean?"

"As I can tell you're busy with your Brazilian translator, I'll be brief... but what's that music I can hear in the background?"

"Brahms!" I shouted, while trying to redirect Miguel's kisses downwards and away from my neck, so that he wouldn't hear Enrique's voice. "Brahms!"

"It sounds very nice. Your translator has good taste. Well, as I was saying, it seems there were a lot of people near the staircase at that time on the morning of the accident. Avril's teacher for example sent her to fetch a book from the library. It's impossible to know the exact time, but it was definitely during the last lesson. Then there's your friend Sofía. She had a free period, and was on her own in the staff room, so she could have been there too. But there is more news, my love: are you still there?"

At that point I undid my blouse, in the hope that Miguel would continue on his way down – the further down, the better.

Whatever it took, I had to keep him away from the mobile. Undo your blouse altogether, and your bra too, if that's what it takes. Let him make love to you in the hallway of a respectable family home, anything to stop them hearing each other...

"Are you still there, Luisa?"

"Yes, but the line's so bad I'm going to have to hang up."

"I'll tell you the rest in bed tomorrow, sweetheart, while I cover you in kisses."

Shi-it! What is it with men? (I asked myself) Now Enrique's come over all lovey-dovey too. I reckon they can smell each other, just like animals. Even over the phone. They sniff each other, and get excited. And egg each other on.

"Tell me whatever it is, but tell me *now*!"

"All right, all right, no need to get in such a state. Well, just so that you'll tremble with fear and won't be able to do any work at all with your translator, listen to this: as we know, at that time of day everybody should have been in their classrooms, but some people, like Avril and Sofía, weren't. And pay special attention to what comes next: it seems your daughter Elba could have been there too. From what my Captain Hastings has been able to discover—"

"Who on earth is this Hastings?" (Help! That's my blouse gone; at this rate I'm going to be naked right here, in the hall. What can have got into Miguel? Perhaps it's true that Thanatos always attracts Eros? I've read about it, but I never thought it could be true, not like *this*, anyway).

"Jesus, sweetheart, I thought you knew about detectives. Who is Hastings? Why, he's Poirot's sidekick. As I was saying, my own personal Hastings somehow found out that Elba asked permission to go to the toilet during her last morning class. We don't know the exact time and, as with Avril, we probably never will. No, don't go yet..." (Yes I will, this is becoming too ridiculous for words, I thought, look at yourself, Luisa: the deserter from the cause of serial monogamy caught in her own trap, and the worst of it isn't that to your great surprise you're half-naked in the hallway of somebody else's home while you're on your mobile to Enrique, who has a well-developed radar. The worst is that if Miguel suddenly decides to move up from my breasts to my face again and approaches the phone, then what do I do? I have to put a stop to it.)

"…Wait, darling, you still haven't heard the cherry on the cake. When you do, you'll fall flat on your back. Because our sophisticated Señor Gasset, your beloved Miguel Gasset, was also in the school that morning. How about that for a coincidence? What d'you think of that, you who are such a lover of the mocking laughter of fate?"

When I heard this last piece of information, I began to think that everything Enrique was telling me was a lie, simply a crude (but very typical) joke on his part. That he had found out about my liaison with Miguel and was making fun of me. What he said couldn't have been true.

"I don't believe you, it can't be true…"

"As true as it's dark outside, princess. If you don't believe me, ask Peñuelas. Your old childhood friend Miguel, who as we know is in the midst of a fourth and very messy divorce, went to the school that morning. He had just learnt he had lost custody of his son and wanted to talk to the headmistress before that viper of his ex-wife did… Are you still there, sweetheart?"

No, I wasn't. I had switched off the phone. Miguel's lips were climbing my body again (Oh my God, not now, oh shi-it) and up my neck, alongside my right ear. I couldn't take any more, dammit. To disguise the fact that I had cut the call off so abruptly, I let the mobile fall to the floor. To hell with Enrique, I thought. Too bad if my strategy made him even more suspicious – or (if he hadn't been suspicious to start with) made him suspicious now. He could think what the hell he liked; I really didn't have what it takes to handle such a melodrama. While I was trying to readjust my blouse before I bent down to pick up the mobile (which had

lost its back when it fell) I couldn't take in the significance of
what the Man of My Life had just told me. I knew now that Avril,
Sofía, Elba and even Miguel had been, or could have been, near
the boy on the day of the accident. It was like something out of
one of Carmen O'Inns's most extravagant novels. I wasn't worried
either that despite my best efforts to prevent it, one of my lovers
or perhaps even both of them had heard the other. And least of all
was I concerned about the number of swear words I had uttered
in the previous few minutes. No, I wasn't thinking any of that
while I deliberately took my time finding my battered telephone:
what I devoted this short, strategic truce to was promising myself
that not even with five Bloody Marys under my belt, not even if I
were crazy or past it, would I ever try to describe a situation like
the one I had just been through in any of my books. Not even the
most suicidal writer could imagine such an outlandish scenario.
"Sorry, Miguel, I'm so clumsy," I said, pretending I still couldn't
find the back of the mobile. Then I added: "Give me a hand,
perhaps you can see it over there, I can't find it anywhere," all the
while telling myself: "No way could you write anything like this.
What idiot would dare mix two people meeting up again after the
death of one of their children, a second lover on the phone, plus
an intense and completely unexpected sexual assault by the first
of them, interspersed with precious information for the thriller
reader as to where the plot is headed? I'll never write anything
of the kind, I swear." And yet, I told myself as I pretended to
look under another chair, the worst of it isn't that reality is such
a dreadful scriptwriter when it presents you with scenes like this.
No, the worst thing is that no sooner has it presented you with
them than it just keeps on going, sweetheart, so now ("Oh, look!"
I said. "Here it is! I've found the back of the mobile, it was under
this sideboard, thanks anyway"), when any writer worth her salt
would put a full stop and start a new paragraph, leaving the reader
to wonder what's going on, I found myself playing out an equally
difficult role: that of concerned therapist to a man who had lost a

son less than a month earlier and who, it appears, was not looking for solace but sex, and not exactly gentle sex either. And you'll have to carry on as if nothing had happened, sweetheart. As if what Enrique said hadn't aroused your worst suspicions. And as if you weren't betraying the pair of them in truly Olympic style. ("Wait, darling, I'll put the mobile away so we won't be disturbed again. Can I have a drink? Yes, a double Bloody Mary please, no, make that a triple.") "My God," I thought as I watched Miguel walking off towards his library – which, by the way, was very fine, full of touches of good taste such as photographs signed by the artist and modern paintings alongside old masters. Tibetan rugs and Swedish neo-classical furniture. Perfumed candles lit to give off the fragrance of Oriental woods that combined perfectly with the Brahms music. Everything was so different from Enrique's apartment, so diametrically opposed, that I forgot all my detective instincts and could think of nothing more than my career as a love cheat. You're out of your depth, sweetheart, you're not someone who can love two men at the same time, you don't have a *bolero* soul. So when Miguel returns with your Bloody Mary, make sure you drink it down in one like a Wild West cowboy. Yes, get as drunk as you can as quickly as you can, because it's going to be a long night and life is a crap scriptwriter who doesn't end scenes where she should, who never gives you the chance to get your breath back. ("Oh, you're here already! Thanks my love, but it's very strong, I don't know whether I'll be able to drink it all, I'm not used to alcohol, I usually only drink wine, though I'll make an exception tonight – you can't imagine the day I've had!") Drink it down, you idiot, and… ("What's that, Miguel? You want me to follow you? I'm coming, my sweet, I'm right behind you. Your apartment's really lovely, I love the way you've decorated the corridor, oh and is this your bedroom? Isn't it nice? It looks out over Retiro Park, just like mine…") Christ, you sound so tipsy, Luisita, let's see if you can put as much passion into this meeting as seems to be required. ("Yes, Miguel my love, I was dying to see you again after all this time, wait, let me do it, let me at least take off... oh well, you do it then.") Go on, kiss him like he's kissing you, caress him as much as he's caressing you. It's obvious you haven't the faintest idea about how human beings react. If you imagined tonight was going to be calm and sexless, with you playing the friend consoling him over the death of his child, then you don't have the faintest idea of how grief operates. Yet again it turns out that the great observer of human nature, the renowned novelist, is so wide of the mark that ("Wait a second, Miguel, wait my love, not so quickly, oh, my tights...") so wide of the mark that if my life were a novel, the only title it could possibly have would be something like *I Only Know I Haven't Got A Fucking Clue.* ("Do you really want me to do that to you, darling? And with this thingamajig? I don't even know what it does...") Goodness me, I told myself – a little too late recovering my old habit of not using swear words, what strange reactions people have. It's obvious my idea this was going to be a chaste night was completely wrong, and what was in store for me ("Yes, my love, more, like that, do it more!") was sex, or rather hardcore porn. So concentrate on the job at hand, even if your head is full of terrible suspicions. Despite the fact that infidelity should have its own rhythm, a pause so that those men (and women) who indulge in it ("Yes. Of course, I love everything you do to me, even that. Of course, I swear I do. There's only you, you know that!") can have a gap between their two loves and don't have to swear eternal love to one of them on Friday, and the other on Saturday. Especially when, like now, their heads are filled with doubts, suspicions and so many other things ("Yes, like that, go on, more, oh, I like it, I love it... You want me to stick my tongue there? Oh, I've never seen that done before, not even on Gay TV, shi-it.") What a rubbish scriptwriter life is, all this chaos, all this mess.

Never Mention the Names of the Dead

What happens when life becomes a play of mirrors and past and present become a parody of each other? What do you do when you start to suspect that a death everyone else considers an accident might not have been so innocent, and that at least four people were close by when it occurred? If you happen to be Carmen O'Inns, it's simple. You undertake a course of action that consists of visiting the possible suspects one by one, making sure you take your assistant with you (this is fundamental, because then you can discuss the case with him, create hypotheses and throw out ideas that will offer the reader important clues). The visits will all follow this pattern: first, an introduction which will give a short sketch of where the meeting is happening. Usually, this will be the home or workplace of the person under investigation. But take note: no rambling, no unnecessary flourishes or digressions; no lengthy descriptions either, or rhetorical tricks: three or four well-chosen lines are enough.

After that, each scene will be a dialogue. Short exchanges, questions and answers, and again, make sure you avoid slowing things down with descriptions such as "he said, staring languidly out of the window with a glass of whisky on the rocks in his hand as he listened to *Das Lied von der Erde* by Gustav Mahler, played by the Berlin Philharmonic Orchestra directed by Von Karajan". No, a thousand times, no. No descriptions of the surroundings. As the famous literary critic Enrique Santos might say: "all the poor reader is interested in is finding out what's going on, so what you need is action, action and more action".

185

Once all the interviews have taken place, the detective and her assistant (who always has to be a bit slow on the uptake, so he can ask stupid questions to which the detective can give scintillating replies) will sit and talk things over. Then at a certain point the detective – in this case, Carmen O'Inns – will suddenly stand up (if they really are sitting down) or slam on the brakes if they are driving, or leave Newton *in medias res* if they happen to be in bed, and exclaim something along the lines of: "I've got it, Newton, my God, how stupid I've been, why didn't I see it before?" With that, she'll rush off to unmask the murderer, taking Newton (and ideally, the reader as well) completely by surprise.

Yes, that would be how Carmen O'Inns would have behaved, also taking great care not to reveal the solution to the mystery until four or at most five pages before the end of the novel, using those last paragraphs to explain to Newton (and the astonished reader) how she came to solve the mystery and discover the truth. This, it goes without saying, ought to be ingenious, unexpected and above all (although it is almost impossible to achieve) *believable* – although to judge by the books that have become best-sellers in recent years, this last requirement may be increasingly irrelevant.

Unfortunately, since I am not Carmen O'Inns and Enrique Santos is even less like Isaac Newton, none of the procedures stipulated above actually took place. There were no separate visits to each of the suspects; no revealing dialogues; nothing of the kind. What happened instead was that Elba had her twelfth birthday.

"It's incredible how much has changed since last year," I told myself as I remembered that for my daughter's previous birthday I had organized a simple tea party with a dozen of her friends, and kept them all happy by showing a Disney video. Now Elba had changed schools, got a new set of friends, went to the gym on her own, dressed as though she were sixteen and spent hours in front of the mirror. Yet when I wondered what to organize this time round, it seemed to me it was still too soon to put on a party with music, dancing and boys, as if it were Elba's fifteenth birthday. What should I do then? It's a very mixed-up age, I told myself, as I always do when I try to put myself in Elba's shoes, they like Shakira and *The Sims*, trinkets as well as boys. Perhaps the best thing would be to organize a party somewhere in between: something that isn't either too childish or too adult. But what?

It was then I remembered that, thanks to a TV show, the search for a hidden treasure following a series of clues had become popular again. What made it exciting was the value or uniqueness of the hidden treasure. It seemed to me like the perfect solution.

"I've been thinking about your birthday party, darling. What if next weekend we have a big party here at home, and invite lots of your friends? We could have music, and games, we could even have a treasure hunt like—"

"Like the one they organized for Miki at his last birthday?" Elba interrupted me, with an odd smile. "That's a silly idea, Luisa. There's no such thing as treasure, in real life you have to create your own treasures and prizes. If you want something, you have to do all the work yourself. That was something I realized that day."

I was left speechless. What could have happened during that distant birthday party to make Elba speak to me like that? I only knew of it thanks to Avril's emails, and she said nothing about any games, only about her own strange search for her past. What else could have happened that afternoon? What did Elba mean? Perhaps I should ask her or, better still, sneak another look inside that folder marked SECRET: KEEP OUT. Doing that had an added advantage: I wouldn't make the dreadful mistake of mentioning that name... "Miki". Over the previous few weeks, it had become taboo to pronounce those two syllables in

any conversation between those of us who had known him. If I
was talking to Sofía, for example, or to the girls, and naturally
if it was Miguel I was speaking to. It was very similar to the
way, years earlier, the name of Antonio had vanished from our
conversation, thanks to the pact of silence that seems always
to be created around naming a dead person, especially if that
person is a child. It was because I had experienced this in my
childhood that I was not so surprised that this strange law of
omerta was followed this time around, so that not only was
someone buried, but their name was buried with them for a
while. This meant that instead we used pronouns: "when *he*
was alive", we would say, or "the last time I was with *him*",
as though uttering the sound of his name was like casting a
dangerous spell we needed to avoid at all cost. Right from the
start, I had been careful to only use pronouns about him when
I spoke to Elba, Sofía and of course Miguel. For this reason,
Miki's name had not cast any shadow over our romantic trysts
– the two romantic trysts we had, I should say, because after
the totally unexpected display of passion he indulged in the
first time we met on our own after the accident, much to my
regret our encounters became rarer and rarer. Every time I
called, he said he was travelling or about to set off on a journey.
("Yes, tomorrow I'm in Zurich, and the day after in Frankfurt;
I promise I'll call you as soon as I get back, on Thursday or
Friday at the latest.") But the days went by, and I spent so long
waiting for news from him that in the end I almost breathed
a sigh of relief, because by then there were too many silences
surrounding a relationship that Miki's death (or at least so I
like to think now) had cut short. Too many words were missed
out, perhaps because censoring one name leads immediately
to the silencing of many others, so that before long it was not
only the two syllables that made up Miki's name that were
a barrier between us. There were also those of Elba's name,
for example, because it is bound to seem like adding insult

to injury if you talk about life, about the mischief and other nonsense a child gets up to, to someone who has just lost one of their own. And soon, two taboo words seem to lead to silencing many more: I soon found it impossible to mention the school to Miguel either, and by extension Sofía as well, or of course the novel I was trying to write, which had schoolchildren as its main characters. Still less could I talk about his other son, Tony, who was inseparable from *him*, and who I had seen for the last time at *his* funeral. I gradually came to realize that the world I shared with Miguel Gasset had shrunk to such an extent, had become so full of pronouns and silenced words, that this was why, in spite of the way he seemed to be forgetting me, I almost breathed a sigh of relief that he was always travelling. In addition to which, although I am no Carmen O'Inns, I could not help but remember from time to time what Enrique had told me about Miguel, and the fact that he had been in the school at the time the boy had died.

As a result, I slowly returned to my old way of life, to my Man Friday and my monogamous existence. This, as well as finding myself unable to write as much as a single further line of the adventures of Carmen O'Inns, meant I was able to revisit an old concern of mine, which passion, sex after fifty, or whatever you like to call it, had driven from my mind: the need to stay at home as much as possible, and to make sure I took good care of Elba.

"What on earth can have happened at... Miki's birthday party?" I asked myself the afternoon I had been talking to Elba about her own party. I said the painful syllables under my breath with all the hesitation and care of someone taking the first step after the plaster has been removed from their foot. Had something happened that day that I should know about? A surprise encounter perhaps? A discovery? What had Elba meant when she said there were no treasures in life, that you have to create your own opportunities if you want to get something?

My daughter has always had her strange ideas; heaven knows what was behind this one. "Sweetheart, if you're worried about something, the best thing to do is to face it," I told myself, thinking naturally enough that what I should do was take another peek in the green folder where the girls' emails were kept. And yet for a second time, I hesitated. I had promised Enrique I wouldn't spy on them. Besides, if I was worried by what Elba was saying, the best thing would be to pay as much attention as possible to her needs, and to keep a close eye on where she went. Even though she was not allowed to go out on her own, except to visit the gym, I often felt I didn't know where my daughter was. I was also worried about the way she broke off phone conversations if I came into her room suddenly, and other things that seem too slight to be worth mentioning here, such as her habit of disappearing to the caretaker's lodge, where she said she liked to play with the cat. The only really worrying aspect of all this was the way I had been neglecting her recently, and not only because of the sudden appearance of death in our lives, but above all due to my brief and apparently failed relationship with Miguel. I told myself that new, unexpected love affairs, outbursts of passion and so on, made one lose sight of one's priorities. But all that was over and done with, and now Mother Hen was coming home to roost.

"I'm sorry darling: when I mentioned a treasure hunt earlier, the last thing I wanted to do was to remind you of anything sad," I said to Elba. "You decide. How would you like us to celebrate your birthday?"

"I'd like us to go to the Natural Science Museum, Mum."

"To the *Science* Museum?" I gasped, because I would have been less surprised if she had asked me to go to a night club than to a museum. And why the Science Museum, which Elba had never talked about in her life, and which I wasn't even sure I could locate. Really, who can understand young girls at that age? But all right, I thought, if that's what she wants. "Fine, my love," I said, then began asking her questions to try to get a clearer sense of what kind of visit this was supposed to be, as well as to try to find out where the idea for this extravagant way of celebrating a birthday might have come from. "How would you like to organize it, Elba? Would you like to invite a group of friends? What do you find particularly interesting in that museum? The dinosaurs, the stuffed animals? Since when were you interested in zoology? Goodness me, I had no idea: so it's reptiles that interest you? Your tastes change so quickly, and... What's that? You want just you and me to go, and it has to be a Thursday? Don't you want to at least invite Avril? Fine, OK, but..."

It was following this conversation that I, Luisa Dávila, who am normally so unlike Carmen O'Inns, decided I was going to emulate my character and take a look in the famous green folder that Elba kept on the top shelf of the bookcase in her bedroom. "It's obvious," I told myself, "that you haven't the slightest idea about lots of things in Elba's life, so put your scruples to one side and see what you can find in that blessed folder. Don't worry, it doesn't mean you're going to turn into a prying detective. You're just behaving like any mother worried about her daughter would. You don't mean to tell me you think you're the only one who behaves like this? Besides, you're perfectly right to do so, because who could be more concerned about Elba's happiness than you?"

Once I had overcome my final reluctance (isn't it incredible how you still feel like that at this age?) I decided to take advantage of one of the afternoons when Elba went down to the gym to make my inspection, despite the fact that I had noticed recently that she was looking for any excuse to skip her classes there. "What's wrong, Elba? This is the third time you've missed your class: if you don't go once more, I'll cancel your subscription," I'd told her only a few days earlier. "OK, don't bug me, I'll go if that's what you want, Luisa, but..." I had insisted, not just because it suited me but from a sense of discipline: it was time Elba learnt it wasn't good to change her mind quite so often.

The first thing that struck me when I went into her bedroom that afternoon was how tidy it was. "Yet another surprise," I smiled to myself. "So now we're neat and tidy, are we? Well, I hope this vogue lasts longer than some of the others." It produced a really strange sensation, because with everything tidied away and the wardrobe doors shut (whenever Elba was in the room, she kept them wide open so that she could study herself in the door mirrors) it had an austere, adult look to it, almost like a hotel room waiting for its guest in order to come to life. It was such a shock that at first I was worried: perhaps Elba had tidied away the folder, or hidden it somewhere under lock and key? That's what I would have done at her age: I wanted everything put away, hidden, as if my life were a huge mystery, and if we are to believe novels, that's how most adolescent girls behave. "All except Elba," I told myself. In this way too, she was different, because at least until now she had always left her letters easily accessible, as if they were a challenge or a provocation. "Well," I said, "that's how girls are," then immediately forgot about it, because there was the green folder where it had always been.

Inside I found all Avril's old emails, plus a few new ones, where above all she was complaining about Elba's lack of replies. "Where have u got to? Its been ages since u wrote. Come back down to earth, Elba" or "Still obsessed with aerobics and biology? Shit, Elba, if I told you know who what yr up to" and "I looked for u on Messenger yesterday, couldn't fund u there either, so Im writing now. What u up to?"

"What a way to waste paper," I thought, then went on searching through the sheets looking for my daughter's replies. I soon realized there wasn't a single message from Elba in the entire folder. They were all from Avril, and were sorted in date order, with the oldest on top. The very first one, for example, was where she talked about everything she had learnt about

Sofía's childhood, then a longer one where Avril wrote about what she had seen in the apartment of the... "Shrimp" I was about to say, until the law of *omerta* silenced the word, and changed it to "in *his* apartment". I glanced through more of the emails and came across three or four I already knew, all of them written in Courier New or in some even stranger type, with that desire young girls have always to be original. "But where are Elba's replies?" I wondered. "Perhaps they're at the very end." I went on looking, but all I found were mails from Avril. "How silly," I then thought, "I should have known: here Elba keeps only the messages she receives. Her own, if she hasn't deleted them, will be on her computer, protected by a password. Now what do I do? I suppose I'd better put everything back where I found it."

I was busy replacing the sheets of paper in the same order I had found them, when suddenly I came across a photocopy of a photographic montage I already knew about, but which I was looking at for the first time. "My God, it looks so real," I thought. There, in the midst of all the emails, was the result of the game Avril had played with *his* photo. Fascinated, I peered at it. There was Avril, sitting next to the fireplace in the Gasset household, with Christmas decorations everywhere. She was in pyjamas, and beamed as she opened a huge present. "What's this photo doing here?" I wondered, but realized at once that Avril must have sent it to Elba as an attachment. Girls tell each other everything, and share everything, so it was only natural she had sent Elba a copy so that she could see the results of her handiwork. Yes, there was the mail that went with the photograph. "What do you think of it, Elba? You can't tell a thing, can you? You can't see it's me rather than that stupid Shrim... (the law against mentioning names, the sacred *omerta*... How ghastly that cruel nickname the girls found for *him* seemed now, I thought, breaking off in my reading and returning to the image). It's amazing, I reflected, as I studied it more closely, at first sight nobody could tell it had been changed. It was Avril, sitting by the hearth in the dead boy's home. A domestic, family scene: a little girl wearing pyjamas on which you could even see the teddy-bear pattern. "It's incredible," I repeated to myself, "that even in such poor quality copies you can see these tiny details." Yet because I knew the photo was a fake, I thought I could detect where the technique was still not quite adequate. Two things gave the game away: the first was the body posture. The top half of the body in the teddy-bear pyjamas were obviously *his* from the original photo: they did not completely match Avril's head. I guess it must be very hard to find two photos in which the position of the sitter is exactly the same: this means that, as in this case, the original body and the superimposed head do not quite fit together. This gave the final image a grotesque, stiff look, like that of a puppet. The other problem was the neck. All I know about photomontage comes from a vague understanding of how Photoshop works, but I do know that you almost have to transfer pixel by pixel tiny bits of the original photo to the new image, and that even so it's almost impossible for the neck not to give away the fact that you're joining a new head to the original. Here, there was a black line right across Avril's throat. It looked just like a scar, like a slit, "a premonition of what was going to happen to *his* neck only a few days later," I suddenly thought. "Twisted, snapped, broken…"

"What does breaking your neck mean, Mum? Is it true you die if you fall backwards like that?"

I remembered the day I told Elba about the death of the first boy. (That was shortly before *his* accident, my God, just a couple of days. Poor little boy: who would have thought it could happen again?) I also remembered, as an icy finger seemed to creep up my spine, how closely Elba had listened to what I was saying, and then all the questions she had asked me about it. "Did you say he fell backwards? So if you fall backwards

194

from a great height, you die? And tell me, did all this stuff that happened when you were a young girl become a secret, so that no one, absolutely no one, talked about it? It's a great story, Mum, it's so romantic. All those fantastic secrets! Can I tell Avril? Please, please, can I?"

Laughing, I said she could, happy to feel that by sharing this old story from my past with her, we had found a way to bring us closer. With the passage of time, even the most dreadful tragedies become fascinating stories. That's why I had told Elba the story of Antonio's death from start to finish. After the mistake I had made lying about how she was born, I was determined never again to keep a secret from her. "Yes my love, you can tell Avril and whoever else you like," I said. "It was a case of really bad luck. Nobody was to blame – he was the uncle of your friend Miki…"

I told Elba all this before "Miki" had become a forbidden word, before the second accident had happened. "Come on, Mum. Tell me it all again from the beginning. It's very dangerous to fall backwards, isn't it?" "Yes, very dangerous, Elba. That's why you should always be careful, my love."

All these recollections of my conversation I with Elba a few days before *his* death came into my mind as I stood in my daughter's bedroom with the green folder open on the desk in front of me. The words flew about, colliding with each other in a way that suddenly made me think that perhaps life isn't so fanciful, so steeped in strange coincidences as I had thought. Because if there was only a remote possibility that two identical deaths happen, or that the present imitates the past to the extent that uncle and nephew should die in almost identical circumstances, there was in fact a much more logical explanation.

"It's imitation," I thought, and felt like laughing out loud for being so stupid. Of course. That was the simple answer to all this symmetry: it may be almost impossible for two identical deaths to take place, but what if someone had deliberately copied the previous one? That was a much more straightforward explanation. And it would have been so easy to copy Antonio's death, in other words to push someone over backwards. Anyone could have done it, including another boy. "Or girl," I said out loud, as if by giving voice to my fears that would somehow make them less real.

Two young girls who tell each other everything, who share even their most intimate secrets: of course Elba was going to describe in full detail the death I had witnessed at their age. She had even asked my permission.

According to the Argentine writer Jorge Luis Borges, life likes symmetries and slight anachronisms. According to Shakespeare, life is a tale told by an idiot, full of sound and fury, but signifying nothing. Where does that leave us? Order or disorder? Causality or casual, random events? "Well," I said to myself, finally putting the folder back where I had found it and leaving Elba's bedroom, just as I heard the sound of a key in the front door of the apartment. ("Is that you, Elba? I'm glad you're back so early. Give me a kiss, I'll prepare you something to eat in a minute.") Well, I thought, as I went to greet her – perhaps in the end both mean the same thing and life may be a terrible mess, but there is order in there somewhere. But now I come to think of it, the fact is that the person who for the moment has given the best description of it is neither Borges and his sense of order, or Shakespeare with his disorder, but Enrique Santos with his Julio Iglesias theory that in this world even symmetries and the sound and the fury sometimes apply... and sometimes don't. In any case (after giving Elba the kiss and following her into the kitchen), Enrique has been right about everything else up to now. He was right to say that the strange things we observe, and in particular the apparently incredible coincidences that occur, often have a much more straightforward explanation than we at first believe. He was also right to insist that as soon as one starts looking for suspects or ghosts, we see them everywhere, and everybody appears guilty. Above all though, he was right about one more thing: this was starting to seem far too much like a Carmen O'Inns adventure. ("What would you like, Elba? How about some milk and biscuits? You look tired, my love, is it true you don't like your exercise classes any more? You change your mind so often... but never mind, drop them if you like, your teacher Sofía says that...") It was then, as I said the name of my former school friend, and faced with the possibility that Miki's death wasn't an accident but a deliberate copy of the way his uncle had died years earlier, that it occurred to me that for once I was going to behave exactly like Carmen O'Inns would do in a similar situation. I was going to pay a visit to Avril's apartment, just like detectives in novels do, and I was going to talk to Sofía. What about? I had no idea: nothing in particular, whatever came up. What she might tell me or what I might ask wasn't that important. What I really wanted to do was to see what the apartment was like, and the feeling it gave me. In other words, to sniff out what the world of that girl with such strange obsessions was like, and to see what twists and turns her life had taken since Miki's death.

That's odd, this time when I thought of the boy's name it didn't shock me the way it has until now. I suddenly realized that perhaps I didn't find those two syllables so hard to pronounce any more because their place had been taken by two even more threatening ones: the ones in the name Avril... "Or April, the month Antonio died in," I told myself, trying to avoid any of this turmoil appearing on my face to give the game away to Elba. Fortunately she wasn't paying me much attention, but was concentrating on her milk and biscuits. Now that I had spotted a further similarity between the two deaths, I couldn't stop myself drifting back to my suspicions. Was the coincidence between Sofía's daughter's name and the month the first accident took place in a question of symmetry or merely sound and fury? Avril had written in one of her emails that she had heard late mothers often gave their offspring names which meant something, and that perhaps she had called her daughter Avril, the Spanish word for April, "so as not to forget the month of her second defeat". What defeat could that be? And what had the first been? Antonio's death, by any chance? So then Sofía…

Speculation, suspicions, clues… I was growing tired of turning all this over in my mind. "It's silly to behave like a character in a novel, even sillier to go to someone's home just to see what I can see," but I really couldn't think of any other way of trying to get a better idea of what was going on.

Sherlock Holmes's Clever Brother, or the Failure of Luisa O'Inns

"D'you know who Mycroft is, Enrique?"

"Not unless he's Bill Gates's long-lost brother, or a clone of one of his computer program… No, I've got it! It's a new brand of cigarettes, isn't it, darling? Could you pass me the ashtray?"

Of course I could. I'd been trying to pass it to him for ages, ever since the ash on the tip of his Ducado had as usual begun to take on the proportions of the Tower of Babel.

"For goodness' sake, Ri," I burst out, "if you make a hole in these sheets, I'm not going to buy you any more. It's not worth it…"

Another Friday night. At home with the Man of My Life. The usual post-coital squabble because of Enrique's filthy habits with cigarettes, and his even stranger habit of buying heavy wooden Castilian furniture: there were several new acquisitions brooding around us. (Oh my God, that Spanish Remorse bedside table, matching the dressing table! That has to be a record! Don't look at it, Luisa, or that's your sex drive finished).

"So who is Mycroft, darling? Was I right?"

Before I put him straight, I couldn't help reflecting on things, even though I had promised myself I wouldn't beat about the mental bush so much, and would try to abbreviate my eternal speculations. But how could I not ponder, if only for a moment, on how incomprehensible loving relationships are, how love (not to mention sex) has reasons of which reason is unaware? With the result that here I was once more installed in absolute monogamy with a pyromaniac smoker, a collector of the most atrocious furniture, a person who likes to test my love by testing my patience. My God, Ri, not the ash again! And no, Mycroft isn't Bill Gates's long-lost brother or a brand of cigarettes. I'll tell you who he is in a minute, but first let me tell you about a visit I made this afternoon.

I then explained how, in best Carmen O'Inns style, I had turned up unannounced at Sofía Márquez's apartment to talk to her. What about? I had no idea – whatever came up. To tell you the truth, I didn't really want to *talk* to her, because what could I say? That I suspected Miki's death wasn't an accident? That it was too similar to the other boy's death for it to be a coincidence? That ever since I had read her emails to Elba, her daughter Avril seemed to me to have serious problems, and she herself didn't appear to be exactly on an even keel? Of course, I couldn't say anything of the kind. In fact what I wanted to do was to get a good look at her flat. You can learn more about people by studying the objects they possess than by talking to them.

"You're right, that's straight out of Carmen O'Inns, honey," said Enrique. "I'm not lucky enough to have read her adventures as closely as they deserve, but I'm sure it must be typical of all the best thrillers that the detective discovers priceless leads simply by looking at the suspect's possessions, and then drawing all kinds of conclusions. So how did your brilliant strategy work, princess?"

Laying aside for a moment the problems I had with Enrique's taste in furniture, there were two glaring failures in the efforts I had made to educate the Man of My Life in affairs of the heart: the first, that he still had so little respect for my literary creations, and the second, his use of terms which to me seemed kitsch, paternalistic or directly vomit-worthy, such as "honey", or "sweetie", or "princess", not to mention the one he seemed to repeat ad nauseam: "darling". (That's the thing about working with words, you end up having such a close relationship with them that when you hear certain expressions you could willingly kill the person using them... But careful, Luisa, don't try to explain that to him, there's not many who can understand that particular neurotic obsession of yours).

"What were you saying, Ri?"

"I was saying, how did your brilliant strategy work, sweetie?"

"Not very well. To tell you the truth, I spent three quarters of an hour waiting for Sofía in her living room – forty-five minutes spent trying to uncover some secret message in what I could see around me and spying on Avril, who was studying in her bedroom just a few metres from me. But I can't say I made any fantastic discoveries."

"Aha, so that's why you decided to come and consult old Mycroft here—"

"So you *do* know who he is!"

"Sweetheart, you writers have the bad habit of underestimating the rest of us mere mortals. I may not have encyclopedic knowledge, but I go to the cinema often enough to know that Mycroft is Sherlock Holmes's elder brother. A reserved gentleman of leisure who Holmes goes to see whenever a case he is on proves too difficult for him."

"And you think you're my Mycroft..."

"With all due respect to your immortal creation, I prefer to be your Mycroft than your Newton."

I curled up in Enrique's arms, and sank into his Michelin Man flab rolls. "Love" – I smiled as I suddenly recalled a phrase I had read in one of Avril's emails – "love which makes everything rose-coloured, which paints shabby walls like new, which lends beauty to furniture (...even High Spanish Remorse)."

"D'you know something, Ri? I love you."

"You say that as though you'd just discovered it... But I don't want to go any deeper into that, I might drown. I love you too, princess, and now tell me what you did see this afternoon at your friend's place, and I'll try to be as 'Mycroft' as I can."

"All right," I said. "For a start, I should say I turned up there without warning, which in itself was quite odd. I don't know how other writers get over the problem of verisimilitude, but nowadays, in the age of mobile phones, there is no reason why anyone should just 'drop in' on someone else without telling them, as detectives in novels still tend to do. How are you supposed to justify your visit? What do you say: I was just passing and saw the light in your window? I wanted to see you, so I rang the bell? Luckily it was Avril who opened the door, and she didn't ask me a thing. She simply told me Sofía wasn't there, but that she wouldn't be long because she had just gone down to the supermarket. I hesitated about asking her if she minded me waiting for her mother, because I know how embarrassed she is at the way they live, but when I finally screwed up my courage she didn't seem at all worried: she only shrugged and said she would turn the light on 'because in that tiny room you can't see a thing'. When she called it a 'tiny room' she sounded to me like one of those ruined great ladies who once lived in an enormous mansion and who can't get used to everything they live in now seeming so small, so beneath them... yes, I know what you're going to say, Ri: 'spare me all the literary stuff'. You're right. From now on, I'll stick to the facts."

So I went on to tell him how for the space of almost an hour I devoted myself to studying the details of Sofía Márquez's world, and what it was like after life had taken so many twists and turns: "Do you know what impression it gave me? It gave me the impression of someone camping out. What I mean is that not everybody can be lucky enough to live in a great house, but that doesn't mean they have to live badly, or precariously, or as if they were only there temporarily. Yes, that's what it was: it's not that Sofía's flat is far from luxurious, or that the furniture doesn't match, or that the walls are sad and in need of painting (which they are), it's that everything seems temporary, as if she believed that life at any moment would take another turn and she could go back to her rightful place. Everything I saw reinforced the idea: for example, a Moroccan spread she had thrown over the settee as if she had been thinking of using it to cover it with, but then had forgotten about. And there were piles of books all over the floor, and unopened packing cases in the corners of the room. Everything had a temporary, provisional look to it, except that is for three magnificent silver photo frames which seemed to lord it over everything else. As you can imagine, I went over to inspect them. It wasn't hard to realize these were the three portraits Avril had mentioned in her emails, and that in them you could still see the kind of life Sofía had led when I first knew her. The biggest showed her father on horseback. Another much smaller one was a photograph of her mother (whom I remember well, she always had an apprehensive look on her face) with Sofía next to her. She was drinking tea from a bone china cup that was so fine you could see the liquid inside. And naturally enough, the third one was of her. Of Sofía, I mean, on her own and smiling as she sat by the fireside surrounded by Christmas presents. And you know what? Perhaps the strangest thing was that when I looked closely at that one, it never even entered my head to compare it with the macabre game Avril had played with Photoshop. Sofía looked exactly as I remembered her: the photo took me straight back to the beautiful, self-assured young girl she once was—"

"Sorry to interrupt, princess, but we'd agreed you weren't going to get sidetracked by any literary descriptions."

"Yes, you're right. Where was I?"

"You were saying that everything in Sofía Márquez's flat seemed temporary rather than poor or messy."

"That's right. What does that suggest to you?"

"Only what's obvious: that people never really get used to reversals of fortune. So much so that many of them think that if they only wait long enough (and I find this quite touching), if they are always on the lookout, then one day everything will come right again. My sister, for example, has a friend whose husband left her six years ago, and who still keeps a pair of his pyjamas under her pillow, just in case he comes back."

"But that's pathetic."

"Pathetic or not, there are people who prefer things to be temporary, because that way they can keep on hoping. Perhaps it's the only hope they have, who knows. But tell me what else you noticed."

"I saw Sofía's face staring at me from her photograph with exactly the same expression I knew from our childhood, and I saw her daughter Avril (who is growing to look more and more like her) peering at me from her room. She kept the door open, as if she deliberately wanted me to spy on her. As I watched her working at her computer, I tried to imagine what Carmen O'Inns would have done, what she would have said or asked, but everything that occurred to me seemed so unnatural, so artificial, so... *literary* in the worst sense of the word."

"Hmm, and at that moment Sofía arrived—"

"Yes, how did you know? She came in just as I was despairing of reaching any conclusion about those three silver frames in the midst of all that jetsam, when it seemed as though Avril at her computer was secretly making fun of me, saying: 'Fine, here I am, Señora Super Sleuth, take a good look at me like in one of your silly novels, and let's see what hidden enigma you deduce from my silence.' And do you know the first thing that Sofía did? She started to laugh. It was very weird. She left her bags of shopping on the table, threw her head back in a way I also remembered from our childhood, and without a word to me, burst out laughing. Quietly at first, but then increasingly openly, until she was chortling so much the tears ran down her cheeks. I stood there not knowing what to say or do. My God, laughter can paralyse you much more effectively than anger or tears, can't it? What had made her laugh? She gave a silly excuse, saying she had been struck by the sight of me in semi-darkness looking so scared, just like when we were little girls playing hide-and-seek in her old apartment. She would always find my hiding place and I would be so startled it would bring on an asthma attack. But I'm sure she meant another kind of game, and another hiding place. She *knew* why I had gone there, Ri. She also knew I hadn't managed to discover anything. Yes, she laughed in the same way she used to as a girl, when she caught me doing something she thought was silly."

"You seem to be forgetting that life takes lots of twists and turns, Luisa. You're the strong one now, the roles have been reversed."

"No, Ri. There are people who can make you behave exactly as you did when things were different. It doesn't matter how much time has passed, or what has happened to you in the meantime; in our case, it is Sofía who will always be in a position of strength. But there's something even worse. I'm sure she *knows* what I'm thinking: she's always had that power over me. That's why she laughed."

"What does she know?"

"She knows everything is happening again, that the present is imitating the past – our past."

"Darling, I thought we had agreed there's no such thing as symmetries, and that if what happened to Miki was something more than an accident, that was because somebody deliberately copied the circumstances of the first death. Because, let me tell you again, that kind of symmetry *does not* exist."

"No, and telepathy doesn't exist either, or at least no one has been able to prove it does, and yet I swear that Sofía thinks the same as me: that Miki did not die by accident. Both of us know it."

"Did she say anything about it?"

"I could tell from the way she laughed."

"The only thing I can tell from her laughter is that she found something funny that I would have too: to find a famous woman thriller writer sitting in her living room trying to carry out an investigation as though she were Carmen O'Inns or Jessica Fletcher, the one from *Murder, She Wrote*. You're the one who's being pathetic now, princess. You think people who sit and wait and don't give in to despair are pathetic, but lots of people might find your attempt to behave like a character from your own novels quite funny. Darling, I can hardly believe that I'm the one who has to remind you of this, but if in thrillers the detectives end up discovering all kinds of precious leads simply by observing objects and searching houses, that's only because the aforementioned thriller writer succeeds in fooling their readers into believing things that they would never regard as believable in real life."

"Oh, so I suppose you're trying to say that this is all just a silly fantasy of mine and that there's nothing strange about Miki's death: all sound and fury, as Shakespeare had it. According to Borges, life likes symmetries, but most of them mean nothing at all, is that what you think?"

"No, you're wrong. What I think is a bit more disturbing: I think that something strange *did* happen surrounding Miki's death, but that it's most likely we'll never get to the bottom of it. And now we're getting to the point I'm most interested in. Have you any idea how many unsolved murders there were in Spain in the last year alone? Or how many murders are considered accidents, without anyone even suspecting they might be something different?"

"I didn't know you were interested in criminology."

"Darling, when you have Jessica Fletcher for a girlfriend you naturally become inquisitive, far more than you might think."

"I thought you didn't even like thrillers."

"I don't, but I am interested in real events, and I try to find out what's going on."

"And what is going on then?"

"I suppose it will come as no surprise to you to learn that it's quite the opposite of what you read in novels. To begin with, here's a statistic you've never bothered to take into account."

("Be patient, Luisa," I told myself, "you may want to strangle him, but it'll keep until after you've heard his stupid statistic.")

"Of course, my love," I said, putting on my most hypocritical smile. "How silly of me not to read police statistics. No wonder I'm a complete imbecile. Thank you Lord Mycroft for pointing this out to me."

"Of course I know you read them, but obviously you only read the ones that are published, in other words, the ones that report solved cases or the ones that mention the fact that nobody has been caught."

"Yes, but of course Mycroft knows about something that doesn't exist: he has a list of perfect crimes, or better still, a list of what we *don't* know, doesn't he? As I understand it, you're not even talking about investigations into deaths it was impossible to prove were murders, but something even more difficult to determine: you're talking about deaths and accidents that nobody even suspected might have been anything else. And I suppose you're going to tell me now that there is a list of this kind of case: in other words, of *what we cannot know*, and that some famous, wonderful criminologist or other has produced a statistic from this…"

"Wonderful yes, famous no. Bustillo Morrazo has always preferred to stay in the background."

"I'm not surprised, with a name like that."

"That's you the novelist talking again: a romantic lead always has to have a romantic name, a supermodel who takes your breath away has to have a supercool one, and of course any self-respecting scholar is forbidden to have a stupid name because it would destroy the novel's credibility. Just so's you know, princess, he may have a silly name, but Bustillo Morrazo has something you novelists would give your right arm to possess."

"I'm all ears, darling," I said, saying that word "darling" with a sarcasm that completely passed Enrique by.

"In Madrid alone, the year before last, there were a hundred and fifty-six; last year a hundred and forty-eight, and in this year, which isn't over yet, so far there have been a hundred and seventeen..."

"A hundred and seventeen what?"

"A hundred and seventeen cases that Bustillo Morrazo thinks could have been murders that no one even suspected: perfect crimes, in other words. I'm sure he'd be really interested in what happened to Miki."

"And I suppose that now you're going to tell me that this Morrazo has been a friend of yours since childhood, or that you play cards with him every Sunday, or both... just like the caretaker at Elba's school who was such help to us. 'Friends in poverty and in wealth, friends even in hell', is that it?"

"You're wrong for once, dear heart. Bustillo M. and I only play canasta on the Internet, so I don't know him in person. That doesn't matter: the important thing is not to meet him, but to read him, and in his blog about unsolved crimes there's a chapter entitled 'We All Know an Assassin'. You'd really like it: he demonstrates that each one of us – you, me, the man in the corner shop – know someone who has committed a murder, even if we don't know we do—"

"That's enough, Enrique. There you go fantasizing again, although you're always blaming me for my literary flights of fancy."

"You can say what you like, but fantasies or not, without going any further than your own life, there are two possibly suspicious deaths – Miki's and the one that happened in your childhood. Isn't that right?"

"That's right. So?"

"What most interested me in what Bustillo wrote is that he reckons you don't need to go looking for clues or spy on someone you suspect may have committed a perfect murder. There's absolutely no need, and for two reasons. Firstly, because logically that kind of criminal, since he is not a suspect, relaxes and eventually makes a mistake. Secondly, for a much more interesting reason. Would you like to hear it?"

"I can hardly wait."

"It's very simple, and responds to what we might call 'creative pride' or, to put it another way, the enormous vanity of the artist."

"What are you talking about?"

"Anyone who knows anything about criminology will tell you that human beings are so vain, such exhibitionists, that a murderer who has created something so extraordinary as a perfect murder is bound sooner or later to leave one or perhaps two small clues, so that someone, at least one other person, will discover their prowess."

"But that's not only terrible, it's stupid!"

"No, it's not stupid, it's only human. What's the point of having done something so out of the ordinary... Or rather, what use is there in being a creator if nobody gets to know about it?"

"What's creation got to do with it?"

"Have you never heard of murder described as one of the fine arts? If you think about it, who could be more like a creator, or even the greatest creator of all, in other words God, than a murderer?"

"Don't be so cynical, Enrique: that's a completely ridiculous comparison!"

"Have it your own way. There's no reason you should take my word for it, or that of Bustillo Morrazo, who's spent his whole life studying murderers. Just remember: when Luisa O'Inns gets tired of rushing round like an idiot, when she finally realizes how pointless it is to go searching for clues in other people's homes, or to try to spot secret signs of guilt in her friends' laughter or their daughters, one fine day she'll come up against something she wasn't even looking for. It might be an object, a letter, some other insignificant detail – something totally unexpected but irrefutable. Then our famous detective will discover that the person she least suspected, man or woman, someone very close to her, is a *murderer*…"

"He's found out for sure," was my first thought. "Enrique knows only too well I had an affair with Miguel and now he's making me pay for it in his own inimitable way. Pretend you haven't noticed…"

"Who do you mean exactly, Ri?" (Be careful, Luisa, put up a smokescreen, use any means you can to distract him.) "For Heavens' sake, Enrique, watch what you're doing with your cigarette ash!"

"Who do I mean, darling? Nobody, of course. Besides, there's no reason why what I've just told you should be true, nothing *has* to be true, no theory is completely correct, so that dear old Bustillo Morrazo's prediction that murderers who get away with it are bound eventually to give themselves away only takes us back to what your colleagues Borges and Shakespeare said. Or more precisely to my Julio Iglesias theory: even something that seems infallible or simple common sense turns out to be true, sometimes yes, and sometimes no."

An Unexpected Encounter

"Careful Luisa, don't look at him like that," I told myself when I almost bumped into him, "remember what you and Enrique were talking about only yesterday, don't look at him like Sherlock Holmes. That's not the way to uncover the truth or to unmask suspects. Smile, don't let him see that meeting him again after all this time makes you feel both nostalgic and upset; what you had was a brief affair that only lasted a couple of weeks. Yes, sweetheart, it was nothing more than a tumble in the hay, good while it lasted, but it didn't last long. Smile, you idiot. (Does my hair look all right? My God, I wish I'd worn a skirt instead of these trousers. I wonder if this blouse goes with them?) Now say hello, nothing too effusive or too brief."

"Hello there Miguel. It's great to see you, I'm so glad we met!" (That's enough, don't go too far, and don't overact. Who on earth would have thought I'd meet him here of all places, at the Natural Science Museum?)

For at least three weeks now, my relationship with Miguel Gasset could be said to have moved from past imperfect to (im)perfect forgotten. We no longer even called each other on the phone, and once I had got over the first flush of wounded self-esteem, and no longer asked myself all the usual things – Why did it finish? What did I do wrong? Was I really just another adventure for him, another item on the doubtless long list of his amorous accounts? Another notch on his gun? Just a bit of a fling? – I also stopped wondering whether what we had would have been different if his son hadn't died. And since I wasn't asking myself any more questions, I didn't even bother to wonder why men are such cowards that they vanish from one day to the next without a word of explanation. In the end, I had managed to convince myself (yes, yes, I had…) that it was better this way. However, it's one thing to be convinced of something, and quite another to find oneself confronted by the reason for this unshakeable conviction. And there stood Miguel Gasset. I wouldn't have been at all surprised to run across him in a fashionable restaurant or somewhere near his apartment – we're almost neighbours, after all. Or perhaps even in a cinema queue: anywhere in fact but in front of a Tyrannosaurus Rex.

"What a surprise! You're looking really well…"

As soon as I had said it, I bit my tongue, because I felt exactly the same as I had done the last few times we had been together: the crushing weight of words that could not or should not be mentioned in his presence. Not just the word "Miki" or the words "accident" or "son", but many others as well, in the same way as when you're with a sick person and it seems equally bad to mention the illness as to keep quiet about it: you have to be careful with what you say and with what you don't say. Yes, words killed (or at least, that's what I like to think) whatever there was between us, and it was obvious that they still kept us apart, to judge by the way he responded to my polite "you're looking well".

"Yes? You think so?"

We stood there staring at each other for a while, separated by the abyss that opens between people who have once been intimate but have never properly got to know each other. Because, as Carmen O'Inns says in one of my lesser-known novels: "The biggest paradox about love affairs nowadays is that you immediately know what a guy's favourite Kama Sutra position is, what kind of underpants he wears, and every single line of the tattoo he has on his arse, and yet you don't have the slightest idea about the most important thing: what he thinks. D'you know something, Newton? Leaping into bed creates so much fake intimacy that if I didn't enjoy it so much I'd probably agree with something my mother's generation used to say: relationships today are only skin-deep, because everything is topsy-turvy. No, don't look at me like that, you know I'm right. Haven't you ever woken up alongside some woman you have slept with ten, a dozen or even three hundred or more times, and suddenly thought: what do I actually know about this person? From what little I know, she might be a thief or a murderer; I don't have the faintest idea of what she is really like."

"What are you doing here?" Miguel asked after a few moments. "I never thought I'd meet you here."

Neither did I. I'd gone with Elba to the Natural Science Museum to fulfil her strange request of a visit there for her birthday. So there the two of us were, Elba clinging to my arm like a little girl and staring fascinated at the specimen of Diplodocus Carnegiei presented to King Alfonso XIII, and amazed by the six-metre tall Megatherium Americanum displayed nearby. I looked at Miguel with a sort of paleolithic astonishment: what I had felt for him now seemed so distant and yet so recognizable, just like the strange skeletons of those extinct animals.

"What am I doing here? Nothing, it's just that Elba wanted to visit the museum. It was her birthday a few days ago, and she got it into her head that this was how she wanted to celebrate. You know what kids are like..."

As I said this, I could sense the shadow of Miki coming between us once more. Miki, who would have no more birthdays, Miki, who would get no more wild ideas into his head. The kid whose father would never be able to take him to the museum again as he used to do. I looked around me. The room was full of men with their sons or daughters. Of course, I should have realized. I'm not especially interested in animals, so it would never have occurred to me to bring Elba here if she hadn't asked me to. But just by glancing round I could tell that the Natural Science Museum was an ideal place for divorced fathers who only see their children on certain days a month. Part-time fathers who benefit from the restricted access imposed by the strict, bureaucratically decided regime of time they were allowed to spend with their children: every other weekend, and one afternoon a week, almost always Thursdays. What other alternatives are there apart from going to the cinema or a café for a man on his own with a child on a Thursday afternoon?

By chance, this was a Thursday, and I could count one, two, three, four men of a variety of ages dotted around the room, admiring the skeletons with their children. I wondered if that was what had brought Miguel here too. Perhaps he was recalling the times he came here with Miki, when he too was a father with the same kind of restricted freedom. But that couldn't be right: Miguel had never been a part-time father to Miki. He had only lost custody of him two days before he died, that same afternoon I almost ran him over as I was coming out of my garage. I could even remember what he had said: "What a day it's been! First the call from the lawyer, and now this scare. But tell me something, Luisa: what was Miki doing coming out of your apartment block?"

It wasn't the part of the conversation about what Miki had been doing outside my apartment block which interested me so much as the first part of what Miguel had said. About the fact that he had lost custody of his son only two days before his death, as well as some of the things Enrique had said about Miguel which brought earlier fears flooding back to me. Absurd fears, of course, and ones that Ri had deliberately aroused, because he always likes to unnerve me.

Instead of looking at Miguel, I ran my eye over the enormous skeleton of the Diplodocus Carnegiei in front of me, pausing at each vertebra. How remote and inappropriate my feelings for Miguel seemed all of a sudden; and yet my fears were not so easily dismissed. Be careful, silly, I told myself, make sure he doesn't notice you're thinking about him: find something to say about the damned diplodocus. Anyway, it's all the kind of nonsense Enrique comes up with to make you feel nervous, to show you time and again the distance there is between real life and novels. Fine... but can it really be true there are fathers willing to harm their children just to punish their ex-wives? We all know that truth is stranger than fiction.

"Look, Miguel! A giant squid! It's enormous!" I heard Elba say. "Our literature teacher told us it was one like this that grabbed Captain Nemo's submarine. Do you think there are squid as big as submarines? And sea snakes? Are there snakes that can swim? Tell me, go on."

"Now look what you've done," I scolded myself. "You seem so far away that your daughter is asking him questions. She's bound to bombard him with more and more, and drag out this painful encounter even longer. Stop all this nonsense – just because a man drops you, it doesn't mean he's a murderer. Don't confuse your wounded pride with something else, as everyone does."

"But of course, Elba," Miguel was telling her, when I finally managed to pay attention to what they were saying. "Nature is far more amazing than we could possibly imagine. It always ends up surprising us."

I saw him put a fatherly hand on Elba's shoulder, then turn to me with a smile he had not deigned to show me before.

"It seems Elba likes all this. Especially the reptiles, she was telling me a minute ago. If that's the case, I'm sure she'd like to go inside, into the library where my son works."

It took me a few moments to realize who he was talking about. For me, when Miguel talked about his "son", it could only mean the one who had died.

"Who do you mean, your son?"

"Tony is a biologist. I thought you knew, but perhaps not. There are so many things we never talked about. He's writing his doctoral thesis on the adaptability of marine reptiles."

No, I hadn't remembered that Tony was a biologist. Although, thinking more closely about it, I did vaguely recall that somebody had mentioned it the day Miki died, when they found all those stickers in his pockets. Someone said they were pictures of snakes, an old collection of his elder brother's. Of course, Tony, the boy who had been so needlessly cruel to my daughter on the night of the vigil. I remembered *that* perfectly well.

"No thanks. I think Elba and I will carry on looking at the dinosaurs, there's no need to—"

"What d'you mean no, Mummy? Of course I'd like to see the library. I want to go inside, to see everything. That's why we came here, isn't it? I need to see what it's like working in a museum. There's so much I want to learn."

"No, Elba, I don't think it's such a good idea."

"But it's my birthday isn't it, Luisa?"

She was so insistent that both Miguel and I turned to look at her. Miguel was inquisitive; I was on my guard, particularly after she called me "Luisa", which meant something only she and I knew. But then the tension eased, because Elba clung to my coat sleeve, just like she used to do when she was much smaller and would tug at me with both hands, begging me to buy her an ice cream or to let her stay a bit longer on the swings. "Please, Mum, I've never seen a museum library. What's in it, Miguel? Is it true it's near the place where they store all the bones of the dinosaurs they haven't been able to put together yet? Can I see them? Are they very big? What about snakes? Are there any snakes in there as well? Is it true that in the past there were snakes that could fly? Is it, Miguel? Well anyway, I'd be happy just to visit the library."

And the miracle happened. Miguel smiled in a way I hadn't seen him do since his son's death, and Elba took one of her hands away from my coat and put it in his, still clutching me with the other one.

"Why don't the three of us go together? It was so lucky we found you here, Miguel," said Elba, "I'm crazy about animals. I've loved them since I was a little girl, haven't I, Mummy?"

When she said that, I couldn't help but recall our arguments when we moved into the new apartment and Elba had insisted on taking in the caretaker's cat. Fortunately that crazy idea seemed to have gone out of her head as well, together with her love of mirrors, the gym and that hideous doll from the pound shop. "So it's reptiles she's into now, is it? We'll soon see how long that lasts," I said to myself with a smile, then reflected how, with the three of us arm in arm, anybody seeing us would think we were a married couple taking their daughter for a visit to a museum. A very close couple as well: it goes to show how deceptive appearances can be.

"Mummy, Miguel has just told me I can go to his apartment one day to look at the reptile books Tony has."

"Don't you think Tony should be the one to decide that, sweetheart?"

"Of course not. Miguel is his father, and Tony has to do whatever he tells him to: isn't that right? Even if he doesn't like it?"

Miguel smiled broadly again at Elba's outburst. The smile of a man who liked children and obviously enjoyed being with them. It was then that I wondered what on earth I had been doing the past few days, apart from seeing ghosts everywhere. I swore I would never pay any attention to what Enrique said, or his irredeemable habit of elaborating stupid hypotheses about other people's behaviour, because to think that Miguel could be one of those depraved people who harm their child just to get back at their ex-wives was as stupid an idea as it was to think that Sofía could have had something to do with Miki's death just to settle an old account from the past. All poppycock, including the possibility that Avril could have pushed the boy out of jealousy or envy. It was an *accident* : that's what the police said, that's what everybody thought; nothing and no one gave the slightest indication it might have been otherwise. "And Enrique is the one who knows that better than anyone," I said to myself. "He's always mocked my novels, and enjoys making fun of me by pretending I behave like Carmen O'Inns. But that's enough of that. From now on, I'm going to forget all the nonsense that's been going through my head recently. Appearances are deceptive, and it's true that nothing is what it seems, but it's also true that in real life the simplest explanation nearly always turns out to be the right one."

"I've heard that in the museum there isn't a single room devoted to snakes. That's really bad, they're my favourite animals. And d'you know something, Miguel? Like Tony, I've got a book all about reptiles. I bought it with my own money, and I keep it in a box under my bed with other important things I don't want anyone to see. Now let's go up to the library. Tony's going to be so surprised to see me: his face will be a picture! And don't worry, I promise I won't make any noise. I'll talk quietly and behave; I know what you're supposed to do in libraries, Tony's explained to me."

"What are you doing here, Elba? Did you bring her?"

This last question was aimed at Miguel rather than at my daughter. Tony didn't seem particularly interested in me either; he glanced in my direction only long enough to say a formal hello. That's fine, I said to myself, greeting him equally coldly: there are people we don't get on with right from the start. Let Elba talk all she likes with him about her new love of reptiles. I had no great wish to join in the conversation with someone I didn't think much of after the way he had treated her during Miki's vigil. So I chose to look at the covers of some scientific magazines on display nearby, whilst Miguel and Elba began to talk in hushed tones with Tony at his desk. I was only a couple of metres away from them, but I couldn't hear what any of them was saying, not only because the library encouraged them to speak as quietly as possible, but above all because what I saw at that moment seemed much more interesting than what was in all likelihood a conversation about snakes or books on reptiles. What I saw was not the covers of the scientific magazines, which in fact were as boring as what the others might be saying, but the remarkable change in Tony's appearance since I last saw him. How long ago had that been? Barely a couple of months had gone by since Miki's funeral. Of course, a tragic death changes everything and everyone. It changes emotions, desires, passions and, as I myself had seen, it could lead to the failure of a relationship, like mine with Miguel. But changes of attitude or emotion are one thing; physical changes are something else, especially when they are as obvious as the ones in Miguel's eldest son.

If suffering can be measured by the physical damage it causes, then Tony must have suffered a lot. It was plain from the signs of ageing that had distorted features which, when I first met him, reminded me of Antonio in my childhood. That was no longer true. This Antonio looked nothing like the other one, as if losing his brother had also meant the loss of innocence. And it must have been grief that caused the long, harsh line that appeared across his forehead as he talked to Elba. It was impossible to make out what they were saying, but I could see she was smiling broadly, and he wasn't. She was talking nineteen to the dozen, and Miguel seemed delighted with whatever she was saying, but the furrow on Tony's brow only seemed to get deeper and deeper, completely obliterating what few traces of childish surprise still remained in his expression. As I stared at him, I couldn't help thinking that one day, in a few years' time, when Elba had left adolescence behind and had experienced her first disenchantments, her face would take on a similar look I would not fathom, just like this boy now. Whereas a few months earlier Tony had looked like his uncle, now he was the spitting image of his father. Of course, that may seem like more nonsense, because Miguel and the first Antonio were twins, so that if the latter had still been alive, he would presumably have looked just like the first. And yet this did not contradict but in fact supported something obvious: the fact that each and every one of us has all the faces of their past in them: not merely that of the child they once were, but those of all their predecessors on both sides of the family. Every face, every gesture, every expression. And it is precisely this collection of identities which gives rise to the strange phenomenon that someone can at times look just like somebody else in their family and at others resemble another person from the other branch. At one stage for example, we can look like our maternal grandfather, and then a few years later, we're more like our maternal grandmother, even if they belonged to different races. Inherited traits are a strange thing, and we are constantly changing and mutating: many people co-exist within us, and that's why one day Elba will no longer resemble me but somebody else I don't know at all, she'll have the face of that boy I met on the island of Elba, who was also called Antonio.

What will Elba's face be like then? Who knows? I had made a deliberate attempt to forget everything that had happened on that island. "That really was a tumble in the hay, sweetheart," I said to myself, inadvertently looking at Miguel again, "it was far less important than what I had with you, and yet it had permanent consequences: one day those same features I've tried so hard to forget will be staring at me from Elba's face. When that happens, will I recognize him?" Inheritance, similarities, genetics... it all comes down to biology. How many books around me here in the library are about these very same topics?

"Look, Luisa, I think we ought to be leaving, don't you?'

Miguel had come up behind me so quietly he startled me. I glanced down at my watch and saw it was already half-past seven. I realized that, despite my firm intention to put aside all my fears concerning Miki's death, there I was yet again scrutinizing faces like an idiot, especially Tony's and Elba's, exactly as I had done at the vigil. Faces that are similar, or not, to other faces. Intuitions we have about people which are impossible to confirm, particularly about Tony, because, although I had seen him once or twice now, we had hardly exchanged more than a few sentences. "There are some people we never get to say more than a few words to," I told myself, "people who will never mean much to us. But there you go again, Luisa, that's such nonsense: the vast majority of people we meet in our lives are like that, nothing more than shadows, or phantoms. That's enough of that!" I looked over towards Elba.

"Shall we go? Come on, darling, it's time to leave."

I had said this slightly louder than is recommended in libraries, and two students turned to look at me. I apologized, and was heading for the door with Miguel, when I saw my daughter was not coming with us.

"What are you doing, Elba?"

"I'll only be a second, Mummy, I just need to say goodbye to Tony. It'll only take a moment, I promise. I'll catch you up before you reach the staircase, you'll see."

"Fine, Elba, but no drawn-out goodbyes, please!" I said, as Miguel held the door open for me and I thanked him. Before leaving the room, I turned back once more to try to encourage Elba to hurry up.

I took a good look at both of them. Tony was standing next to my daughter. Side by side, they made an odd-looking couple: he was so tall that Elba had been forced to stand on tiptoe to give him a peck on the cheek, and then, with a childish display of affection, clung to his neck as she glanced towards me.

"I'm coming, Mummy…"

Happy birthday, darling, I thought, smiling back at her. My daughter's clear, perfect forehead showed she still had a long way to go before her face took on the harsh mask of unfulfilled desires.

Writer's Block

Writer's block is a kind of paralysis when faced with the empty page that can happen at the start of a book or at any point in it, and results in the author being incapable of writing a single wretched line.

Although I myself have only suffered writer's block in its mildest forms, I know it comes in many guises. There are the temporary ones, which last at most a few days and are the result of either small structural problems in what you are writing, or emotional problems that have nothing to do with your creative work. The best answer to this kind of paralysis is to ignore it, and even to give yourself a few days off. Then you can go back to the text, read it again from the beginning, and sit at an empty, flashing computer screen for hours, in the hope that today, tomorrow or at some point in the future the miraculous mental click will occur and everything that seemed awkward and unconvincing will suddenly become clear as day. "Goodness me, the answer was so easy, how silly of me not to have spotted it before," you say to yourself, and the writer's block has suddenly disappeared.

But I also know, though it has never happened to me, that there are much worse kinds of writer's block. The first of these, which could be called "the winner's paralysis", happens to people who have had an enormous success with a book. In cases like this, the pressure to write something equally successful becomes almost unbearable, and if you are not careful you turn into someone like Salinger, or more modestly Patrick Süskind. The second kind of block is even worse, because it isn't even helped by having a previous triumph. It happens when the writer loses what could be called the Ariadne thread in the middle of the labyrinth. In other words, when you reach a certain point, you realize that the slender connection that should run all through the book to give it its internal coherence has somehow snapped, making the whole work a complete disaster.

There is also a third kind of block, which I had heard about, but until now had not really known of in detail. It happens when real life bursts tragically into your fictional world, either due to a death, a huge emotional upset or, as had happened to me – damn it – because one fine day you discover (or think you have discovered) that life is parodying what you are writing, because you see coincidences everywhere. "That's the moment when what happened to you in the past few weeks occurs," I told myself, "first you find it impossible to make any progress with your novel, then you turn to someone like Enrique for advice. After that, you start snooping around like a character from one of your own books, spying on Sofía and her daughter, until one fine day, just as in the case of writer's block, the magic click takes place and you can once again see everything in a clear, reasonable and perfectly sensible light." That moment of sudden lucidity also has a name in literature. It's called an "epiphany". That's something like what happened to me yesterday in the Natural Science Museum. The moment just before we met Tony, when all of a sudden, for no apparent reason, I became convinced that all my fears were groundless, and that an event which everybody else but me saw as an accident was probably nothing more nor less than that. My epiphany therefore was to realize that the truth is always simpler than one imagines, because, although life is full of chance occurrences and the oddest coincidences (which give rise to all the conspiracy theories we gullible people tend to believe in), by far the greater part of them are nothing but "sound and fury".

And so it was, with my head full of sensible literary advice from Shakespeare and company, that I, Luisa Dávila, decided to take up my novel once more, convinced that the writer's block I had suffered following Miki's death must be about to disappear. I knew it was simply a matter of sitting down at my computer and waiting for the famous magical click to occur so that I could return to the adventures of Carmen O'Inns, the murderous children, Señor Beil and Señorita Duval.

That's what I was doing one stormy afternoon more or less at the start of winter. I've always enjoyed dark, sad days that offer no temptation to go out, because they are good aids to productive work. It seemed like a perfect situation to try out sentences on the computer according to the old method of "I'm not getting up from my desk until something has happened", a method that in the past has often stood me in good stead. It's an extremely simple method, which consists in writing one sentence after another, and to go on however bad they sound – go on, keep going, because at any moment an idea, or simply a word showing the way forward might suddenly appear. "Come on, try your method again," I told myself, "it doesn't matter if what you write seems rubbish, there's no such thing as inspiration, only perspiration." Keep going, keep going – and I was almost starting to think that this time I would find my way out of the accursed writer's block, when the noise of the phone made me jump.

I usually don't take phone calls when I'm writing, but even so I keep my mobile to hand just in case it's something to do with Elba. I looked at the screen: yes, it was her school number. Before I took it, I made sure I pressed "save" on my computer.

During the first weeks following Miki's death, the mere fact of seeing that number I knew by heart on my mobile caused me repeated anxious moments. Little by little though, the fear that fate was on the prowl again gradually diminished as everyday reality reasserted itself. I had received four or five calls from Elba's school in that time, all for different and trivial reasons: one to inform me that the date of a parents' meeting had been changed; another to tell me that because of a computer error I had been overcharged for the previous term's fees; and two or three times because Elba had forgotten something at home: her gym bag, a medical certificate and this time:

"Señora Dávila? Sorry to disturb you yet again, this is Esther speaking."

The tone of the secretary's voice made it sound like a very routine call, so I immediately felt reassured.

"It's little Elba," she said, "her head's more and more in the clouds…"

"What's she forgotten this time?"

"Her file, Señora Dávila. Normally when a pupil leaves something at home that is their direct responsibility, such as homework or their school file, we simply give them a poor mark and that's the end of it. But on this occasion I'm going to have to ask you to get it to school today, because we need it urgently."

Esther explained that today was the last day to put Elba down for the Lower Cambridge English exam, and that they needed some signed forms which Elba said were in her school file.

"She can't remember where she left it. At first she said it must be on the school bus, but it isn't there. Could you please check whether she left it at home?"

With Esther still on the other end of the phone, I made a rapid mental calculation. On a day like today, there were bound to be traffic jams, and the school was on the outskirts of the city, which meant quite a journey. "Farewell to my day's work," I said to myself. I looked down at my watch: a quarter to four, which meant at least that by the time I reached the school it would be almost the end of lessons, so I could pick Elba up while I was there. That was a good idea, because recently, even though I had forbidden her to do so, Elba had twice somehow managed not to come home on the school bus, but had taken a regular city one instead – according to her, with a couple of friends. I saw this as one of those small demonstrations of freedom that are so natural in early adolescence, but which nonetheless drive every father or mother wild with worry. I could recall having done similar things at her age, but nowadays I wasn't so keen on little escapades like those. "So many things can happen these days," I argued to myself, "you hear about little girls who go places on their own without their parents knowing, and by the time they find out, it's too late. You can never be too careful with that wonderfully pretty word, freedom."

Elba's School File

Since my last foray into Elba's room in search of Avril's emails, I had not been back inside. I suppose that was why I found the impersonal aspect it took on whenever she wasn't there so surprising. It was quiet and tidy, the exact opposite of the rowdy den it becomes as soon as she shuts herself in there with her music and computer games. The rainy, dark afternoon made even the window where Elba had the habit of sitting and gazing out into the street look slightly sinister. "I'd better switch the light on," I thought, quickly seeing that the file I was after was not in any of the most obvious places, such as on the bed or on her desk. I took a few steps further into the room, until I was close to the bookshelves, where another folder had pride of place: the famous green one with the warning "SECRET: KEEP OUT" on the cover. "Keep Out" – of course I wasn't going to search in there, though a quick glance in its direction showed me it was still there, as stuffed full and accessible as it always had been. Would Elba keep her school file with the other one? At first glance, it didn't seem so. I looked on the higher shelves to make sure it wasn't there. The one I was after was easy to recognize. It was very different from the green folder because it had photos of pop stars all over the cover, and before I started to look in any of the other rooms, I decided to check quickly that it wasn't kept in one of the desk drawers. They are so big and heavy Elba doesn't seem to use them much, so I wasn't expecting to find the file there either. Yet in the third drawer down, which was wide open and contained a jumble of things that were in stark contrast to the rest of the room, I finally came across it. "That's Elba for you," I smiled, as I began to leaf through the contents. There was a bit of everything: handwritten sheets, others that were computer printouts, drawings, notes, some maths homework. What about the forms I was looking for? Yes, there they were. It was a few seconds later, as I was readjusting the elastic bands round it after I had put everything back, that something on the inner cover of the file caught my attention. In the top right-hand corner, between a photo of Shakira and one of Alejandro Sanz, there was a rectangle about five centimetres long, with a drawing of a cobra in it.

I am sure that if we hadn't been talking about reptiles just the day before, I wouldn't even have noticed it. But considering Elba's recently discovered fascination with natural science, it made me pause. It was an old drawing: where had I recently seen something similar? Just as I recalled: "in Miki's house, the night of his death", my eye caught more and more of these rectangles, as if the inside cover of the file had once been covered with those old stickers, and more recently someone had stuck on top of them pictures of a whole host of singers like Shakira, Alejandro Sanz, Coti and the whole Canto del Loco group...

The first thing I told myself when I saw the drawings was: "No, Luisa, don't start imagining things again, like 'what is something that belonged to Miki doing in Elba's file?' Or 'is this symmetry or sound and fury?' No, Luisa, that's enough of that. You can't for ever be digging up the memory of a dead person you weren't even close to emotionally; there must be some perfectly reasonable explanation for this latest coincidence."

I really tried, but it was impossible. There in front of me were all those reptiles, like an evil omen: a cobra, a salamander, a chameleon, several lizards, more and more slimy things. As I looked, I couldn't help remembering something Elba had laughingly said to Miguel the day before in the museum: "I love reptiles. I've got a book about them that I bought with my own money and keep in a box under my bed together with other important things I don't want anyone to see."

On the left-hand cover of the file was a black mamba, and a boa eating a mouse… "On your own head be it, Luisa," I said to myself. "It's up to you to decide whether to go on like a crazy writer who ends up confusing her own novels with real life." I was even heading towards the door, clutching the forms the school had asked for, telling myself it really didn't matter that Elba was so fascinated by reptiles, and about to close the folder and to put it back where it belonged, when something I had not noticed before leapt out at me. It was just my bad luck that I was still wearing my reading glasses, because otherwise my usual short-sightedness would have prevented me seeing the opposite inside cover. It was plastered with more photos, but this time they weren't of singers, but blurred print-outs of images taken on a mobile phone. They were poor quality, but still clear enough to make out who the person photographed in all of them was: Tony Gasset. One showed him asleep in bed. In another he was getting dressed half-naked in what might have been a gym changing room. A third showed him in the shower. And finally there was one more, in which Elba was with him, and between them was Miki, whose face a talented but cruel hand had obliterated with what looked like the drawing of a rat or perhaps a shrimp. His body was covered in letters and syllables which at first seemed meaningless, but which gradually formed a single, obscene word that was so hurtful I would never have dreamt my daughter even knew it. When I saw that, all thought of where the photos might have been taken, or when Elba could have been in a men's changing room, or so close to the sleeping Tony, went out of my mind. I wasn't even worried about what else Elba was up to that I was unaware of, what secret escapades she was mixed up in, or who she was involved with without my knowing it. No, instead I stupidly regretted my bad luck for still having my glasses on: otherwise, that myopia with which wise mother nature blesses us after the age of fifty would doubtless have prevented me seeing something I wished I had never seen.

Epiphany

When I think back now to that afternoon in Elba's room, I seem to recall that what happened next was heralded by a clap of thunder and a flash of lightning. It was a stormy afternoon, so perhaps this really did happen. That is what we read in novels and films: all of a sudden there's a blinding light, a crash, and then everything one didn't understand suddenly becomes crystal clear. But rather than an epiphany, when everything suddenly falls into place and you feel triumphant, what I felt that afternoon was more like defeat. I couldn't deceive myself any longer, close my eyes and pretend I was completely blind to what was going on. I couldn't sustain my earlier suspicions either: I had invented them all (I now realized) over the previous weeks, pointing first to Avril, then to Sofía, later on still to Miguel... an accumulation of fears and speculation I had created so carefully with the sole intention of *not seeing*. The fine but dense threads I had spun around Miki's death with the aim (there was no point trying to hide it now) not of catching the suspect, but simply of hiding all the self-evident clues which pointed time and again to my daughter. When did I start to spin this web of deceit? Cobwebs, even those spun unwittingly, are very effective at covering everything. Possibly it began on the night of Miki's death, when I had been wondering (very much against my own will) why two days earlier, just before I almost ran him over outside the garage, I had seen Miki coming out of the front door to our apartment block sobbing his heart out, with a smiling Elba only a few paces behind him. Or perhaps I started spinning the web slightly later, when I saw how Elba, on the night of Miki's vigil, clutched at his elder brother and whispered: "Now I'm the only one you've got." Or perhaps not. Possibly I started a few minutes later when Elba, pushed away by Tony and with another "I'm the only one you've got" on her lips, had suddenly had that spectacular nosebleed. And since then, Mother Spider had spun a huge web, not only to protect her daughter from everyone else, but also (or above all) to protect her from my own suspicions, the ones whispering to me there was something odd going on between her and Tony, who was so much older than her he could almost have been her father (and who coincidentally or not had the same name). So successful had my efforts been that for a while I had also succeeded in covering up other such obvious clues as the lengthy periods Elba spent staring out of the window at the nearby Calle Alfonso XII, the few snatches of phone conversation I had overheard without meaning to, or the visits to the gym which had first been so frequent and then had ended equally abruptly, not to mention a host of other hints I now preferred not to recall, while all the time I kept spinning and spinning my suspicions in any direction but towards her. And my web was so perfect, so dense, that I had been unable to see what even the most obtuse readers of thrillers must have worked out ages ago. Unlike in books, in real life murderers are not the people who arouse the least suspicion; they are the most obvious ones, the ones who are most easily uncovered by anyone with a minimum of "little grey cells". For anyone, that is, who is not too busy spinning lies.

Another lightning flash rent the darkness, lighting up the room and me standing there with Elba's file in my hand. If I were braver (or more spontaneous, which usually amounts to the same thing) I would have plucked up my courage and looked under the bed at the box where Elba apparently kept her other secrets. I would have learnt what little more I still had to find out about Miki's death: the how, and above all the why. To judge by what she had said at the museum the day before, it seemed more than likely that the box (whose existence until then I had been completely unaware of) could contain a diary where Elba, with that passion of hers for writing everything down, explained in great detail what had happened. Yet as far as the question of "how" was concerned, I had no need for anybody to tell me something I had always known despite the cobwebs: that Miki's death was a deliberate copy of the one that had happened forty years earlier. Something so simple, so easy to carry out that even a young boy (or rather, a young girl) could do it: "*What does breaking your neck mean, Mummy? Did it really seem as though nobody had pushed your friend? Tell me all about it again, from the start.*"

That's why the more I thought about it, the more convinced I was it would be better *not* to look under the bed. I was terrified that in addition to this "how" I already knew about, I would also find the "why". Why would I want to know something that would in all likelihood be the confirmation of what I had imagined for quite a while now, something I had always known, despite pretending not to: Elba, my little Elba's disturbing, fragile personality? Although Sofía had once declared that children are perfect strangers to their parents, nothing could be further from the truth: we always know the worst about our children, because they are part of us, especially their sins, which we seem to visit on them like a biblical curse. How long, I asked myself, would I have to go on paying for the one great mistake I had made in my life? Is there really no forgiveness? That was why I had no wish to look under Elba's bed. I preferred not to know her "whys". Did she do it to win something or someone she didn't have? Out of jealousy or envy? Whatever the reason, I didn't want to know. Why did I have to go in for all the useless breast-beating that seemed to be part and parcel of being a mother or father? – Where did I go wrong? What mistakes did I make? and so on – all to become part of that vast chorus of right-thinking people who argue that everything bad someone does, especially if they are a child, can be explained and even justified by their personal circumstances: their needs, and above all, their fears: they did it because they needed love, or because of some deep-rooted lack. In Elba's case, the lack of a father offered the perfect explanation. It was easy to imagine, for example, that given the circumstances of what happened and all the coincidences involved, Elba did what she did in order to monopolize the affection of a man who by a ridiculous symmetry happened to have the same name as the father she never knew. Such a simple explanation, a typical case: archetypal, a psychiatrist would say.

But none of that was true. In spite of all the signs pointing to this conclusion, there was another far more powerful reason for me not wanting to look under the bed. At that very moment I began as quickly as possible to spin another web that would hide this second reason for Elba doing what she did: a reason even worse than the previous one. I preferred a thousand times the explanation that, in the end, it was all my fault, rather than to have to face this new suggestion. So I spun a web that was so thick it would cover the stupid, absurd idea that occurred to me when I thought of the name of that lad I had met on Elba, the one whose features I couldn't even recall. "All I do remember is that he had uneven teeth, which means they were completely different to my daughter's, so stop even thinking such nonsense, Luisa," I told myself, "don't allow yourself to contemplate the silly, completely politically incorrect notion that might lead you to believe that Elba has the capacity in her blood or in her genetic make-up to commit a crime. That an eleven-year-old girl like her has it in her to dispose of someone else's life, just as Miguel probably did forty years earlier, when he disposed of his brother's life. Killing can sometimes be so easy, nothing more than a push when someone is standing with their back to a flight of stairs, or not reaching out to stop a brother falling, letting him crash to the ground. It's so easy that if I myself know of two unpunished crimes, it's impossible not to imagine there must be hundreds, perhaps thousands, of similar cases. And the reason in this case could be in the half of my daughter's blood I know nothing about, her father's blood, a perfect stranger, someone I'll never know anything about."

Even as I was thinking this, I could sense my brain spinning and spinning yet another web to conceal the thought. It was essential to cover it up as quickly as possible, because it offered a fresh and even more terrifying explanation for what my daughter appeared to have done: that it was all down to genetics, the inexorable law that governs us, and which can be made the scapegoat for everything. Who knows, perhaps Elba's father was a criminal, maybe even a murderer, why not? After all, what did I know about Elba's dark side? "My God, how often do I have to pay for the same mistake: ten, twenty, a hundred times? Hurry up, Luisa, spin your web so we can forget this new possibility as quickly as possible. It's politically incorrect to say that someone is born evil; nobody accepts that idea any more. There has to be a motive for all the bad things that happen. A perfectly reasonable explanation that takes into account a person's circumstances, their way of life, not that of their parents. OK, all right, fine, that's how it is in novels, everything has to have an explanation so that the reader can feel satisfied, but what about life? Is life politically correct?"

Not to look, not to see, but spin, hide, cover up, forget. That's what must be best, or even the only thing we can do when we find out something like that about the person we love most in the world. Am I wrong? "Just think," I said out loud, as if I were confronted by an invisible interlocutor or reader, "what would you have done in my place; how would you have reacted? We're talking about a young girl here. My daughter."

But there was no one with me in the room. Nobody to hear me or to put the question to. I was completely alone. I didn't even have the consolation of seeing my image in the welcoming mirrors of Elba's room. She wasn't there either, and her bedroom, intermittently lit by flashes from the storm, seemed utterly impersonal and distant, its wardrobe doors shut like closed eyelids. Inside them were hidden the invisible looking glasses in whose depths my daughter so often lost herself as she danced her secret dances, or tried out adult poses, kissing their cold surface with cherry-red painted lips, imagining herself in love. She's only a child, a small child, Elba, my love, my only life.

Not to see: to forget, hide. We always think we know how we will react at crucial moments. The brave think they'll face up to things; cowards suspect they'll run away. They're both wrong: the commonest response is to pretend nothing has happened; and that is almost always the only possible way out.

That was why that afternoon I decided to leave the unknown box and its hidden secrets exactly where it was. Also to leave behind the file with the intimate photos of Tony and the drawings of reptiles stolen from a boy who no longer needed them. A boy who no longer needed or would need anything at all, not even justice. It's a lie that the dead clamour to be avenged. The dead don't talk. As everybody knows, the most significant thing about the dead is that they're silent: as silent as the grave, and how fortunate that's how it is, because that means nobody has to find out about something known only to the dead and us.

"I was sure you'd find it, Mummy."

It sounded like Elba's voice, but at that time of day surely she was at school, or ought to be. And yet:

"Is that you, Elba?"

By the flickering light of the storm I could make out my daughter's slight figure in the doorway. I felt my throat tightening, and gasped for breath, just like I used to as a child when I had to stop playing with Sofía because of an asthma attack.

"Elba?"

"Yes, it's me, Mummy."

She looked so much of a child in that red-and-grey uniform of hers, so similar to the one I had once worn. In those days I was not allowed to come home from school on my own or to take a city bus. Elba is not supposed to either, you hear so many stories, it's so dangerous these days, young girls shouldn't be out on their own without their parents knowing where they are, who they're with, who they're seeing. When I saw her standing there, my first reaction was to go up to her, put my arms round her, and ask: "What are you doing here, Elba? How did you get here? What else don't I know about your life, my love?" and "What did you get up to during all those days (my God, it wasn't even a fortnight ago) when I wasn't so close to you? *What* have you done, my love?" That was my first reaction, but I didn't do it, because a warning voice inside my head told me: don't mention anything, keep quiet, be careful.

Another lightning flash tore apart the darkness with the stubborn tenacity of something being born. For some reason, the thought came into my mind that the blue flashing light was very similar to strobes in discos: they both slow people's movements down so that they look like slow-motion scenes from a film. Could they possibly have the same effect on thoughts? That seemed to be the case, because before I asked my daughter the perfectly reasonable question: "What are you doing here at this time of day, Elba?" I had time to reflect on what she had just said: "I was sure you'd find it, Mummy". That's what she had said, but what was she referring to? What was that "it"? The box? The file? Or could she have meant "the truth"?

Then, by an inevitable association of ideas, I remembered the comment Enrique had made about how in real life there was no point searching for the guilty like detectives do in novels. One day, when you are least expecting it, he said, you would come across a piece of evidence that would implicate the guilty person. Anyone responsible for a murder that is seen by everyone else as an accident – in other words, someone capable of committing the perfect crime – needs to have at least one witness to what they have done.

My daughter was still standing like a dark shadow in the doorway, looking at me with her head tilted to one side in that way of hers, as if she was waiting or silently asking me a question. I could see a strange gleam in her eyes. She stood there so still that, despite feeling the same shortage of breath I had experienced a few minutes earlier, I had to look carefully at her again to make sure I wasn't just imagining things. To make sure that Elba had in fact come back and that, although it seemed to me it had been a very long time, in all likelihood the previous scene had lasted only a couple of minutes at most, because the lightning flashes slowed down movements and possibly time as well. So I had the chance to think a bit more. To think that even though I was sure (I could tell from the way Elba was staring at me) that she knew that I knew, it was best not to say a word, and to calculate as carefully as possible what I did next. Another bolt of lightning helped me understand one of Enrique's comments about the way that someone who is capable of taking another person's life might act. Elba smiled at me again, but I had to force my aching muscles to respond, because it's one thing for a girl like her to have pushed a child in a moment of jealousy, anger or loneliness, and it's quite another to want to boast about their achievement to the point where she wants me to find out. There's no doubt the first of these is terrible, but the boasting is even worse, because it shows… My God, just what does it show?

Yet another lightning flash. It's a ghastly sensation to feel that life can imitate thrillers to the extent that it accompanies each dramatic discovery with a blinding flash of light. But the next lightning fork brought me the instant conviction that nobody, and still less Elba, should know that I knew; what some people call instinct and others prudence convinced me this was the right course to follow. Enrique had not told me what happened next to people who had been on the receiving end of the confession to a crime, but I had read more than enough thrillers to know. "Oh come on," I laughed to myself, "life doesn't imitate art to that extent," and yet, even though the next day I might discover everything I was so afraid of at that moment had been completely groundless, still that old instinct was telling me to be careful, that the best thing I could do was to pretend, to behave exactly as I would have done if I had not known what I did. Act normal, Luisa, don't let her see anything odd about you: and the most normal thing you could do would be to scold her for leaving school early, so I said:

"What are you doing here, Elba? You ought to be at school. How did you get here? Who brought you?"

(Careful, don't overact, and be careful what questions you ask. You don't want to say something you'll regret. Like the question that is making it so hard for you to breathe: why, Elba, *why?*)

"What I mean, my love, is what are you doing home so early?"

Elba immediately responded:

"I asked someone coming into Madrid if I could have a lift. I had such a bad headache, Mummy."

Of course I thought she was lying. Two things raced through my mind. First, that Elba's early return was not innocent. She had come for some reason, but what? And second, that from this moment on the relationship between her and me was going to be one long lie. What would have to happen for me to trust her again, for me not to see in everything she did or said some ulterior motive, some inadmissible desire?

"...So you have a headache do you, Elba? Why didn't you go and see the school nurse? Come here, let me feel your forehead, perhaps you have a temperature. I'm sure it's nothing."

It was yet another revelation in an afternoon full of surprises. As I brushed against her forehead, I found it was burning.

"My goodness, Elba!"

So she hadn't been lying. That strange look on her face... that weary smile... they had nothing to do with anything inadmissible. Of course not, my poor little girl had a raging fever!

"I'm so sorry, Elba, I should have realized as soon as I saw you. Are you all right, my love? Come on, the best thing for you is bed; I'll help you put your pyjamas on..."

As I went to get them under her pillow, I realized I was still holding Elba's school file under my arm, an awkward witness to what I had discovered. She also saw it and gave another of her tired smiles.

"No, it's me who's sorry, Mummy. I forgot to take it this morning, I didn't mean to—"

"That doesn't matter now, darling, none of that matters... what's important now is to find out what's wrong with you."

Elba was still standing there, staring at me. Another lightning flash lit up her feverish eyes, glittering like a cat's in the night. Her head was tilted to one side again, and her glassy gaze seemed to lose itself in the contemplation of the pop stars stuck on the back of the file I was still holding... as if she were seeing them for the first time, or as if they didn't belong to her. While she let me undress her ("Here, Elba, don't catch cold, let me do the buttons up properly for you, that's right, my love") one of her fingers reached out to touch the top left corner, where a sticker of Miki's showing a cobra had been placed. As she did this, it happened again: a low, animal noise, the slightest coughing sound, and Elba's nose started to bleed – so heavily that at first I thought she was vomiting blood. A stream of red gushed down the front of her pyjama jacket, the carpet, the file with its photos of Shakira and Miki Gasset's faded stickers.

"Help me, Mummy, please help me!"

Then once again the haemorrhage of blood swept everything away. It splashed onto my cheek as I embraced my daughter, as I kissed her, laughing and crying, protecting her from her own blood, from so much blood.

"Don't worry, my love, your Mummy's here to make sure nothing happens to you. To make sure nothing ever, ever happens to you, Elba."

Chicken Pox

The days that followed were some of the happiest I can recall. Happiness that triumphs over anxiety is unimaginable for those who have never experienced it. How could I describe it? Possibly like the unexpected, welcome breath of someone trying to warm a pair of frozen hands, or the disconcerting sight of a flower poking up out of ruins. That's what the next few days I spent beside Elba's bed were like. "Chicken pox," the doctor ruled as soon as he saw her and, after explaining that although there was a particularly virulent outbreak going round, it did not require any special measures, he prescribed antipyretics and lots of patience. As he was leaving, he gave me a further warning. "You're the one who has to be careful, Luisa, especially if, as you say, you never had it as a child. Although it's not a serious illness for children, it can lead to complications for adults, and may even result in pneumonia or encephalitis. How long has it been since your last asthma attack?... Well," he said after I told him I hadn't had one for ages, "even so, you ought to get someone in to take care of Elba; that would be safer."

I said I would, but did nothing about it. This was because after coming home with a high fever that first afternoon, Elba spent a delirious night calling out for me time and again, begging me not to leave her. "Do you love me, Mummy?" "I adore you, my love, now go to sleep, make sure you get some rest." She finally fell asleep with her little face in my hands; I could feel her breath warming my frozen hands: just like happiness. The happiness of knowing that, for the moment at least, there was nothing to think about beyond seeing her well again. Her chicken pox, with its high temperatures, the uncomfortable but superficial feeling of being ill, offered a blessed pause that seemed to suspend time, and with it time's tyranny. The world and all it signified did not exist beyond the four walls of Elba's room. My daughter was ill, and nothing else mattered until she was better again. The only thing I had to do regarding the outside world was to call Sofía so that her school knew and could take whatever measures it felt were needed.

"No, really," I said when Sofía insisted she wanted to come and see Elba, "there's absolutely no need... the doctor says it will take five or six days, and that I'm not to worry if her temperature goes very high. I'll give you a call tomorrow to tell you how she's getting on."

I didn't call her, because the next day Elba still had a fever and cried out to me: "I knew you'd understand everything, Mummy. I love you so much. Nothing's going to happen to me, is it? I'm going to get well, aren't I?" "Of course you are, my love, you're a lot better already. Try to get some rest now." "Will it soon be over?" she asked me again and again. "Promise me it will." When I did, she fell asleep contentedly in my arms.

The second day passed, and the third arrived. Another day of glory when it was impossible to think of anything but Elba's body – which, when I took her pyjama top off to rub the ointment the doctor had given me on the tiny red spots on her back and front, looked so defenceless that all my fears seemed completely absurd and improbable. Her slender shoulders, the beautiful but still childish line of her collar bone, and above all, her tiny young girl's breasts, all seemed to prove them groundless. What could make my daughter evil? It was impossible. I kissed her feverish body and told her: "Mummy will always be with you, my love."

More than once during that third night it occurred to me to take advantage of her being asleep to sneak a quick look in the box apparently full of secrets that lay so close to her. Perhaps then I could finally lay all my doubts and fears to rest. After all, I tried to convince myself, everything I thought concerning

Miki's death, all the reasons behind it, and even how it had happened, were nothing more than speculation on my part. My sleeping daughter's frail little body and the smile on her half-open mouth told me I must be wrong, and the best way to make sure was to see what was in the box. Probably there was nothing in it but the sound and the fury.

"Go on," I said to myself in encouragement, "just a quick peep and all your doubts will be forgotten; don't forget, this wonderful parenthesis will soon be over. By next week at the latest Elba will be better, and daily life and what is so cruelly known as 'reality' will take over again. If you sneak a look and don't find anything suspicious, then there'll be no more room for doubts, fears or worries." "Of course, Mummy, open it, look inside and you'll see I'm not lying": that seemed also to be what the sleeping Elba's smile told me. "There shouldn't be any secrets between us, Mummy, so do it."

And yet I didn't. While it was true that Elba's smile and her gentle breath on my hands seemed very like happiness, something told me I shouldn't tempt fate because, if you thought about it – or so I told myself – however dreadful a doubt may be, it is always preferable to a truth you have to live with for the rest of your days. Only fools prefer certainty to certain kinds of doubt.

This sense of complete happiness lasted another two days. Hours of fitful sleep in which Elba muttered incomprehensible phrases. She seemed to be talking first with Avril, then with Sofía, sometimes she appeared to be calling out to Tony, more often to Miki: *Come on, Miki, why are you looking like that? It's as though you had seen a ghost, be brave, come on, show you're a real boy. And you, Mummy, don't worry, look, nothing's happened to him, it's only a scratch.*

All this time my hand was there to soothe away any pain, to calm her anxiety. "Sleep soundly, Elba, your mother's here. She'll always be with you, my love."

There was only one moment, one tiny shadow that was cast over us in those three days. That was when the caretaker's cat appeared: I saw it through the window, but simply catching sight of it made me short of breath, as if I were having one of my old asthma attacks. That damned cat; I'd almost forgotten it existed.

The third day of fever gave way to a fourth, and this brought Sofía's first visit. She appeared without warning, without so much as a phone call. She'd brought Elba a present.

"It's not much," she said, "just a little something, and yes, I do know I can't see her, that would be acting irresponsibly to all the other children, but you can give it to her from me, can't you Luigi? I'm really fond of her."

"I'm really fond of her" was what Sofía always added when she talked of Elba. It sounded slightly childish to me, in a way which only served to reinforce my belief that however intelligent or capable they may be, people who work with children eventually regress until they start thinking, behaving and of course expressing themselves exactly like their pupils. Perhaps that was the most logical explanation why whenever I talked with Sofía, I ended up back in the relationship we had as little girls.

"I really miss Elba," said Sofía. "She reminds me so much of me when... When d'you think she'll be able to go back to school?"

I told her the doctor thought it advisable for Elba to stay at home two or three days after her fever had gone down – and this hadn't happened yet.

"So what with one thing and another, I suppose I'll have her with me all week," I said. Then, to change topics, I asked her: "But tell me what's going on in the big wide world: how's Avril?"

We talked about Avril, about the classes Elba would miss, and how it would soon be the holidays. It was pretty much a

248

routine conversation, in which I only said the strictly necessary, because all I wanted was to get back to my daughter as quickly as possible. Elba's illness seemed to have negated the strange hold that Sofía had over me, and the way she always took me back to my childhood. But this truce only lasted for her first visit. Sofía came back the next day, and before we had even said hello I could tell that everything was back to normal between us.

That day, Elba's temperature had dropped and she was sleeping quietly. It was another stormy afternoon. Yet another one in the wretched winter we were having, and when I saw Sofía come in with wet face and hair I suddenly felt we had already lived a similar scene. When could that have been? "You're soaked," I said, "let me help you," and it was only a few moments later that I remembered. As she handed me her mac and umbrella, the latter slipped from my grasp, and I was suddenly reminded of another distant and equally rainy afternoon in Sofía's old apartment. It was a grey day, and it must have been soon after the first boy's death because, as we both ran in soaking wet from the rain, Sofía had noticed my face and said, laughing, "Come on, silly, don't tell me you're still crying for him. What's the point? What did you do that day for you to cry like an asshole?" I may have only recently arrived in Madrid, but I knew that word was one little girls shouldn't use, unless they were very beautiful and brilliant like Sofía, with a home as pretty as hers, where I always felt so out of place, small or stupid. "Come on, Luigi," she repeated, "Don't cry. You didn't do anything. I did, and look at me." So I looked at Sofía in the way I always looked at her in those days, with a mixture of fear and admiration, with no idea what she had meant by that "I did".

"I'm not crying, it's the rain," I had said on that occasion, before the umbrella had slipped from my grasp and fallen to the floor between us as if to prove yet again that I really was an asshole. For further confirmation, Sofía laughed once more with that laugh of hers that sounded so deep and grown-up in a twelve-year-old girl. "That's what people trying to hide it always say, Luigi: they're not tears, but raindrops. *Rain & Tears*, like in that stupid song."

The oddest thing about this memory was that I had stared closely at Sofía as she was making fun of me and hummed that song, which was all the rage at the time – and wasn't stupid, but very beautiful – and it seemed to me that despite the rain, it was *her* face that was covered in tears, even though everything about her mocking attitude and her laughter seemed to contradict the fact, as did what she was saying. "What are you waiting for, Luigi? Pick up that damned umbrella and let's get our wet things off. What's wrong, are you just going to stand there staring at me all day?"

This was what I remembered. A memory that had been buried by other more painful ones in that unforgettable month of April. Such as, for example, the first days back at school following the boy's death, and the fact that Antonio's name was wiped from all our conversations and replaced by pronouns: "The day *that* happened", "the last time I was with *him*", "that was *his* desk".

"Wait," I said to Sofía, finally emerging from my daydream. "I'd better go and find you something to dry your face with."

Sofía turned towards me with a "Thanks, Luigi" on her lips. It was when I saw her face, lined now by the years that had passed, but just as wet as on that other distant afternoon, that I suddenly thought that *Rain & Tears* might be a pretty song, but that its words did not ring true at all, because faces wet from rain are nothing like faces covered in tears: *Rain and tears all the same. When you cry in winter time you can pretend it's nothing but the rain.* It wasn't true, it was impossible: I knew now that even a silly girl such as I had been then could not have confused rain and tears. But if what I had seen on Sofía's face that afternoon (so similar to this one) had in fact been tears, what could she have meant by "You didn't do anything, Luigi, and I did"? There was no doubt that tears on the face of a little girl who never cried meant something: but what exactly?

"How is little Elba today? Better? It's raining cats and dogs out there, I'm soaked to the skin. What's the matter, Luigi? Are you going to fetch something for me to dry myself with, or what?"

It was at that moment, even though Sofía's mocking tone suggested everything between us was back to the way it had been in our childhood, that I decided that for once our conversation wasn't going to be casual chatter as it had been the day before as we watched over the sleeping Elba. It was just the two of us again, as it had been on that rainy afternoon soon after the first accident, when Sofía had told me that rain and tears were all the same. That too had been a lie.

"What happened that afternoon, Sofía?"

"Which afternoon are you talking about, Luigi?"

"Come on," I said, "I'll give you something to dry yourself with, and then we can have a drink: do you like Bloody Marys? There's a question I've been wanting to ask you for ages."

A Confession

I looked down at my drink and then at Sofía. She had chosen to sit on the sofa by the window, so that her silhouette and dishevelled hair were lit from behind by the declining afternoon light and the sudden streaks of lightning. She didn't want a Bloody Mary. "You're the only one who drinks a mishmash like that these days," she said. "Is it because it's bloody, sweetheart? Wasn't it Agatha Christie's favourite drink? For goodness' sake, Luigi, you're like a compendium of clichés." She served herself a coke ("Julie Andrews' favourite drink, honey, but don't count on me singing for you"). She took two sips then peered at me. She was wearing her perennial grey woollen dress, and I suddenly wondered how, in spite of her obvious ageing and lack of dress sense, she still had an almost animal attraction, like a cat.

"Well then, fire away," she said, "although I think I know what you're going to ask me: yes, you're right, every rainy afternoon makes me think of Demis Roussos."

That was it: he was the one who had sung *Rain & Tears*. So Sofía also remembered that other rainy afternoon and the tears. Now all I had to do was find out exactly what it had meant to her.

"It didn't mean anything special. Everybody remembers at least one rainy afternoon in their lives, and that's the one for me."

I was thinking of saying this was yet another stupid lie, but I didn't, because although the vodka was starting to work its usual wonders on me, I also felt the onset of another slight asthma attack. An attack that told me the balance of power established between us in our childhood still held sway. If possible, it was even stronger, because the semi-darkness prevented me seeing Sofía's face, so that she once more became the brilliant, perfect young girl who had such a deep laugh and spoke with an attractive lisp I'd always wanted to copy.

"No, it's not that afternoon I want you to talk to me about, but the other one: you know the one I mean."

"Yes," she replied, "I can imagine; but are you really sure you want to talk about it? As a novelist, you must know the reason why we spend our lives saying let's talk about this and that, everything under the sun, all the past, present and future nonsense you can think of. Because when people use that word 'talk' they don't really want to *say anything*, do they?" She took another sip from her Coke, setting the ice cubes chinking in her glass. She went on: "I suppose that's exactly why we spend all our time chewing the fat. I'm sure the great Carmen O'Inns would agree with what I'm going to say: we talk so much precisely in order to avoid saying anything. But if you want to break the universal rule that we only talk about what doesn't matter, if you really want to *talk*, I will, even though you might be sorry I did. We are always sorry about what we know, never about what we don't know. A*w*en't I *w*ight?"

That wonderful lisp again, accompanied by the chinking of ice in her glass. The cat curled up by the fireside once more, and everything was as it always had been between us. I didn't see the point in admitting I was (and how!) in complete agreement with her theory: I'm all in favour of not knowing, or at least of keeping a reasonable doubt; may the good Lord deliver us from all kinds of certainties. Yet I had just thought of a very strong reason for trying to find out, after all these years, exactly what had happened that afternoon the first boy had died. In other words, to choose, at least this once, to know rather than to remain in the dark. And that reason had almost entirely to do with Elba. The scene with the tears and the rain had demonstrated something that had occurred to me more than once, each time with a renewed sense of surprise: the way that memories (and not simply memories, but the version that two or more people have of a single event) can be deceptive. Wasn't it obvious for example that, as I had read in Avril's emails, Sofía and I had seen two very different kinds of death that first afternoon? I needed to know what Sofía had seen, because if our versions were so different and what happened then was not what I thought I had seen, it was also possible that something even less obvious than an event we had witnessed together, for example the suspicion I had about little Miki's death, could be equally mistaken. I told myself this was a perfectly logical possibility, because there were symmetries and slight anachronisms in both cases, and if I had been wrong about the first death, I might also be wrong about the second one.

"What happened that afternoon, Sofía? I need to know."

"You were there, Luigi, you saw it the same as I did, the same as Miguel. All three of us saw what happened."

"No, that's exactly what surprises me. The evening we met again here after all those years – d'you remember? I got the impression that, if we had forgotten what you call the universal rule of only talking about what doesn't matter and had described what we had seen, there would have been three very different versions."

"I see. Let's start with Miguel then. What do you think he saw?"

"What makes you think I know what he saw?"

"Darling, that universal rule we were talking about is smashed to pieces as soon as two people climb into bed together. So don't tell me that in at least one of those lovemaking sessions our man is so expert at, he didn't open up. You know what I mean, one of those delightful nights of tantric sex you shared, with Brahms playing in the background and a few oriental bouquet candles spicing up the atmosphere. Did he nibble at your ear as

255

well if he caught you on the phone? Don't look at me like that, Luigi: how do I know all this? Men are so uninspired in their habits that I'm sure over the past few months you and I have shared exactly the same decor, the same rituals and the same soundtrack; not to mention the same pillow, of course."

"Miguel and I never talked about his brother," I replied, not just to refocus what we were talking about on what I wanted to ask Sofía, but also, and above all, to give me time to refocus my thoughts, to get over my renewed dismay (my God, how is it possible???) at my lack of perception, of how I – the Supercool, the superduper, etc., the great expert in human nature – had been wrong yet again. Wrong when I decided that Sofía not only had no interest in Miguel but detested him, as I had read in Avril's emails, and so could not even imagine any love affair between them. Wrong when I thought that night when we met at home, Miguel had only been interested in me and not in the cynical and plainly ageing Sofía. In me, the superstupid, who not only thought that nobody knew of our romance but, to add insult to injury, had even felt all sorts of scruples and remorse about hopping between Enrique and Miguel's beds. I reproached myself (what a whore you are!) for betraying them both. Betraying Miguel! When all the while he had been sleeping with me and Sofía at the same time. For heaven's sake, how blind can you get! What else could be happening right in front of my nose without me realizing it? Could Enrique be sharing me with someone else too? With whom? Perhaps it even was with Sofía because, as Enrique had once said, nowadays infidelity is more like endogamy, incest or, worse still, musical chairs. Why not, after all? While I thought about it, I seemed to remember that the day I introduced them, after Miki's funeral, they got on very well. That's more than enough, I suddenly told myself, halting my interior monologue and lapsing into what for me was the unusual habit of swearing, you really are an asshole, aren't you? Who on earth gives a damn what things *seem* to you? Forget once and for all those *seems*, it's obvious that what you see, or think you see, is always wide of the mark, shi-it.

I took another long swig of my Bloody Mary. God bless vodka, I thought, and peered again at Sofía's profile against the light. The stormy afternoon had turned into evening, so that I could hardly make out her features. Much better that way, I thought. That way I wouldn't have to see her ageing face or the plump outline of her menopausal body, so different from mine, the Pilates queen, the superslender, the... (wait, before you go on with your self-flagellation, look at the bright side to all this, because now it's more obvious than ever that nothing, absolutely nothing is as you think it is, and therefore your fears about Elba must be misplaced as well).

"What were you saying about Miguel, Luigi?"

"I was saying... I was saying he never talked about his brother, with me at least." I was about to ask: "How about with you? Did he ever tell you what he saw that afternoon?" but stopped myself, because there was no reason whatsoever that what Sofía *thought* Miguel *thought* about that accident would be true either; nobody should trust what they think others think. But then how do you find the truth, if indeed it does exist? In fact, the only sensible question you can ask anyone is "What do you think happened?" or "What did you see?" and in the end that's what I asked her, mentally hoping she wasn't going to lie. What if she did? That's always the danger, but at least it wouldn't be a second-hand version, which meant it would be distorted right from the start.

"All right, Luigi, if what you want to know is my view of what happened that day, I may tell you later; but first of all, tell me: what do you think happened?"

"To me it's quite clear. We were playing cops and robbers. Antonio and you had climbed onto that crumbling stone urn. Miguel and I, who were the cops, were down below. From up above, you began to shout: 'Let's see if you can catch us! I bet you can't catch me!' Then I saw how Miguel jokingly began pushing at the base of the urn and saying: 'Leave Antonio and come with me, Sofi—'"

"Yes, I hated being called that—"

"After that, the crumbling urn started to topple, and Miguel decided to catch you and not Antonio. It was an accident, it all happened so quickly, it wasn't true that he deliberately let his brother crash to the ground, it's not true at all..."

"Who said it was?"

"I thought that you..." I began, hoping against hope I would not have to reveal how I knew it, "that you had thought all these years it was Miguel who—"

"Wrong again, Luigi: you never get it right, do you? I'm not the one who thinks that; he is."

"Miguel thinks he killed his brother?"

"Why else do you suppose he's made a completely insulated life for himself? All that sophistication: expensive works of art, four ex-wives and a new woman every week, money and more money? Because wealth, spent as frivolously as possible, is an (almost) perfect shield to protect ourselves against horror. Isn't that what Carmen O'Inns would say?"

"I've no idea what Carmen O'Inns would say, but I know what I think: that nobody knows what anyone else believes or thinks, and so we can't and shouldn't speak on their behalf."

"That's very true, but for the moment I'm not going to tell you what I think, but what I know of what Miguel thinks, and he thinks he's the guilty one. He told me so in tears the day his son died. And do you know what I did then, Luigi? I left him with his guilt. Yes, there's no need to look at me like that, it's what I did. It was one of the few times in my life I've played the Good Samaritan. If fate had been so cruel as to imitate something that happened forty years ago, then I wasn't going to be the one to deny him that consolation."

"What consolation?" I asked, recalling how I had seen Miguel sobbing in Sofía's arms that night, without guessing (once again, the super-short-sighted) what was going on between them. "I don't understand a thing. What consolation?"

"It's hard to understand if you haven't lived it, but when you suffer such a terrible blow it's somehow a consolation to know that what has happened is to pay for something equally terrible you have done in the past."

"I still don't get it…"

"Then you really are lucky, Luigi. You always were the one with the luck. But I can assure you that when something terrible happens, it's better to think that God, fate, or whoever you believe may be in charge of this chaos, is vengeful or demands justice, rather than to go mad wondering 'why did it happen to me?' Isn't that the question everyone asks themselves as soon as anything goes wrong? Why am I a failure when he isn't? Why am I poor and she's rich? Why, why me? Personally I've never found the need to ask it, but I'll bet it's really high up on any list of the most common phrases in the world. When anything tragic happens, our first thought is: why me? So you can't imagine how great a consolation it can be to have a ready answer, such as: this death pays for the other one."

"But that's monstrous. Besides, how do you know how it feels?"

"Everything is monstrous, Luigi. But you get used to even that, and sometimes it gives meaning to things, believe me."

"So do you think it's true or false? I mean, did Miguel deliberately let his brother fall?"

"Truth and falsehood: they're such slippery words. What was it we learnt at school, those lines everybody repeats without knowing where they come from? Nothing is completely true or false; it all depends on the colour of the glass you see it through. That old poet Campoamor had it spot on. And so you can see just how right he was, listen to another possible version of what happened that afternoon."

Another heavier clunk told me Sofía had finished her drink. I could feel the effect of the vodka coursing through me; sometimes it's good and even necessary to feel slightly tipsy.

"Let's suppose things didn't happen as Miguel saw them, but not the way you saw them either. Let's suppose that Antonio didn't fall, but that it was me who pushed him."

"Oh come on, you don't mean to tell me that—"

"I said 'let's suppose', Luigi; humour me a while and you'll see all that you can learn about human nature. To begin with, let's suppose something it won't be hard for you to remember: that in those days I was used to having everything I wanted just by stretching out my hand."

"How could I forget? I've never known anyone as strong as you, you were so capable of making sure things turned out the way you wanted."

"Yes, and look at the twists and turns life takes… let's also suppose that someone like I was as a child came up against a person who refused to let me do that. Someone (Antonio, for example) who was a symbol of everything I most desired and couldn't have."

"But I thought you had everything…"

"You thought… Didn't we just agree that all those 'I thought's didn't mean a thing? What does anybody know about what motivates or stirs anybody else, what makes someone behave in one way rather than another? Other people's motives are always incomprehensible for those listening to them. We always think we are good, better than anyone else, that we would never commit certain little infamies. And yet, when it comes down to it, Luigi, no one is innocent, we are all criminals. Just supposing it were true I pushed Antonio that afternoon – something I haven't yet said is true or not – I can easily tell you the reasons why I could have done it. For example, because he had something I wanted."

"Perhaps, but that's no reason to—"

"Am I talking or are you?"

"You are."

"Let's just say I was the girl everybody loved, but he didn't. He didn't even admire me, which for someone like me in those days was even more important than being loved. Let's also say that sometimes the most terrible things aren't exactly planned, but are a spur-of-the moment reaction: a hand you should hold out, but don't, a look the other way when you could have helped somebody. And everything happens so quickly it seems it wasn't you who did it. Yes, that's the best part about it: 'It wasn't me,' you think, and yet it happened. Who was responsible for it then? Who knows? Fate, luck, chance: you can always find a good explanation. And d'you know what you feel once it's all over, Luigi? You feel a sense of power—"

"Power? But that's monstrous too."

"Please! Don't be so clichéd, so petit bourgeois, so politically correct. Do you want to know what happened next or not?"

"Yes, I do."

"Everybody thought Antonio's death had been an accident and began to be worried about us: the three poor children who had witnessed a tragedy. I don't know about you, Luigi, but the reward I got was a week off school. My mother... do you remember her?"

"Of course, she always stuck in my mind, I don't know, she seemed so frail, so scared all the time."

"That was later on. At that time, my mother wasn't the insecure person she soon became. Then she fussed over me the whole time: poor little Sofía, do you feel all right? Are you sure you aren't having nightmares? What would you like to do, my love? Would you like to talk about it? I suppose that when she asked that, she didn't really know what she was letting herself in for, but one fine day I took her at her word and told her what I had done: we always need someone to confide in. No, perhaps what we really need is a witness. There are some things we need somebody else to know, one person at least..."

At this point I again heard the clink of ice in her glass, but this time it was a soft, liquid sound as if somehow her glass had been refilled, even though that was impossible, because we were still sitting there in the evening gloom without either of us having moved. But everything was unreal at that moment, as unbelievable as what she then went on to say:

"I told her how it had all happened so quickly: how warm Antonio's body had been next to mine up by the urn, how I had longed to touch him, but how he had rejected and scorned me, my pain at his rejection, his laugh and then – it's only a second, and then you feel free, you feel stronger than everybody else, much stronger – just a second and it's done. It's simple; child's play, as they say."

"I can hardly believe you! It's too horrible and it doesn't make any sense. I knew you well in those days, and—"

"You're reacting in the same stupid way as before. What on earth does it matter that you think what I've just told you makes no sense? And what on earth does it matter what you thought then, or now come to that? My mother believed me. My mother did know me well. That was why she never asked me the question everyone asks when something like that takes place: *Why, Sofía?* She never asked me that, because she knew."

"What did she know?"

"Let's just say she knew it was better not to ask, and so our lives continued as before, until she started her love affair with Johnnie Walker."

"With whom?"

"Oh please, Luigi, don't play the fool: until she started drinking whisky. And it's bad to drink, isn't it? That's why Coke is the only drink I'm addicted to. Drinkers don't think, or even worse, they think everything is simpler than it is in reality. They even get to believe that things that have no solution can somehow be fixed, and that's not only false, it's dangerous. A sober person knows there are reasons why it's better not to know, and also knows there are details it's better not to tell even their own shadow, and confidences that should never be revealed. But when you're drunk, all that goes by the board. It's so sad, isn't it? Although in my mother's case it wasn't that important, because she died soon afterwards. Yet another accident—"

"You're crazy, off your head. I don't believe a word of it."

Sofía's guffaw, exactly the same as in our childhood, and then she said:

"D'you remember how this interesting confession began? It began with a 'let's suppose'. If you like, you can forget everything I've said: Antonio's death, and my mother's… Let's just say I simply wanted to demonstrate that you should never trust what you imagine, nor even what you see. Isn't it true that this is yet another possible version of events? It *could have been* that way."

"And I suppose that now you're going to tell me it wasn't that way after all."

More chinking of ice cubes, and another childish guffaw.

"It's an old, old story Luigi. Nobody cares about it any more. Too much water under the bridge: isn't that what they always say? If you like though, we can carry on playing TRUE or FALSE, and see what more we discover. It used to be one of our favourite games, didn't it? And look where it got us. Look what's become of me, and look what's become of you. Life has so many twists and turns."

Vodka

No, life doesn't have that many twists, I told myself half an hour later. Sofía had finally left. I was sitting alone in my living room with a "Virgin Mary" in one hand, and the bottle of vodka within reach in case I felt like baptizing Mary (which wasn't very likely: I only drink at moments of crisis, and as far as I was concerned, those were all behind me). It was two in the morning. I had just checked, and Elba was fast asleep. All the lights were on, to mark a difference with the previous scene, and I took a long swig at the drink, because I suddenly felt as though I had succeeded in winning a game with Sofía and myself that had been going on for years. It might have been because I felt so tired, but what I sensed was that everything was in place. Yes, in place, because now I knew what had really happened that far-off afternoon in our childhood, and that Sofía was the guilty one, I didn't feel disgust or repulsion. No, I felt a strange sense of calm. How typical of Sofía to have prefixed her story with a "let's suppose"; it was such a classic ploy to leave room for doubt. But there are no doubts any more, I thought. And it's not true, I told myself again, life doesn't have that many twists. In fact, it only changes enough to put people where they belong: Sofía had been right about that, of course. What happened to Antonio was terrible, cruel, and the motives behind his death were incomprehensible, unless we put it down to wounded pride or simply to that strange phenomenon it seems everyone is finally beginning to acknowledge: the perverse and always inexplicable cruelty of children. But whatever the explanation, my friend had also been right in saying it was all water under the bridge. There were lessons to draw from it, though. The first lesson was that it confirmed once and for all my complete lack of awareness about how things really were. I was completely useless at seeing what was going on, totally blind: it must have been some sort of a record for someone who lives (and lives well) from their supposed powers of observation and portrayal of human conduct. Possibly any future novels I write were going to suffer from this sudden revelation, but who gave a damn about literature? To hell with literature: the good thing was that if, right from the start, I had been wrong in my assessment of everyone around me, from Avril to Miguel, from Sofía and even to Enrique, it was obvious I must also have been completely wrong about my own daughter. Wasn't it for precisely this reason that I had questioned Sofía about our past? The need to confirm that nothing is at it seems? Well, the saints be praised, it turns out that nothing is as it appears, I said, taking another sip from my tomato juice. Our intuition fails us, so do our eyes, to say nothing of the suspicions we fabricate. So now I could even tempt fate or that universal rule which says it is better to harbour doubts than to be sure about something. I could, if I liked, open the famous box under Elba's bed, sure in the knowledge I would find nothing there.

After another sip at my Virgin Mary (thank goodness I hadn't slipped any vodka in there this time, it's dangerous to drink, it even fools us into believing we can solve problems that have no solution. Sofía had said that about her mother, but what do I have in common with Sofía's poor mother?) I found it hard to understand how I could even have thought such stupid things about Elba. Let's see, I told myself, what scared you so much? That you found some stickers that had once belonged to Miki in Elba's file? Why was that so important? All it proved was something that in fact ought to help reduce my fears still further. Because, I reasoned with my new-found clarity, it was easy to see that if I had been so alarmed by this discovery it was because, as the Man of My Life was always telling me, literature was forever leading me astray, so that sometimes without even realizing it, I behaved like a character from one of my books. You ought to be ashamed of yourself, I thought. It was only according to the logic of crime novels that finding something belonging to a dead person in someone else's possession was proof of guilt. All right, I told myself, let's examine my other fears: what was the other "damning" evidence you were so worried about? What was it about Miki's elder brother? Oh yes, the fact that you found Elba had spied on Tony, taking photos of him without his knowledge, including one or two which were more intimate than was strictly decent. Out of this completely harmless adolescent behaviour, I turned into the ineffable Carmen O'Inns, and came to the worst, most outlandish conclusion: that Elba saw in him the father she had never known because there was a vague resemblance between Tony Gasset and the description I had once given of that other Antonio on the island of Elba. Two men who vaguely resembled each other and shared the same name: it was a nice symmetry, with that wonderful added "slight anachronism" that Borges wrote of. Of course, once you have symmetry and a slight anachronism to boot, then it's easy to add further elements to the drama, such as Elba's obsession about having no father, as well as the phenomenon so well-known to psychologists that all children who feel the lack of a father as keenly as Elba did end up trying to find one among the people they know, who they then feel the need to monopolize, to keep for themselves. "Now I'm the only one you've got," Elba had told Tony the day his brother died, which my befuddled brain of a guilt-ridden mother (because we mothers always feel guilty for everything, absolutely everything) had interpreted in the worst possible manner, as if it hadn't simply been one of those empty phrases we all say at some time or other, which mean nothing more than sound and fury.

All at once I felt a slight shortness of breath, as I had done when Sofía had been here. I must be catching a cold, I told myself. What else could it be? It's raining too much this year, as much as in that month of April forty years ago. This time it was winter rather than spring, but there was as much rain as there usually is in April. By the way, I thought, since we are so busy sorting out all the "mysteries" in this story, why could it have been that Sofía called her daughter Avril, like the name of the month in Spanish? Was it because it reminded her of the month of her defeat? Yes, it's true, I said to myself with a laugh, throughout these years Sofía has suffered every possible kind of defeat, as many as I have had victories. It's not true that life gives so many twists and turns, in the end just enough to make sure everyone ends up where they deserve to be. And I won all along the line. In everything, because the fact was that my talk with Sofía had succeeded in dismantling yet another symmetry, the one that for me was the most important one: the symmetry between the deaths of the two boys, Antonio and Miki. That similarity was the most worrying of all, and yet now it was plain it was entirely coincidental. What was common to the two accidents? A lot less than might appear at first sight. For a start, the two boys were not similar, but completely unlike each other: Antonio was brilliant, Miki totally insignificant. Then there were the motives for Sofía doing what she did: the rage that a young girl who had everything felt when she found she couldn't force someone to love her. In what way was that similar to Miki's death? There was absolutely no symmetry there either: nobody had ever been in love with the poor shrimp; on the contrary, he was a shy boy who didn't even have any friends.

I sipped some more Virgin Mary. There was no getting away from it: at first, I had seen the two deaths as identical, simply because fate enjoys itself by leading us to believe it repeats itself. Who hasn't felt that to some degree or other? But it's not true, nothing is bound to repeat itself, it's nothing more than superstition. So now, if you like – I told myself – now you can open that famous box, Luisa. Without any sense of fear. A doubt may usually be better than a certainty, but when you know what that certainty is, who doesn't prefer it?

I got up from my chair and walked towards Elba's bedroom. As I passed through the hall, for some reason I came to a halt between the two mirrors. That small mirror – infinitely reflected in the bigger one – had also played its part in our story. For example, when Elba, after I had told her the truth about her birth, spent hours staring at herself in it, clutching her doll and searching for who knew what distant shadows. I had also stared at myself in it, as that time when I had discovered that success is the greatest and most subtle form of revenge. What do they say in French for this optical phenomenon when a mirror is reflected in one opposite so that they repeat each other to make an infinite gallery of images? *Mise en abîme* I think it's called. Yes, I now realized, that was what our entire story had been like: a series of images reflecting each other time and again. But mirrors can deceive: it looks as though they are offering us an exact image, yet we all know that in fact it's quite the opposite.

I tiptoed as quietly as possible to Elba's door and opened it. The very first thing that struck me was the familiar smell her bedroom had, which at that time was a mixture of the sharp smell of her medicines and ointments and my daughter's own body smell. All mothers recognize and love the smell each of their children has, and I could pick out Elba's among thousands: cinnamon, a woody odour, a hint of liquorice. That was what my daughter's room smelt of – the smell of happiness. I took two steps closer to the bed. Elba was still scared of storms, and went to sleep with the bathroom light on and the door ajar. Even so, it was so dark in her room that I opened the door to the corridor in order to see more clearly. Thanks to the influx of light, I could admire the beauty of my sleeping daughter's face. "Elba, my love," I said, kissing her on the forehead to make sure her fever had completely gone. "That's good, sweetheart," I added, "sleep soundly, your mummy's here." I hesitated for a second, then knelt down to feel under the bed.

Just as I had imagined, the box was underneath. It was a large, blue box, one of those they sell in superstores on the outskirts of the city. I had never seen it before: where could Elba have got it from? How had she bought it, and who with? To know or not to know... to see or not to see... There was still time for me to pull back, but that special smell of my daughter was so intense and seemed so much like happiness that I pulled the box out with both hands, and lifted the lid.

There was still not much light in the room, so I took two or three steps back towards the door to get a better look inside. As I carefully moved away from the bed so as not to wake Elba, I noticed how light the box was. It didn't seem as though there could be much inside. Open the door a bit wider, I told myself, and when I did so, I could see the box was completely empty. Or rather, at the very bottom, like a princess abandoned in the heart of a vast castle, there lay the ugly doll Elba had bought at the pound shop. I remembered she had wanted to give it to me on the first day at her new school, for me to throw away, but then had changed her mind and said she would do it. That unpleasant, absurd image of herself that she had fantasized about in the days before I told her she hadn't been adopted but really was my own daughter, those days when she called me Luisa and not "Mummy". I almost burst out laughing; all there was in the box was the sound and the fury or, what amounted to the same, another deceptive image from the play of mirrors. Clutching her pillow in bed, it almost seemed as though Elba too were smiling in her sleep, as if to say: "You see, Mummy, I told you so. How silly you've been!"

Child's Play

Anyone who knows the so-called "Proust questionnaire" will know it consists of a set of questions aimed at compiling a portrait of the person answering them. Among apparently trivial questions such as "Which is your favourite flower?" or "Which is your preferred historical moment?" There is one I've always found very easy to answer: "What is your greatest virtue?"

"The ability to laugh at myself," I always respond. Sometimes when the question is part of a longer interview, I amplify my answer and say that knowing how to laugh at myself is the only attribute I share with the most outstanding representatives of great literature. It's completely false to say that all the great writers knew how to laugh at themselves, but it sounds good in interviews, and so far nobody has taken the trouble to check and contradict me.

Be that as it may, it is my greatest virtue, and I'm glad of it. Not only because taking yourself seriously must be an endless source of unhappiness (to spend the entire day thinking you deserve more recognition, more tributes, etc.), but also because for a writer, it's a very useful quality. Everyone's life is full of mistakes, failures and stupid, groundless fears, and it is these shortcomings, much more than the successes, which provide an invaluable source for literature.

It was precisely my mistakes and failures that I intended to use as literary material in a few minutes' time, when I wiped from my computer memory everything I had written for the latest Carmen O'Inns novel, the one I had made so little progress with.

All right, here goes with the "delete" key. Now to start planning afresh. What should I call my new novel outline? Perhaps it's best to spend some time, half an hour say, playing with ideas to see what happens.

Of all my most recent errors – making love to Miguel Gasset, my lack of awareness when it came to Sofía's guilt, my misjudgement of Avril and, above all, the mistake I had made regarding my own daughter – this last was by far the worst, and therefore the most interesting from a literary point of view. Yet I would be lying if I said it was the first one I started to analyse. The first that came to mind was my mistake over Miguel; it popped up no doubt out of a desire for revenge.

That's why I'm sitting here now at my computer. It's six in the morning, still too early for the outside world to disturb my work with phone calls or text messages wishing me a nice day from the Man of My Life. Too early as well for Elba to come and give me a kiss, to show she doesn't have a temperature any more. And above all, too early for me to start writing properly: that requires a bit of warming-up, of trial and error, and what better way to do that than to think of Miguel Gasset?

To think of him, or what amounts to the same, to think of my lack of awareness not only as a woman but even worse, as a writer, incapable of understanding what was right before her eyes. What do psychologists call that blind spot which leads us to think that someone is interested in us, when in fact it's our rival they are focused on? I don't know, it must be one of the most common failings, but in your case, Luisita, it's unforgivable. Pink socks (I wrote furiously), music by Brahms, neo-classical Swedish furniture and tantric sex!

Curiously enough, I had tried to incorporate all these elements of Miguel's personality into my previous novel by making them part of one of my central character's attributes, yet out of elementary politeness towards him I had only sketched in them briefly, without being vicious in any way. Now though my body was demanding I spend at least a chapter making fun of his socks. And what about tantric sex, that masculine desideratum? (Bravo for men – I thought as I typed that word "tantric", that's a great step forwards for your species; so finally you've succeeded in emulating us when it comes to faking it: join the club, boys.) That particular desideratum, I told myself, was worth not just a chapter but an entire book, which I could call something like "T-Sex with Raspberry Socks".

I wrote down "T-Sex With Raspberry Socks" as a possible title to develop, then let my fingers roam over the keyboard, writing whatever nasty thoughts came into my head. Because if the ability to laugh at oneself is a help to creativity, then a desire for vengeance is even more helpful. In fact, if you take a close look, I told myself with a smile, because I was already imagining a thousand ways to ridicule the guy, in general the arts owe far more to mankind's base passions than to their more lofty side. After all, wasn't it personal vanity that led to the construction of the pyramids? Wasn't it Pope Sixtus VI's envy that paid for the painting of the Sistine Chapel? Carry on, Luisa, it serves that conqueror in raspberry socks right if you lampoon him in a novel, if you write about all his tics and manias. You could even suggest that he let his brother die. That's what he thinks, isn't it? Possibly he's right, because no one is innocent as far as little Antonio's death is concerned. "No one is Innocent" I jotted down as another possible book title, then let my fingers continue their crazy gallop over the keyboard. It's gratifying to feel you are entering that state of literary grace where one idea flows naturally into the next. I have to admit that literary grace is a rare thing, so I must make sure I take advantage of it: let's see what I can make of it. So all of a sudden I found myself sketching out another idea, one that Enrique had suggested and which I thought might be useful from a literary point of view: according to that friend of his who has a blog called "We All Know an Assassin", the world is full of unsolved crimes, and therefore of unpunished murderers. I personally know about not only Miguel's story, but Sofía's too, so why not take a few notes about them? What writer needs imagination when they have so much real experience so close to hand?

I closed down the folder I had called "Miguel" and opened one I intended to devote to Sofía. If finally I preferred to tell her story, it was not to take my revenge – life had already done that for me – but because my friend's past contained several interesting literary elements which were worth setting down in black and white. My fingers needed only the slightest encouragement before they set off again, and so, completely forgetting "T-Sex and Raspberry Socks", I started sketching how I could tell Sofía Márquez's story. I wrote "We All Know an Assassin" as a possible title and then, in a different way to what I had written about Miguel Gasset, I took some time to describe my characters. These are a young girl with a pronounced lisp, a girl so beautiful it took your breath away just looking at her. Then there are two identical twins, one of them in love with Sofía, the other not interested. I note down these details and immediately add other remarkable points in the story, such as a game of cops and robbers, a stone pond that the wind and rain have filled with dry leaves and stagnant water, and then the sudden irruption of a murder which everyone sees as an accident. As I am writing this, I recall Sofía's words from the night before, here in my own living room: *When a death like that happens, it all takes place far too quickly. So quickly it seems as though it wasn't you who did it. And do you know what you feel when you kill someone without meaning to? A sense of power, Luigi, power.*

My fingers come to a halt. There's no doubt this could easily form the basis of a good novel, but the fact is, Sofía's story now has a second part to it, an interesting "sequel" as they call it nowadays. "Remember Señora Márquez" I jot down, because I have had the sudden mental image of the photo of Sofía's mother, in which she is drinking a cup of tea while her daughter looks at her with a smile. I have often thought that photos of dead people sometimes offer us a premonition of how they are going to die. At others though, they seem like mere sarcasm. Who would have imagined, to see her looking so frail like that, raising her tea cup with her daughter smiling at her side, that one day this image could somehow foretell the way in which she died? She may have died of drinking, but as Sofía had said, it wasn't exactly tea.

"Johnnie Walker" I write in capitals, then begin a short resumé of what I remember from all that Sofía had said. About how once Antonio was dead she had confessed what she had done to her mother because (and this was another of Enrique's ideas, but it fitted perfectly into the way Sofía had behaved) anyone who commits a perfect murder needs at least one person to be aware of what they have done. I also recall what she had said about the way her mother had started to drink and how drunkards are incapable of controlling what they say. "Although in her case that wasn't really important, because Mummy died soon afterwards," Sofía had said. "Yet another accident."

You don't of course have to be a genius to understand the meaning of those words, and I suppose it was an association of ideas that had led me now to think of something that has nothing to do with my life, but with what I've read. I've remembered the climax of that thriller with a child's lullaby for a title which I read many years ago. There too the young girl who was the protagonist ended up killing her mother after telling her what she had done to a school companion. A case of reality imitating fiction? No, the most logical explanation, I tell myself, is that this is a very common human reaction: confidants, like prophets, always come to a sticky end. We have only to turn to our own experience to know the truth of this: somebody tells you a secret and then shortly afterwards starts to do you down, to mistreat you. How ungrateful, we think, how bad of them, but it's not that, it's more like a survival instinct. It helps to get things off our chests, but then the witness to our misfortunes becomes a nuisance.

I'm short of breath again. I feel the same unpleasant sensation I had last night in Elba's room, which I then put down to tiredness. Now though I can also feel a slight pain at the back of my neck. I hope this doesn't mean I've caught her chicken pox, I say to myself, and stop typing. Perhaps I should have listened to the doctor and found someone to look after Elba. But what mother would do that? Besides, I'm fine: we mothers, I tell myself with a smile, have a natural immunity against falling ill when a child needs us. I write "Chicken Pox", although for the moment I have no idea how I could turn that into literary material. At that moment, a slight noise makes me glance out of the window. Even though it's dark outside, I spot him. Perched on the balcony rail is the caretaker's cat, staring at me with those yellow eyes of his. That damned animal: fortunately there's no way of it slipping in unless somebody opens the window, so I return to what I was writing on the screen. I think it was Agatha Christie herself who pointed out that the biggest virtue of this exercise of throwing up ideas at random is that at first they are never really productive but that all of a sudden, thanks to some input from the world outside, a perfectly rounded idea that has been prowling around (like a fox, she used to say) finally slips into the hen house. "Elba", my fingers type. I suppose that it is seeing her name next to those of my childhood friends which makes me realize that of all the possible stories I could write, the one that has the most literary potential is not Miguel's or Sofía's, or Avril's, which I hadn't even begun to think about, but my own daughter's.

I feel dizzy again, but this time I don't worry about it. Instead, I'm convinced it's the kind of giddiness you feel when you've hit exactly the right note on the musical scale. I had my theme: I was going to write the story of a mistake, or rather, the story of a girl whose mother has made the mistake from her earliest years of telling her a lie that confuses her dreams. I would write about a pre-adolescent at that awkward age around eleven or twelve, who dreams of a father she can never meet, and whom she searches for among those around her, until she commits a crime that nobody discovers. Nobody discovers it quite simply because there is no motive. Without a motive, there can be no crime; therefore nothing has happened, and this is another of those perfect crimes which according to Enrique occur so frequently.

But this story would also have another important protagonist: the girl's mother, a successful novelist who – not for any objective reason but simply out of literary superstition – starts to think right from the opening chapters that an accident which happened in her childhood has repeated itself in her daughter's life, because, as she sees it, fate plays games and likes to look at itself in mirrors. The most remarkable thing about this (and Heaven knows how I'm going to be able to explain this) is that this woman, whose profession directly involves trying to interpret human conduct, is completely unaware of what is going on around her. She notices the symmetries and the coincidences, but cannot see that the people she considers as secondary characters (Miki and above all Tony) are the main ones, whereas the main ones (Miguel, Sofía and Avril) are merely extras. She is so used to the deceptive world of fiction, where everything is made so obvious, that she does not even see that her daughter has fallen in love, because, as happens with the majority of parents of adolescents, she knows only one or two scattered pieces of the puzzle that is her daughter's life: a random fact here, a strange look, a fleeting suspicion. What do other unconnected pieces mean, such as an ugly doll her daughter claims resembles her, or the girl's obsession with mirrors, or the way in which she uses the name "Luisa", her mother's Christian name? What can their significance be? That's impossible to tell, since Luisa believes that what she sees is reality, when in fact it is nothing more than her subjective (and very limited) view of things. Fine, I say to myself at this point, let's not twist the knife in the wound any more, the characteristics of my beloved alter ego are more than clear; let's look at other elements the story should contain, other conflicts. Towards the end of the story, two or three chapters before the climax, and without the writer going in search of it at all, she discovers an object – some photos, anything at all – which tells her what her daughter has done. But then another interesting point of conflict arises: what does a mother do in such a case? Anything but give her daughter away, of course. A mother would even be capable of accusing herself rather than let her daughter be implicated in a crime. Would you do that, Luisa? I wonder. That's nonsense, I tell myself dismissively, there's no need for me to do anything of the kind. But of course during those three or four days when I was filled with doubt, I never even thought of telling anyone anything. This raises another theme that could be developed: whatever has happened, a mother won't talk about it, which automatically makes her an accessory. My fingers are still flying over the keyboard. It's still pitch black outside, which means there is some time to go before a new day dawns. Within a few hours, two at the least, Elba will wake up and I'll have to leave my computer to look after her. I'll have to take her temperature, prepare her breakfast. Then some time later, around half-past nine, Enrique, displaying a diplomatic punctuality entirely out of kilter with the rest of his behaviour, will give me a call. I haven't seen him since Elba got chicken pox, but he rings every morning regular as clockwork to ask how we are getting on. How is the girl? And what about you, princess? This morning I'll be able to reply for the first time in many days, and without any kind of lie: "Fantastic, Ri, and longing to see you. Oh, and by the way, I'm hard at work at last, I've just had a great idea. I'll tell you about it later." Of course I won't: I'm not going to tell him or anybody else, for the moment at least. First I have to plan it from start to finish: so what comes next?

I begin to describe exactly what I felt when I thought my daughter had imitated the first Antonio's death forty years on. All my suspicions and fears. Aren't you worried, writing about something so intimate, so autobiographical? I wonder for a split second, but I know it's nothing more than a rhetorical question. In spite of what everyone says, literature doesn't consist of real elements from an author's life. It's made up of what might have happened, but didn't. More often than not it's created out of passions we will never fulfil, of frustrated desires, of unanswered prayers. Or, as in my case, from fears, which fortunately have proved groundless. So let's go on: where was I? I scroll up the screen to make sure I'm linking up with my original idea, and then come to a halt: now comes the hardest bit, inventing the grand finale.

It occurs to me that in order to delay the ending somewhat, after the scene when she discovers her daughter's guilt, there has to be a slight, unexpected pause in proceedings: the daughter falls ill, for example. That illness can be put to a double use. On the one hand, the girl can talk in her sleep, confirming what the mother and by extension the reader already knows: that she is guilty. On the other, it can be used to bring in the necessary narrative elements for there to be another surprise death.

Right from the outset I knew the story had to have a tragic resolution. Not so as to punish the mother for having lied to her daughter about something that was so important to her. Nor to contradict Hollywood or Walt Disney happy endings that I find so boring. No, simply because real life does not have Disney endings or, at best, sometimes yes it has them, but almost always no, it doesn't. Fine, so you're going to have a disturbing ending, when most people seem to prefer the other kind. But go on, what new twist can you give to the plot? I suppose that by a tragic resolution, you mean that the daughter, just like Sofía and her mother...

At this point my hand shakes with a silly, superstitious fear, but of course it would make the perfect end to the novel. "An accident," Sofía had said, but what kind of accident? In a case like this it's best to use the elements that are already there. These are: the girl's illness, her mother's refusal to get anyone in to look after her, and... what else could it be?

"Cat" my fingers type, and then come to a full stop. I've just had the idea that I can add the caretaker's cat to the mix: that black beast with its shiny yellow eyes that disturbs me so much. If my protagonist catches the illness from her daughter and also suffers from asthma, the fact that the girl lets the cat into the apartment would add a sinister touch to the plot.

After this, my fingers start to shape the last chapter. It occurs to me to write that when the girl has almost recovered, one morning her mother wakes up and finds she has trouble breathing. She remembers what the doctor told her about the complications chicken pox can bring for an adult, especially if that person is also asthmatic. It's in the early hours, and the very first thing she feels is surprise, because people never think that the worst could happen to them. I'll then go on to explain that as it is years since she has had an asthma attack, Luisa no longer keeps an inhaler close to hand. I'm fairly good at creating scenes of panic, so I don't think it would be too difficult to convey to the reader the mixed feelings someone in a situation like that experiences: at first she tries to calm herself, to deny the fact that she is having trouble breathing. "It's nothing," she tells herself, "I must be catching a cold." But when she looks at herself in a mirror (mirrors have to play an important part in the story, just as they do in Elba's life), she sees from her face that something is wrong. The fever has started to cloud her ideas, but so far she doesn't realize this. She calls out to the girl asleep in her bedroom, but Elba doesn't reply. The woman's surprise grows. There's nobody else in the apartment, it's nowhere near dawn yet and, added to the sense of unreality she has from the fever, she has a growing sensation of uncertainty. She wonders how she might call for help, but finds she can hardly move. Fortunately, the choking feeling is not constant, but comes and goes, which means that there is a quiet moment. She tries to stand up, but falls. She stretches out her hand, but where's the phone? She has forgotten she's left it in her daughter's bedroom. Why doesn't she come? Could it be she can't hear her mother calling out? Each wave of fever brings with it the echo of the words Elba repeated time and again while she was ill: "Promise me nothing is going to happen to me, Mummy", "Nobody is going to know, are they?" At the time, these sounded like innocent phrases, but now she is not so sure. Time crawls by; she has another choking fit. "My God, it's nothing, I'm fine," she tells herself. "Breathe, Luisa, breathe," she tells herself, "it'll pass. It's nothing more than your fears: you're like a little girl scared of shadows. Everything is fine; you'll get over it, you don't need an inhaler. Besides, Elba will wake up in a minute and come to help you." Then you'll be able to tell her: "Look in the medicine cupboard, sweetheart. Bring me that small plastic thing on the top shelf. Yes, Elba, you've seen it before. Help me, my love, but above all, don't be frightened. Your mother's just fine."

Eventually the sleepy girl appears, still in pyjamas and barefoot. Luisa sees (thanks to another flash of lightning, because there's a storm this early morning too) her daughter's silhouette in the living-room doorway. What's that she's holding? It looks like that doll which for Elba symbolized everything she thought she was: a child with no family, no past. I thought that ugly replica of Elba had been thrown away long ago, that it no longer meant anything in her life.

"Is that you, Elba? What are you carrying? It's so dark in here, come closer so I can see properly."

The bluish glow from the computer screen only lights my face; the rest of the room is in semi-darkness. Show me what you've got there, Elba. Come closer, sweetheart, this is no time to play childish games.

I can't see my daughter's face, but do catch sight of a dark shadow that flits between us like an animal in the night.

"Who's that with you, Elba?" I ask. "What is it?"

"Nothing," says my daughter. "Can't you see? It's just you and me, alone together. As always, Luisa."